The Future is *Now*

"You are dead, and I am your master."

"No! No, I don't remember—anything—"

"That is your final good fortune. You must go soon. But first you will answer me."

"Answer what?"

"You have the gift. Tell me what you see!"

"It was you I saw coming! Death and violence and burning, they come with you, and the wolves and the wind. You've come to meet the comet!

"The comet is the Great Circle—the worm that devours its tail. It passes and returns, and what was may be again."

"Yes! Yes!"

"The Sword is nearby. Even now it is being forged."

"I must have the Sword, but it's the Spear I must know about! Tell me how I'll get the Spear!"

"Three times you've tried to use the Sword, and three times you have failed. It does not show itself yet, and it can be bent. But if it were easily bent, it would not be the Sword."

"I can bend the Sword."

"Bend it, and you will have the Spear. If you cannot, the Spear will have you."

"What more?"

"Nothing more. What I see I've told."

"Tell me where the road leads!"

"It leads a hundred ways. It leads nowhere. But the Wolf waits at the end. Whatever way you take, it leads at last to the Wolf."

BAEN BOOKS by LARS WALKER

Erling's Word
Wolf Time

Wolf Time

Lars Walker

WOLF TIME

This is a work of fiction. All the characters and events portrayed in this book are fictional, and any resemblance to real people or incidents is purely coincidental.

Copyright © 1999 by Lars Walker

All rights reserved, including the right to reproduce this book or portions thereof in any form.

A Baen Books Original

Baen Publishing Enterprises
P.O. Box 1403
Riverdale, NY 10471

ISBN: 0-671-57815-4

Cover art by Gary Ruddell

First printing, June 1999

Distributed by Simon & Schuster
1230 Avenue of the Americas
New York, NY 10020

Typeset by Brilliant Press
Printed in the United States of America

DEDICATION
For Dad and Pauline

Axe-time, sword-time—
Every shield shattered.
Wind-time, wolf-time—
Then the world is wrecked.

—from *The Voluspá*
(Sigfod Oski's translation)

Prologue

April, A Tyr's Day

The tractor backed, roaring, and the log chain went taut.

Old Jack Tysness opened the throttle of the rust-orange Allis-Chalmers and clenched his teeth. The oak had been tough, but he had her now. He'd felled her with the chainsaw and grubbed her roots with spade and axe, and now the stump would come like a tooth. He always pulled his own teeth.

Men with machines could be hired to clear land, but that would have been the easy way, and a waste of money. He'd had that lesson from his father, who'd had it from his own father: first you get the work done, then you can look to your comfort.

Jack's great-grandfather had built the barn that still

stood on the farm; raised it while his wife and baby muffled one another with love in a lean-to. The baby had died that winter, but there'd be other babies, and where would they be if they lost the cows?

So Jack in his turn had looked to the stock, looked to the fields, from year to year. It would have been nice to have finished high school, but dangerously comfortable and a temptation to get above himself. The house was lonely and run-down—it needed paint and a woman's hand, but there had always been another job to do; the time for comforts was always next fall or next spring.

And now he was old and alone, shunned even by neighbors, and neighbors in the country were farther between than in the old days. The Twentieth Century had decamped with the small farm in its baggage. Jack's sole heir was a niece somewhere out in California, who would certainly sell the 160 acres to an agribusiness when the time came, and that would be that.

Jack still hated his father, but did not see the irony.

The stump cracked, groaned and moved. Snapping she came free, and the tractor raced back a few yards. Jack flipped in the throttle and cut the engine.

He walked to the stump and spoke to it. "That's it then," he said, and spat. "I been grubbin' the trees along this row for thirty years, and you're the last. You shoulda growed across the fence there, in Troll Valley. That's woods—this is farm. I don't suppose you coulda knowed that a hundred years back, when you was an acorn, but that's how it turned out. Anyway, what kick you got? I'll never see a hundred."

"What's this here?" The corner of a flat, squared stone stuck up from the dirt and roots. Jack hadn't seen its like in his fields before. He bent closer and brushed with hard fingers.

"By God, there's writing here!"

The sun was going and Jack's eyes weren't what they'd been. He got his axe and chopped at the roots.

He'd nearly severed the thickest root when his axe slipped. It struck the stone, spitting sparks, and there was a sharp crack. The stone fell in two pieces.

Jack cursed. A carved stone could be valuable, and he might have spoiled it. He was kneeling to look at the damage, dreaming of a Florida vacation, when he heard footsteps in the grass.

He peered up to see the craziest man he'd ever set eyes on, except for some of the college kids in town. The man wore a wide, floppy hat and some kind of dark blanket. He had a long gray beard, and in one hand he carried a stick taller than himself. He stopped a few feet away and fixed Jack with one bright eye. He swung his stick up and held it chest high and horizontal, as if offering it for inspection.

"I don't take no tramps here," Jack said, getting heavily to his feet.

The crazy man smiled, his teeth very long and white. Jack saw that his stick was wildly carved with snakes and crawling things, and weighted with iron. The crazy man spun the stick like a baton twirler, but with both hands. He flipped it around his back, danced it from hand to hand. He threw it high in the air.

Jack watched, fascinated, as it soared and spun and fell.

It was the last thing he saw.

Chapter I

Odin's Day

Carl Martell was frightened.

He locked his office door, creaked down the hallway, down the steps and out through the lobby of the Old Main building. The student essays on his desk would wait. Most of them would have to be scored on VQs anyway, and grading them under the present conditions seemed a little unsporting. Not to mention futile.

He wondered if he should grow a beard.

It was almost 6:00 P.M. The committee had told him to come back by six and they'd probably have a decision for him.

It was October, cool and clear, with a fresh breeze. Martell stopped a moment to see if Cerafsky's Comet was visible yet, but it was too early. He'd taken a personal interest in the latest comet, feeling somehow that it had a message for him, like the Star of Bethlehem. He wouldn't have admitted this to anyone of course. Unless they'd asked him.

Martell headed down the sidewalk, dark under the shade of tall firs despite the moonlight and street lamps. He decided to take an alley shortcut to the Campus Center and turned between the library and a storage building.

He'd gotten about fifty feet when sudden footsteps pounded up behind him.

Martell looked over his shoulder and ran from bulky shadows, his chest tight, his mouth open.

Hands clutched him from behind. An arm went around his neck. Another pinned his right wrist. He smelled sweat and aftershave.

"Don't make any noise," said a big young man, only a shape in the dark, who came around in front of him, holding up a hunting knife which caught a gleam of light. "I'm a friend of Julie Anderson's. I want to have a little talk with you in private."

"I didn't do anything," Martell said, between gasps. His voice sounded thin to him, almost squeaky. He'd always wondered how he'd react to violence. It was as bad as he'd feared.

"That's what you keep saying, Carl-baby. But you know you're lying and we know you're lying."

"I'm not lying."

"I'm gonna get the truth out of you, Carl-baby. Maybe those fat-butts on the committee can't get it out of you, but I will. Give me the hand, Billy."

The man holding Martell stretched out the arm that gripped his wrist, proffering Martell's hand as if for inspection. He was strong as a backhoe.

The young man placed the knife edge against Martell's palm. "Now you're gonna tell the truth or

I'm gonna cut you. You forced Julie to sleep with you, didn't you? You promised her you'd pass her in History if she put out, right?"

The knife edge was a slice of supercooled interstellar vacuum against Martell's flesh. He floundered in his mind for words, but the only one he found was, "No."

The shock of the slash took his breath. He mouthed, "Oh, God," and the young man struck him twice across the face with an open hand, so that stars flashed under his eyelids.

Then the blade was against his cheek, and he could feel the warm blood. "I don't want to kill you, Carl-baby," the young man said, "but I'm gonna get the truth from you."

"It is the truth, I swear!"

"You're asking for this! Don't make me cut your face!"

"I never—I never touched the girl."

"Then lie! Just give me the satisfaction! I need to hear you say it!"

"Nothing happened." Martell clenched his eyes shut.

Crack! Something burst above them, exploding in bright light and shouts. The knife blade was gone, and the hands that held him were gone, and Martell toppled to the sidewalk, striking his head. He was out for a moment, and when he came to he pushed himself up to a sitting position and found that the two young men were now lying on either side of him. He feared for a moment they were dead, then heard them breathing. Something like a movement at the edge of his vision made him turn his head, which got him woozy again, but when his vision cleared he thought he saw, running away towards the street, a man in a long, dark coat and wide hat, carrying some kind of stick.

A sharp pain in his hand reminded him of his

wound, and he fished a handkerchief out of his trousers with his left hand to wrap around it. Only then he remembered what they'd wanted of him. . . .

"I couldn't lie," he murmured. "I couldn't lie to save my life."

He went on his knees in the grass and vomited. Then he lost consciousness again.

If I grew a beard, Martell thought, *maybe things would be all right.* He'd always thought he would one day, but his came out red, and it contrasted so with his white-blond hair and pale skin that he knew people would stare. Besides, if you grew a beard people wondered if you were covering a weak chin. Martell was rather proud of his chin.

He could hear Elaine, teasing him, saying, "You know, people wonder if you're an albino. Or a half-albino, if there is such a thing. The skin around your eyes is as white as paper." And he had answered, "My beard grows red."

Flashing red and blue lights. Voices. Muffled, distant. "I ran for a pay phone and called 911 as soon as I found him."

"Did you move him?"

"Didn't touch him."

"Well, let's get him on the cart. That collar secure . . . ?"

"Of course we have every confidence in you, Carl," the Dean of Instruction had said to him. *"You can count on a completely objective and open-minded hearing."*

Martell would have recognized that speech as the Kiss of Death even if he hadn't sensed she was lying. He felt the lie as a kind of double vision of the mind, a vertigo. It made his stomach queasy.

The Dean had said, "You know we're on your side, don't you, Carl?"

And Martell had stood there and looked at her, white-faced, unable to make the politic response.

Someone was shining a bright light in his eye. A voice said, "No sign of concussion, but let's run a couple tests. . . ."

"How long have you been teaching here at Christiania, Carl?" the Dean of Women had asked.

"About eight years."

"And you've been happy here?"

"Yes."

"You came here from University of Minnesota, didn't you?"

"Yes."

"Why did you leave there?"

He had said, "Because I was afraid of a man," and everyone had looked away or cleared their throats, embarrassed by the naked candor. A mistake. One he couldn't avoid.

Maybe he should grow a mustache. No. He wasn't the mustache type. Either a full beard or nothing.

"You've never married, have you, Carl?" the Dean of Men had asked.

"No."

"And you don't live with anyone?"

"No."

"How often do you date?"

"I never date."

"You have a number of attractive young women in your classes, don't you, Carl?"

"Yes."

"Isn't it true that you had a live-in relationship

with one of your students at the University, a woman considerably younger than yourself?"

"I've talked it over with Sally," Roy Corson of the English Department had said, sitting on a corner of the desk in Martell's office, plump and bulky in his uniform tweed jacket with elbow patches, stroking his little beard and looking serious. "She says she'll play along. All you've got to do is say you spent that evening at our place. We'll say we played Trivial Pursuit or strip poker or something."

"I don't think I can do that," he had answered.

"Come on, Carl—you didn't do the deed, did you?"

"Of course not."

"Don't you see? I might have. Anybody else on the faculty might have—those who could and those who swing that way. You're the only man I know I'd trust with my virgin sister, if there is such a thing anymore. That's why we've got to get you off. It's the grossest possible miscarriage—another show trial for the sexual harassment gestapo. Sometimes you've got to give justice a little nudge."

"I'm sorry, but there are reasons. I just can't."

"Okay, have it your way. But Jesus isn't gonna come down on his Harley and pull your butt out of this."

"I don't believe in Jesus."

"Sure."

Maybe he should grow a half-beard like Roy's. No. Tall, thin men with half-beards look like Don Quixote.

"You make enemies, Carl," Elaine had said once, over breakfast. "You think it's your responsibility to right all the wrong in the world and correct everybody's mistakes, as if humankind was your History 101 class. People aren't bad just because they're wrong. And they're not always wrong."

❖　　　　❖　　　　❖

"Carl, is it true that on the 18th of September last, you interrupted a student's report in class by shouting, 'Lies, lies, lies!' threw a chalk eraser at him, and ran to the men's room?"

"Yes."

"Why did you do that?"

"I didn't want to be sick in the classroom."

"WEEP News, Sid Edelman reporting for Huset Motors. Unless you've been in labor for thirty-six hours, you've probably heard that Epsom is expecting a celebrity. Sigfod Oski, winner of the Nobel Prize for Literature, announced on arrival at Twin Cities International Airport this morning that, instead of making his expected visit to the University of Minnesota, he has decided to come immediately to Epsom where, he said, he will make his first public statements at a meeting scheduled for Thursday. President Saemund Lygre of Christiania College told WEEP News:"

"Yes, we have known about Mr. Oski's plans for a couple days now. But he made it very clear that he didn't want any announcements made before his arrival, and of course we were eager to cooperate with him in every way."

"We were able to contact a spokesperson for the University, who asked to remain anonymous, for the administration's reaction. All he was able to say was that they weren't very happy about it.

"Turning to national news, the Supreme Court is set to hear a challenge by the One Nation Under God Foundation to the Definition of Religion Act. A spokesman for ONUG described the new law as 'a frontal assault on the First Amendment,' while a spokesman for the Justice Department stated that 'We're trying to get the American people to understand that not only is DRA not a threat to freedom of religion, it's the greatest boon this country has ever seen to true religious conviction.'

"And now a word from Huset Motors. Tired of the high prices and runaround you get from those big city dealers? Ted Huset says—"

The Reverend Harold Gunderson of Nidaros Lutheran Church, a heavy, red-faced man with tangled, thinning hair and a gift for getting the wrong button into any buttonhole, pulled his Oldsmobile into the parking lot of the Epsom Area Medical Center and flipped the radio off. He was excited by the news about Sigfod Oski, and slightly disturbed by the entire DRA business (although the bishop had assured them at the last convention that there was nothing to worry about) but he had work to do. He turned the key off and opened the door to get out, dragging his prosthetic right leg.

The lighted brick front of the building illuminated graffiti that shouted (all graffiti is a shout), MICROBE MURDERERS—SPESIESISM SUCKS! and NO MOR BREEDERS! But, like everyone else, Harry hardly noticed graffiti anymore.

He never limped into the cramped, '80s style lobby of the medical center without a twinge of remembrance. He'd left a limb here, and something infinitely more precious.

"It's my cross," he said silently. "Help me to bear it for You. By Your grace we'll make good of this."

He was surprised to find Carl Martell at the front desk, his overcoat over his arm, a gauze bandage on his forehead, signing out awkwardly with a bandaged hand.

"Six stitches in it," Martell told him when he'd finished his story. "About my head they're not sure yet, but then what else is new? They'll want me to come back for more tests."

"It's appalling," said the pastor. "You've talked to the police, of course?"

"Sure—they deserve a laugh like anybody else.

Whoever attacked me was gone by the time they got there. 'Did you recognize either of your attackers?' 'No.' 'Were their voices familiar?' 'No.' 'Is it possible that they were your students?' 'I suppose so.' 'Anything else you remember?' 'Well, there was this mysterious rescuer with a stick . . .' They liked that part a lot. Am I an absent-minded professor, Harry? I didn't think I was bright enough."

"They hear stranger stories every day. Believe me— I hear some of them too."

"That's right, you're like Father Brown. The underworld has no secrets from you."

Harry's face went grave. "Any word from the disciplinary committee?"

Martell gasped. "My God. I forgot all about it. I was on my way to find out when all this happened. Where's a phone? I've got to call the Dean."

Harry followed him to a pay phone and picked his pocket for him when he couldn't get at his wallet for his credit card. Martell pushed the buttons slowly, reciting each digit as he did. "You'll have to forgive me if I'm a little vague, Harry. They gave me some kind of painkiller and I feel like I've been flogged with shaving cream."

He reached the Dean at home and made his explanation. Harry could hear a voice from the receiver, and then Martell said, "Thank you," and hung up, his face whiter than usual. "Well?" Harry asked.

"It's been dropped. Julie withdrew the accusation."

"That's wonderful!"

Martell shook his head, then winced. "It's over. All the fear. All the sleepless nights. Over. Just like that. And I still don't know why. I don't know why it started, and I don't know why it stopped. I've never felt so powerless in my life."

"I was sure you'd be vindicated, Carl. And now I

think what you need most is a good night's sleep. Go home and go to bed. Then you'll be fresh and rested for the reception tomorrow."

"Reception?"

"For Sigfod Oski. I assume you've got a ticket, as a faculty member."

"Of course. I got a pair of them this morning, but I hadn't thought much about them with all that's been going on. Which just shows you how far out of things I've been—I mean, Oski after all. I've dreamed of meeting him for years."

"Do you know who you're taking with you?" Harry was fishing, but he often had to, with Carl.

"Taking with me? Oh, the second ticket. No, I hadn't thought about it . . ." He turned to walk away, then turned back. "You want to come to the reception?"

Harry beamed. He'd caught his fish. "Why thank you, Carl, how thoughtful. I'd be delighted."

"I'll pick you up at six then."

"Splendid. Will I see you at church Sunday?"

"When my time comes you'll be the first to know." Martell struggled with his overcoat, and Harry helped him get it on and watched him drift towards the doors. The pastor watched him go. A fine looking, tall man, he thought, but strangled inside by some private worm.

He went to the desk and asked for the printout of Lutheran patients. As usual it was a long one, but only about half of them were his responsibility. The Lutherans of Epsom, in the proud Norwegian-American tradition, believed there was no such thing as too many, or too small, Lutheran churches. But like the Good Shepherd, Harry Gunderson knew his own. He noted the Nidaros church members.

He called on a new mother, an old woman dying of cancer, a farmer with a broken hip and three STDs. On his way out he found Livingston Berge, the church custodian, signing out just where Carl Martell had been, and having the same trouble.

"How in thunder's a fella supposed to sign out with a bandage like this?" he was demanding of the nurse. "These kid doctors don't know nothin' about finishing a job!"

"Stoney!" the pastor said. "What happened to you?"

"I was attacked by a vicious beast," said Stoney in the voice of a soul purified by suffering.

"He was bitten by a mouse," said the desk nurse.

Stoney gave her a "he jests at scars" look, which she ignored. He was a round-headed, stoop-shouldered man in his sixties. He spoke in an immigrant's brogue although he had never been in Norway in his life—he was the last of a breed.

Harry tried to look concerned.

"You know those new humane mouse traps the government made us buy?" Stoney said. "Well, I had a plastic bucket with a lid I was keepin' the little buggers in, so I could take 'em out and release 'em in the country all at once—"

"That's against the law, you know," said the desk nurse, who didn't seem to have a lot of work to do at the moment. "You could be charged for cruelty under the Animal Rights Act. You're supposed to release them within six hours."

"I don't recall sayin' how many I had or how long I'd had 'em. For your information our church is infested with mice, like every other place in America, includin' this hospital." The nurse looked sulky and turned away.

Stoney held his hand up. "Mouse bite is just like rat bite, they say. And everybody knows rat bite is as bad as rattlesnake. They wanted to keep me overnight for observation, especially after all these plague scares, but I wouldn't stay. Got too much work to do. I could be dead tomorrow though. You could be preachin' my funeral Saturday."

"I suppose my text could be, '*I fought wild beasts at Ephesus.*'"

Stoney looked as if he was thinking that one over. They moved towards the brown, ovoid vinyl chairs in the waiting area.

"I saw a bandage just like yours on another friend of mine right in this lobby, about an hour ago," Harry said. "Carl Martell from the college."

Stoney snorted. "I don't see why you hang around with that perfessor. All them college teachers is atheists and acrostics."

"Carl's not exactly an atheist."

"I remember a day when they hired Christians to teach at church schools. But nothin's been the same since they shot all that hardware up on the moon."

"Nothing ever stays the same, Stoney."

"Ain't that the truth? You know what the problem is? I think I worked it out yesterday afternoon while I was rakin' the leaves.

"Meat. We don't eat enough meat anymore. All those animal rights nuts got us eatin' salads and beans and silage, and it's messed up our heads. They won't admit it, but there's a vitamin in meat helps you think straight. Never was a vegetarian in the history of the world could use his brain.

"No, you think about it. You know what Hitler was? He was a vegetarian. I seen it on TV. He didn't die in the war, you know. He lived on for years in Argentina, or Venezuela, or one of them places. My friend Ellsworth swears he saw him when he was on a package tour to Rio D. Whatever. It was Hitler started all that vegetarian propaganda, you know. It was revenge was what it was, for us beatin' him in the war."

Harry narrowed his eyes and looked at him closely. "But Stoney," he whispered, "how do you know it hasn't affected you? Maybe it's not the vegetables at all. Maybe it's—pizza!" Stoney squinted at him. "Yes! Pizza from Mussolini's Italy! Whoever ate pizza in America before World War II?"

Stoney pulled himself up straight in his chair. "Now you're laughin' at me," he said.

Harry shook his head. "I'm sorry, Stoney. Maybe it's the vegetables after all."

"An' green fire plugs! Ain't nothin' been the same since they started paintin' the fireplugs green."

Later, swinging his unmatched legs into his Olds, awkwardly lifting the plastic one over the center console so he could control the gas and brake with the left, Harry felt the wave of panic he sometimes still experienced in an automobile. It took all his control to put the key in the ignition.

If I had started out ten minutes earlier, or ten minutes later that night.

If I had driven slower. Or faster.

If the truck driver hadn't been eighteen hours without sleep, propped up with pills. If I had let Joanna drive, then I would have been the one thrown through the window and under the wheels. She could have managed without me a lot better than I can without her.

And underneath, the nagging fear that, if really given the choice, he might have grabbed for his own life.

Useless thoughts. He pushed them down. "It's my cross. Help me to bear it for You. By Your grace we'll make good of this." And he said a prayer for the driver of the truck, four years in a wheelchair.

Driving home he turned on the radio and listened to Rory Buchan.

Chapter II

MEMORANDUM
FROM: A. Carnegie Hall, Station Mgr.
TO: WEEP Announcers
RE: Pay raises

I am unhappily saddened to here that there
has been a continual of discussion re: pay
raises for announcing personels.

WEEP has been very outgoing and generes,
I think, in it's tradition of raising salaries
whenever the Minimimum Wage goes up. Apparently some consider this sufficiency not
enough.

I trust you all realise and understand that
we would really truely love to increase the

remuniation and pay to all our personnels.
But, economical conditions being what prevail, there's only so much money to go
around. Also, resent expences encurred in
the renevation of our Executive Offices have
proved more prohibtive than expected.

I might remind you, however, that if everyone
would only put out a little more dillingence,
sales people selling more time, announcers do
better shows to increase our market share,
making posible a small encrease some time.

Remember, your hear to work for the Lord,
so you've got to work very hard.

But, you're working for the Lord, so you can't
expect much money.

A.C.H./cak

Rory Buchan read the memo twice while he waited
for the prerecorded program to finish. It was a few
minutes before 6:00 P.M., when his shift would begin,
but he'd told the afternoon man to go home. There'd
be nothing to say on the air before the station ID
at the top of the hour.

At least two memoranda a week showed up tacked
to the studio's walls. Mr. Hall felt strongly about
memos, and no one was allowed to take them down
but he. And since he never visited the studio—some
of the announcers had never met him at all—the slips
of paper had pretty nearly crowded out the acousti-
cal panels. How they got posted in the first place was
a Sacred Mystery.

Rory cued up his first two CDs and pulled his
commercial carts for the next hour. He went into the

news room—news closet, really—and cleared the wire service machine, pegging the stories, and waited for the weather forecast, which was due any minute.

Predictably, the forecast started printing about two minutes before air time. Rory rather enjoyed the suspense of standing over the old black machine, tensed to rip and run, while the printer leisurely clacked its lines out.

He made it to the mike with three seconds to spare. He pulled on the earphones and said, "The Righteousness Abounding Hour has been brought to you as a public service by WEEP Radio. It's six o'clock, and you're tuned to WEEP, AM and FM, Inspiration and Country Music for southeastern Minnesota. America can still be saved, and we're here to help. I'm Rory Buchan, and I'll be with you till midnight, keeping you company on a Wednesday night. Stay tuned for more music on the Country side, but first the weather.

"The National Weather Service reports a strong cold front moving south from Manitoba. We can expect temperatures to drop during the next few days, with increasing winds. Freezing temperatures and snow are also possible by the weekend, so you farmers will want to get those combines out and bring in what's left of your corn. This is Minnesota, folks, the Theater of Seasons. And as fast as they're bringing winter on, fall's box office must have been really lousy.

"Look for northwesterly winds tonight, around eight miles per hour, increasing tomorrow. Temperatures tonight will be in the upper 30's to low 40's, tomorrow's highs in the upper 50's. Chance of precipitation 20% tonight, 30% tomorrow.

"Currently in Epsom, we're looking at winds from the northwest at eleven miles per hour, and our temperature an ominous 46°. No wind chill factor, but it won't be long.

"And that's the weather, brought to you by WEEP,

the voice of decency in southeastern Minnesota. I'm Rory Buchan. Coming up, Sally Crocker with, 'You Cheat On Me, I Cheat On You.'

"But first a WEEP public service message: 'There'll be a special prayer meeting on the steps of the Minnesota Capital in Paul City—which we still like to call St. Paul, no matter what the courts say—to pray that God will guide the Supreme Court in Washington to overturn the Definition of Religion Act.'" He gave a telephone number for people who wanted to arrange for a ride.

He started the CD and took his earphones off. The red telephone light was flashing, but the line hummed when he picked the receiver up. Many callers thought the time to telephone an announcer was while nothing important was going on—while he was announcing.

"God bless you anyway," said Rory.

He loaded his carts for the next break.

Rory was a tall, beefy young man with a lot of curly brown hair and a Buffalo Bill beard. A short upper lip gave him a pleasantly rabbity look. He wore blue jeans and a flannel shirt with cowboy boots, and a bronze cross hung from a thong around his neck. He was that fiercest form of Country Music fan, the converted Rocker.

The phone light blinked again, and he picked up the receiver.

"*Hi, Rory, this is old Pontoon. How you doing?*"

"Just fine, Pontoon. How's yourself?"

"*Not too bad, not too bad, except for the arthritis. Couldn't hardly get out of bed this morning.*"

"I'm sorry to hear that."

"*Well, be glad you're young.*"

"I enjoy it."

"*Hey Rory, I sure do like that Righteous Rebounding Hour. That's a real good show. I listen to it every week, except when I miss it.*"

"Glad you like it, Pontoon."

"And I sure do like that music you folks play. Can't stand that Rock and Roll junk. Dirty, immoral Say-tonic music that Rock and Roll is."

"That's a fact, Pontoon; that's why I got away from it."

"Hell yes. Can you play 'Wakin' Up With Some-one Even Uglier Than You'?"

"I think I can do that for you, Pontoon."

The first number was fading out. Rory potted it down and started the second, then ejected the first and turned to search the CD rack, the receiver tucked between his shoulder and ear.

"I sure appreciate it, Rory. You're a good guy. I listen to you all the time. I like good music, none of that nigger rock and roll."

Rory hung the phone up, but he continued look-ing for Pontoon's song. He'd promised.

The phone lit up again.

"Listen, Rory, you're a good kid, but you've got no idea what's goin' on in this country. Say-tonic powers is at work, and it all comes from those— BLACK—savages—"

Rory hung up again.

The phone rang again.

"I don't take any offense, Rory, because I know you young folks all got brainwashed by the schools, but where do you think all this Satan worship is com-ing from? Cows mutilated, right here in our own county, and their owners is too scared to tell the cops, scared the hoodoos'll come and take their kids next.

"And what about old Jack Tysness, him whose farm that W.O.W. cult owns now? They say wild dogs ate him. Well, I ask you—whoever heard of a body ate up that bad in one day? People saw him alive in town that same morning. And I never heard of no wild dogs killing no man, anyhow."

"Look, Pontoon—"

"This used to be a decent, God-fearing town, Rory. That was before the college started bringing in them— BLACKS—on football scholarships—"

Rory hung up. The phone didn't ring again, and Rory took a moment to say a prayer for Pontoon. Then he broke for commercials and started the request. When he was done the phone light was blinking again.

"WEEP. God loves you."

"Hello, Rory," said a woman's voice. *"Do you know who this is?"*

"How are you, Violet?"

"Can you play, 'You Cheat On Me, I Cheat On You,' for me Rory, dear?"

"I just played that one, Violet."

"I know, Rory, but I'd really like to hear it again. It has special meaning for me."

"I'm sorry, that's against the rules. You know that."

"Well then, you know what my favorite song is, don't you?"

"I'm sorry, we don't have 'My Shy Violet.' We only play Country."

"Couldn't you get it? If you asked the manager?"

"We only play Country, Violet. I'm sorry."

"Well, play something by the Beaurivoir Brothers for me, won't you, Rory?"

"Yes, I can do that, Violet."

"Thank you, dear."

"You're welcome." *Click.*

Rory was always happy to play something by the Beaurivoir Brothers. They were his favorite group. Once they had been a Gospel group, and Rory was convinced that they had only pretended to cross over to mainstream Country. He knew in his heart that there was a secret message in the Beaurivoirs' songs. He was sure he could figure it out if he listened to them enough. Then he'd find his own Calling.

For Rory, the line between this world and the next
was a very thin one.

Rory's shift ended at midnight. As he was clear-
ing the teletype in the newsroom before his shift
ended the phone rang. In that room it rang audibly.

"WEEP. God loves you." Rory hoped it wasn't
anything that would keep him late.

"*Is this Rory Buchan?*" a man's voice asked, and
Rory said it was.

"*I've been told you're somebody who's concerned
over what's happening to destroy our country today.*"

"I sure am. Lots of people are."

"*That's right. But you know and I know that most
people aren't really serious. Are you serious, Rory?*"

"If you'd seen what I saw back in California—if
you'd been through what I've been through—you'd
know I am."

"*Were you a drug user?*"

Rory took a breath. "I was a drug user, and a drug
runner, and a thief and a mugger and every other kind
of bad thing. Praise God, He delivered me from it
all."

"*They said you'd say something like that. That's
good. It means you understand—you're not just talk.
Do you know the Vinland Motel?*"

"Out on Highway 60."

"*There'll be a meeting there at 12:30 tonight. Some
people who see the danger and are willing to be
counted for the Lord. We'd like you to be there.*"

"A meeting? Who are you?"

"*Just sinners saved by grace.*"

"How do I know you're not some kind of crazies?
There's lots of crazies around. Just saying, 'Lord,
Lord,' doesn't make you right with Jesus."

"*Matthew 7:21. Come and see. That's what Philip
said to Nathaniel. John 1:46.*"

"Well, you know your Bible. Okay, I'll be there, but I'm not making any promises."

"*That's fine. Come to Room 12 and knock.*"

When Carl Martell left the medical center he walked back to his office. It wasn't far. He felt disoriented by the painkiller, but he'd decided not to take the next day off. He'd let things slide the last few weeks, and it was time he took control again. He didn't have an early class on Thursdays, so he'd be able to sleep in. And maybe he could grade papers with his left hand.

He climbed the worn cement steps of Old Main, between the wooden pillars of the portico, painted white in homage to marble. He turned his key, awkwardly, in the heavy lock. Old Main had been built in Victorian grandeur as a hotel before 1900. Failing, it had been acquired by an association of Norwegian farmers who wanted a place where their children could learn business skills and the Word of God. It was still possible to learn business skills there.

In the high-ceilinged lobby he paused for a moment to clear his head. Even in the dark, he almost felt the stares of the college's founders, Oskar Frette and Haldor Bendikson—affectionately known as Moral and Hardy to the students—from their gilt-framed portraits on the wall. Then, creaking across the hardwood floor, he made his way to the stairway that led to the second story, where the History Department lived. He took the steps with deliberation—his balance was off, and it was dark. It hadn't occurred to him to turn a light on. He struggled to unlock his office door for a full minute.

Inside he fumbled to the desk and switched the lamp on. The light stabbed his eyes, and he switched it off again. He sat a few minutes with his left hand over his eyes, feeling just as the doctor had told him he'd feel now and then. Maybe working tomorrow wasn't such a good idea.

He lost track of time. Footsteps in the hallway roused him. The old boards creaked, and somebody was giggling. There were voices, a boy's and a girl's *Correction*, he told himself, *Young Man and Young Woman. "Boy" and "Girl" are pejorative terms which infringe on basic human dignity*. This was a universal truth, set forth in a memo from the President's office. The fact that Christiania College no longer taught the infallibility of Scripture did not mean it had abandoned the concept of infallibility. Nowadays infallibility didn't have the shelf life it once enjoyed, but it was *ex cathedra* while it lasted.

"Can we use one of the rooms?" the Young Man said.

"I don't know," said the Young Woman, "whose offices are these? Henrich, Fosse—here's Carl Martell, the sexual harasser."

"I hear they let him off on the Julie Anderson thing."

"Well sure, they protect their own. The man's a known sexist."

"Yeah, but be fair. He's also known not to sleep with students. How many profs under sixty can say that?"

"So he's gay."

"Gay profs sleep with students."

"Then he's a closet gay. A hypocrite."

The Young Man began to recite:

"I do not love thee, Carl Martell;
The reason why I cannot—uh . . ."

The Young Woman laughed, "You can't use 'tell'!"

"On the reason why I cannot dwell!"

"Oh, God."

"But only this I know full well:
I do not love thee, Carl Martell."

The footsteps moved further down the hall. "Here," said the Young Man. "This door's warped. I think I can get it open with a credit card."

"You think we'll get in trouble, breaking and entering?"

"Don't worry about it. I've got a suitcase full of VQ points."

A door opened and closed. Martell smiled, oddly moved. It wasn't often one got epigrammatized in the modern college. And the young people's bigotry had been sincere, as the bigotry of the young always is.

There was no question of interrupting them. If, as the Young Man had said, he had plenty of VQ points, he was essentially immune from prosecution for anything less than a gross misdemeanor before the law, and for anything less than murder within the school.

A law passed a couple years back had required each U.S. citizen to fill out a questionnaire, under penalty of perjury, along with his or her annual income tax return. The answers to the questions on this form—*What is your ethnic background? Have you ever been sexually molested? What was your parents' estimated annual income?*—formed the basis for the awarding of Victimization Quotient points. These points were used to increase or decrease welfare benefits and adjust tax obligations, and were taken into consideration in judicial sentencing.

Anyway, the kids were probably just looking for a place to have sex, and thought it would be kinky to do it in a teacher's office. If you wanted to get into real trouble with civil rights lawyers, you couldn't do better than trying to prevent a teenage couple from copulating.

He tried to remember what he'd come up to the office to do.

Finally he left, moving as quietly as possible so as not to disturb the young burglars. Martell had a nice sense of personal honor, and to let them know he'd heard them insult him would have smirched it.

His feet knew their way home. His apartment wasn't far, nothing was in Epsom, but he wasn't usually medicated when he made the walk. There was such a thing as a taxi in town, but the driver would be long asleep by now.

Some people were awake though. Here and there, on lawns and rooftops, comet watchers sat out in parkas and stocking caps, peering through telescopes and binoculars. It was the best time of night to see Cerafsky. Martell looked up too. After all, he had a message coming.

The comet shone bright as a neighbor's TV set seen through a window at night, a straight, white blade in the southwest, stretching between the constellations Pisces and Pegasus.

"*A ball of space garbage,*" some science writer in a magazine had called it, as if that ended the matter. "*Justly less famous than Halley's, though admittedly more spectacular this time around. Judging from the records, most of its passes seem to have escaped all notice.*"

Phooey. There was more to a comet—to anything—than could be learned by analyzing its composition. We have only five senses, after all, Martell reasoned (it was amazing how clearly he was thinking tonight). Suppose we had six or seven? What would we learn that would seem fabulous to us now? Think about that, astronomers and journalists! Think about that, Professor Forsythe!

No, best not to think about Professor Forsythe.

"Hey, Carl!" Martell lowered his face to see Roy Corson walking toward him. Although Roy belonged to the English Department, his office was along the same hall as Martell's. He'd lost a game of musical offices, he liked to explain, and History had had a room available. Martell thought that the two Young Persons could be doing unspeakable acts in Roy's office even now.

"Out kind of late, aren't you, Carl? Celebrating your vindication? Good for you. But how come you didn't invite me along? What's with the Band-Aid?"

"I had—I got hurt. Stitches." Martell held his hand up. "You'll have to excuse me—the doctor put something pretty heady in my veins and I don't think I'm tracking real well."

"You'd better get home and rest."

"My very plan."

"You want a lift?"

"No. It's not far now."

"You sure?"

"I'll be all right. Thanks."

"They give you pills?"

"Yeah. They're here somewhere." Martell patted at his pockets.

"Don't bother. Just make sure you take them. You should take drugs whenever you can, Carl. Good for the character."

He strolled away, a '70s revolutionary trapped in history as in amber. Martell wondered what he was doing out walking at midnight. One? 1:07 by his watch.

His apartment building stood on a corner. He paused at the intersection and studied it as if he'd never seen it before. There was his building, and a handsome clump of firs on another corner, masking a house, and a parking lot, and another house.

He'd never noticed before how large a space an intersection took up. But there it was, bathed in brave halogen light from a street lamp. You could teach a class in that space. Or hold a dance. Christiania had once had a rule against dancing. Some in the community still pointed to its abolition as the beginning of the downhill slide.

Martell stepped out into the intersection, thinking it wasteful to let so much paved space go unused. He walked around in it, like a man in a new house. There was no traffic, yet he felt bold standing in dead center, temporary occupying force in automobile territory.

The painkiller was affecting him. No question.

And it must have been the painkiller that made him think he heard a rumbling overhead. Thunder? No. It was a fair night—perfect for comet watching.

The rumbling grew louder, and he looked wildly about for its source. In sudden panic he started for his apartment.

Glancing over his shoulder just as he reached the door, he thought he saw a line of clouded shapes in the sky, not quite blotting out the stars. They looked like those "Ghost Riders In the Sky" Vaughn Monroe had sung about once upon a time. There seemed to be hundreds of them, on horse shapes, riding an unseen terrain high above the town; fading in, fading out, defying focus like cheap film stock. Black they were, and their horses were black, and at their head a gigantic black figure rode, who screamed and waved a spear, and his black cloak flapped like ravens' wings.

"Bed. Bed is the thing," said Carl Martell as he poked his key at the lock with his left hand. He felt naked at the back.

In her little house, once a country schoolhouse, the witch laid her cards out on the kitchen table, one at a time.

She didn't look like most people's idea of a witch. She wore her brown hair in a pleasant shag, and her shirt and jeans came from L.L. Bean.

The witch was a charlatan, but not merely a charlatan. Most of her business was carnival tricks, and

it kept the customer satisfied. But now and then the
Patterns appeared, as they had ever since she was a
little girl. From time to time, unbidden. Exciting,
when it happened, like fast driving. And frightening
in the same way.

She sipped a cup of herb tea, still buzzing from
the joint she'd smoked to calm her nerves. The Patterns were back tonight. The strongest ever. No
matter how she shuffled the deck, the message came
out the same.

Death. Violence. Fire.

The witch was troubled. She was not a woman of
ill will. She considered herself a White Practitioner.
She had never poisoned a well, or stolen a child, or
gone about invisible to pinch her neighbors. Or
wanted to.

Death. Violence. Fire. The faces of the cards looked
past her with the idiot depravity of 18th Century
woodcuts. The witch did not wish these things for
herself, and she did not wish them for others.

The knowledge had been growing in her for weeks.
The leaves spoke of it as the trees shed them, and
the cold breeze out of the north was full of it. Something was coming, for good or ill, and it was not
something she could control.

"I'm out of my league here," she whispered.

It was the secret fear of all her Order—that the
forces, unseen and inscrutable, which obeyed her by
whim would turn, like goaded bulls, to crush her. She
had cultivated her gifts, knowing the risk, in the hope
of doing good.

Now, as the turning approached she wondered
about that long-ago choice. Could it be that Good
was not, as she had been taught, an elastic, gauzy
thing you groped for in the dark, but something hard
as iron, big as a planet, something you ignored at your
peril, like clean air and healthy food?

No. That was what the Puritans had thought, and the Puritans had been vicious burners.

The Patterns were clear. Some kind of turning was coming.

The witch felt very alone.

Chapter III

Rory Buchan swung his rusty green VW Golf into the motel parking lot, the pink neon of the ship-shaped sign reflecting in his windshield. There were plenty of places to park, and he found Room 12 easily. He knocked. He was wearing a fringed suede jacket and a cowboy hat because of the chill, but the fresh air smelled good to him after hours in the studio.

The door was opened by a man wearing a sweat-shirt, jeans and a ski mask, who put a hand on his shoulder and pulled him in. Rory almost moved away. He didn't like the ski mask. The room was stuffy, a lot like the studio.

"You're Rory Buchan?" the man asked when the door was shut. He was about Rory's height, but leaner. He looked like he worked out. His mask was black with red stitching.

He gestured to three other men, also in ski masks, who sat on the bed and two of the three chairs.

"I wish I could introduce you, Brother Rory," he said, "because you're never going to meet a finer bunch of Christian guys than these right here. But we're keeping our identities secret for your protection. We do special work under special conditions, and our work depends on absolute secrecy. Maybe you'll decide to join us, and then we'll get acquainted.

"But I can tell you who we are as a group. We're the Hands of God. That's the name of our organization. I'm the spokesman. You can call me Thumb."

"Thumb?" Rory wanted to laugh, but was afraid to.

"Thumb." There was a smile in the voice.

Rory thought the Hands of God looked a little silly, not to mention uncomfortable, in the overheated room. One of them, in a bright red mask, had a finger up under his ear, scratching hard. They all looked fit though.

"Sit down, Rory, so we can talk." Thumb pointed to the empty chair, and Rory sat in it. Thumb sat facing him, on the foot of the bed.

"First of all, let's pray."

Thumb folded his hands, lowered his face and prayed aloud, a prayer rich in "thees" and "thines." Rory noted approvingly that he knew how to use the "-eth" and "-est" suffixes properly. That had been a rare skill for some time.

Voices said, "Amen," and "Yes, Lord."

"Brother Rory," said Thumb when they looked up again, "we have a story to tell you, but first of all we need to hear your own witness. You told me a little on the phone, but it's important that we hear the whole story."

"I'm always glad to tell it," said Rory. "But it's not a nice one."

"We've heard ugly stories before, Brother Rory. And we've seen ugly things."

Rory slipped out of his jacket and put his hat down on the floor. "I come from outside Chicago, but I ran away to Los Angeles pretty young. Its name was still Los Angeles back then, not just L.A. I was a street kid. I hustled, I mugged old ladies and broke into cars and apartments. I was hungry, I was dirty, I was scared all the time, and I was stoned most of the time. It's amazing I still have a brain left, or that I'm alive at all. Most of the kids I knew back then aren't. At one time I thought seriously about male prostitution. If I'd done that I'd be an AIDS statistic today."

Thumb asked, "What about your folks?"

"They looked for me. They registered me with some national search service. Once I saw my picture on a milk carton, while I was sleeping in a dumpster."

"Why did you run away?"

Rory frowned. "My folks were really conscientious. It was painful to watch them, they were so conscientious. Sometimes when I'd been bad, I'd hear them talking on and on, trying to figure out what kind of discipline wouldn't leave me emotionally scarred. I think the tension of listening to those discussions scarred me emotionally.

"And of course they both had their careers, so they were big on quality time. You know what I think of quality time?"

"What?"

"I think if you really believe it doesn't matter how much time you spend with your kids, just so long as it's quality time, then you shouldn't worry about letting them stay up past midnight every night either—just as long as the sleep they do get is quality sleep."

The Hands of God laughed.

"Then there was the marching. My folks were very sincere environmental activists. And one day they had

me marching along with them carrying a little sign
they'd made for me that said, 'I Want To Grow Up,'
and suddenly I realized what that sign meant, and
the next day I hopped a bus to California."

"Then you came to yourself in the far country, like
the Prodigal Son?"

"Not exactly." The fellow in the red mask was
bothering Rory. He was scratching harder than ever.
Watching him made Rory want to scratch too.

"No, the fact is I kind of liked it on the street.
It was like skating near the edge. I cast no thought
upon the morrow.

"No, what happened first was that I met a girl. She
was older than me—about eighteen, I guess. It's hard
to tell in that world. She used cocaine, but she was
young and pretty enough to turn tricks for good
money, and somehow she managed to keep independent. She took me into her apartment—a little bitty
place in a building that went back a couple earth-
quakes. She probably saved my life, because if it
hadn't been for her I probably would have gone into
prostitution myself. Her name was Heather, or at least
that's what she told me. She was always glad to see
me when she came home, and she fed me—her idea
of a meal might be jellybeans on a taco shell or
peanut butter and cabbage sandwiches—and I loved
her. She didn't make demands. It's funny, because if
you asked me what she was like I couldn't tell you.
She never gave an opinion about anything that I can
remember. I wish I knew what had happened to her
in her past. I wish I could have told her what I know
now."

Rory paused and glanced at the scratcher. The man
looked frantic, and Rory wished he'd take the mask
off or leave the room or something before blood
started coming.

Who were these guys anyway? Ski masks, for pete's

sake. They could be first cousins to the Klan, or frat boys down from the Cities to embarrass a fanatic.

"You want a soda or something?" Thumb asked. Rory said thanks, and felt a little more comfortable. He now knew that Thumb was not a Minnesotan. Minnesotans say "pop"—a soda to them is a fountain drink with ice cream. Somebody got a can from a cooler and handed it to him. He said thanks again and drank.

"So what happened?" Thumb asked.

"When I say I loved Heather, I don't mean we were regular lovers. Okay, she took me to bed sometimes, but more like a stuffed animal than a man.

"But Rowan ended that.

"In that world, there's a whole different power structure. It's not exactly organized crime, although some of them are into that too. But they might just as easily be city councilmen or postgrad students in the straight world. On the street, though, they're the system.

"There was a guy called Rowan. I never heard him called anything else. He had a lot of juice. He owned some of the police, and he smuggled drugs and ran prostitutes. He scared people—bad. They'd look around before mentioning his name. Some people said he was a warlock. And not the kind who mixes herbal potions and chants to Mother Earth. I mean the kind you hear about in stories—the kind who sticks pins in dolls, or turns into a wolf, or eats babies. Rowan got lots of respect.

"I remember when a little Puerto Rican kid I knew just stopped showing up one day. I asked around and they said, 'He got Rowan mad.' End of story.

"Anyway, somehow Rowan met Heather, and he liked her, and that was it for her independence.

"That's anarchy. I ran into some prof from the college once, and he told me he was an anarchist, and I said, 'Brother, you don't know what you're talking about.' You know what anarchy is? That's where the meanest, baddest headbuster gets whatever he wants. You know who were two of the all-time great anarchists? Hitler and Stalin.

"I'm getting off the story. One day Heather came back to the apartment with two bodybuilders in warm-up suits. She looked at me and said, 'Sorry, Sweetface, the ride's over,' and she packed her toothbrush and they left. She had the saddest look on her face."

"What did you do?"

"What do you do when you're fourteen years old and in love for the first time? You make a fool of yourself and get people hurt.

"A junkie who was too far gone to know what he was saying told me where Rowan's ranch was. I cleaned up the best I could and hitched up the Coastal Highway. I lived for a week in the woods on the ranch, watching the house. I was used to scrounging. The garbage was good.

"It was quite a place. Stables, vineyards, swimming pool, tennis courts, a private marina. The house was a big redwood thing, poking out over the ocean, hundreds of feet up—the kind of place that slides into the sea when the rains get heavy.

"I watched what went on. During the day there was lots of business, with heavy hitters in big cars coming and going, and Rowan's bodybuilders patrolling with guns. At night they held ceremonies. I suppose that was the witchcraft part, but it looked like plain orgies to me. Sometimes I spotted Heather through the windows. I couldn't come up with a plan to get her out of there. It was the first time I'd been clean in months, and I spent a lot of time just shivering.

"One night a couple of the bodybuilders caught

me going through the garbage. They pulled automatic pistols and locked me in a weight room for the night.

"Next morning they marched me out to the sun deck where Rowan was having his breakfast. He was sitting at an umbrella table in a bathrobe, and there were lots of men and women at tables all around, mostly wearing swimsuits. Heather was at his table, in a bikini, and she acted like she didn't see me. It was a beautiful morning. You could see for miles and miles out on the ocean.

"I can't say how old Rowan was. He looked like he'd reached forty, then stopped, maybe a hundred years ago. He had black eyes, colder than rain in March.

"He said, 'I believe this is your pet, Heather.' She just nodded, not looking at him or me or anybody. Her face was white as cocaine.

"He said to me, 'You've invaded my sanctuary, little urchin. That's not permitted. You understand what I'm saying, little urchin? You understand who I am? Heather, stand up.' She did. She looked beautiful in that morning light, with her blonde hair moving a little in the breeze, and the sky and sea beyond, but it was like a horror movie. Rowan stood up and slapped her face. Then he pointed out to sea.

"Heather walked to the railing, and climbed over, and jumped.

"I screamed and struggled, but the musclemen held me.

"Rowan came close to me and held my face with one hand and shook it back and forth until I stopped crying. He said, 'You go back to your gutter, little urchin, and you tell them what you saw. You tell them that Rowan is the Devil—Satan himself—and that you play like I say or you don't play at all. Remember to be afraid.' Then he let me go, and the musclemen carried me off and stuffed me in the trunk of a car, and a few hours later they dumped me on a sidewalk in L.A.

"I remembered to be afraid. I snatched a purse and got enough money for a bus ticket to Fort Worth. A soup kitchen preacher led me to Jesus, and I never looked back. Or wanted to."

"What a terrible thing for a kid to have to go through," said Thumb.

"I can't stand it!" the red ski mask cried, and he bolted for the bathroom. Thumb got up to follow him inside.

Rory heard a voice saying, "I told you I'm allergic to wool!"

"I told the guy polyester," Thumb's voice said.

"Look at my face! I look like a piece of steak!"

"Well, try splashing some water on it. We'll pray about it later." Thumb came out and looked at Rory. "I guess the masks weren't such a good idea."

"You really need them?" Rory asked.

Thumb sat down. "We're not from around here," he said.

"I figured that."

Thumb took a deep breath. "What would you say if somebody asked you, 'Why doesn't God come down and stop all the bad things in the world?' "

"I don't know. You can't have miracles going all the time. It would be . . . a kind of anarchy."

Thumb nodded. "That's pretty good. But there's another answer. God *is* in the world, and He's working all the time. Through His Body. You know what His Body is?"

"The church."

"That's right. All real Christians. *'Now ye are the body of Christ, and members in particular.'* 1 Corinthians 12:27. The Bible says we're all parts of Christ's Body: eyes, ears, feet—and hands—and Christ is the Head."

"And you're the hands?"

"We are. Not the only hands He's got, of course. There's all kinds of hands—comforting hands, healing hands, building hands. We're the hands that bear the sword."

"I thought Caesar bore the sword."

"Christ also said that he who has no sword should sell his cloak and buy one. Besides, our Caesar's no help.

"Do you believe in Evil, Rory? Not just sad, mistaken people, but foul, hellish wickedness in the world that's got to be stamped out?"

"Yeah, I do. I've seen it."

"That's our calling. We stamp it out. We fight Evil head on. It's not fun, and it can be pretty ugly, and a lot of people just wouldn't understand. That's why we have to work in secret. Someday everything done in secret will be shouted from the rooftops, Luke 12:3, and then everybody'll understand; but for now we've got to keep our light under a bushel."

"And what is it you do, exactly?"

"I'm not sure you're ready for that knowledge, Brother Rory."

"Well, what brought you to Epsom?"

"Things are beginning to happen here. We've had a Word of Knowledge on it, and we know it to be true. You know what a Word of Knowledge is?"

"I guess so."

"You've heard of the Way of the Old Wisdom?"

"That group on the old Tysness farm, out by Troll Valley. The girl who inherited it gave it to her cult."

"Right. Well W.O.W. is nothing but a witch cult. They're Satan worshipers, although they probably wouldn't admit it. Now who's gonna protect this community from the infection of these people?"

"You?"

"That's right."

"But you won't say how."
"We can give you a demonstration."

There were no ugly smells in the wolf's world.

There were bad smells—smells of things that mustn't be eaten—and danger smells, like bear and man. Especially man. But there were no *ugly* smells. Smells brought precious information, keeping the wolf healthy, keeping it far from danger, deep in the northern woods where the hunting was best and the men fewest.

Its world was an ecstatic symphony of smells, fluent of news—around on the breeze, down from the sky, up from the earth. The wolf could see, but paid little attention to sight. Vision was too colorless.

The wolf barely knew it was hungry, for hunger is a wolf's way of life. It had forgotten losing its place as head of the pack, being bloodied and run off, yipping, by a young rival. It felt vaguely its loneliness, an incomprehensible thing without a smell.

But hunting alone was hard. And the wolf was slower than it had once been. It had not eaten in more than a week.

All wolves know that beasts easily killed live to the south.

But to the south the man-smell grows stronger.

The wolf was moving south.

There was a wind that blew at its back. Somehow the wolf could not turn its face to that wind.

And there was a smell, somewhere, on that wind too. It was a new smell, but once sniffed not forgotten. It rode deep up inside the doggy brain, entering a chamber till now unreached. It was a new thing—almost as if the wolf were the first poet of its race.

And the song of the smell told of the meal of a lifetime, waiting somewhere to the south.

"This isn't the W.O.W. farm," said Rory as Thumb stopped his rented Chevrolet at the end of a long country driveway. The house windows shone like tesserae of gold leaf.

"No, this house belongs to a young woman named Leslie Prill."

"What's she have to do with us?"

"She's a witch."

"Yeah, I heard there was a witch living somewhere out here. She's pretty quiet about it though. Just fortune telling and spiritual healing, psychic readings, that sort of thing."

"Typhoid Mary was an ordinary, middle-aged woman who worked as a cook. But she carried a germ that killed people."

"Hey, I'm not defending witchcraft. I just don't understand why we're here."

"Why don't you walk up to the house and talk to the lady, Rory?"

"What?"

"Talk to the lady."

"What about?"

"Tell her about Jesus."

"I just walk up to her door at two o'clock in the morning and witness to her?"

" *'Be urgent in season and out of season.'* 2 Timothy 4:2. It's always good practice, and you'll learn something."

Rory took a deep breath and got out of the car. It took him a couple minutes to walk up the driveway, past the mailbox and the windbreak pines and some bare young mountain ash trees. All the lights were on in the little house. Rory knocked on the door.

A handsome young woman answered it. Her brown hair was cut in a shag and she had very soft brown eyes. She didn't seem surprised to see him.

"I'll do you a free reading if you'll spend the night," she said. She seemed a little unfocused.

"I—I don't—"

"Look friend, I'm having a bad night. If you want bed, we'll go to bed. You want to talk, we'll talk. But I can't be alone. There's reasons. Please."

It was the voice of a child locked in a closet.

"I can't stay the night," said Rory. "But I'd like to talk."

"Sure. Come on in. Twenty bucks for a reading, thirty for the cards. Horoscopes are a hundred and fifty, and I need a week to cast them right." She led him through a little porch into the linoleumed kitchen. The tiles were worn but clean, like the appliances. She leaned against the sink and faced him, arms folded.

Rory unbuttoned his jacket, and her eyes fell on the bronze cross that hung from his neck.

"You didn't come for a reading," she said.

"No."

"People who wear big crosses like that don't ask for readings. Little jewelry crosses, yeah, but not big ones like that. You want to talk to me about my soul."

"People with crosses do that often?" She hadn't asked him to sit, so Rory leaned against a counter.

"Now and then. You want me to open my heart to the love of Jesus so I can become the kind of sweet gentle Christian who burns people like me at the stake."

"I haven't burned anybody at the stake all week."

"Cute. 'I was never a Nazi, I just voted for Hitler.' "

"And witches never judge anybody."

She looked at him and shook her head. "Sorry. I don't even know you. But that's just it, you see? You don't know me either. To you I'm just the Wicked Witch of the West. A target you shoot holy words at. You'll say your little speech, and then you've done your work for God, and if I don't buy it, too bad, off to Hell. But you don't listen. You don't care what I care about. You don't care how I feel."

"How do you feel?"

"I'm scared!" She shivered visibly. "Everything's turning around—I set the stones rolling, and now they're rolling back at me, and I don't know why!"

"Stones? What do you mean?"

"Stones! Rocks! You roll them out of the way to build a road, or plant a garden. Or you pile them up to build a house. But if they roll back down on you they crush you."

"You're talking about spirits? The powers in heavenly places?"

"Forces. Fate. Patterns. The Mother Goddess. The vitality of the earth, and growing things. I love them all. I served them with love, and now they're crushing me. I can feel it coming, and I don't know why!"

Rory said, "How can I say it so it doesn't sound like preaching? There's a Power greater than those powers, Leslie. A . . . rock that doesn't roll. He loves you, and He'll never turn His back on you. He'll protect you and He'll help you, if you let Him."

"*Him!*" she spat back, hugging herself. "It's always a Him, isn't it? Father and Son—no mother, no daughter, no goddess! Your heaven's like some private men's club, and if they let me in, it would probably be to do the dusting. You can't stand to leave anything for us—that's why you burn us! You've perverted love, and you've polluted Mother Earth, and you've killed everything gentle and kind in the human heart, and when anybody—especially a woman—has the guts to use the powers of the earth to relieve pain, you burn them! Burn at the stake! Burn in Hell! Burn, burn, burn, burn . . ."

Rory walked toward her, but she moved away from him and picked up a knife from the draining rack.

"Get out of my house!" she cried, tears running down her cheeks, knife pointed. "You're no comfort— you're just another slap in the face I don't need tonight! Take your bloody cross and your bloody Bible and your fire, and get out!"

"Jesus loves you, Leslie."

She told him what he could do with his Jesus.

"I'll pray for you."

"Do I have to call a cop?"

Rory went out.

He walked down the driveway, hands in his jacket pockets, shaking his head, praying as he'd promised.

The explosion's force knocked him on his face.

When he opened his eyes he could see his own shadow on the gravel, etched sharp as broken glass.

He rolled to look back. The little house was a torch, its flames clawing at heaven. The nearest trees flared like tissue paper.

"Leslie!" Rory ran back. He couldn't get within a hundred feet.

He ran to Thumb's car.

"We've got to get to a phone!" he said, jumping in.

"Right," said Thumb, and he started the motor. "We can't let a thing like this spread."

They raced to the next farm where Rory roused the farmer and his wife, and the call was made.

Then they drove back toward town.

Rory sat silent for a while. After a few minutes he said, "You blew up the house, didn't you?"

"It's possible."

"What does that mean? You admit it?"

"I don't admit a thing, Rory. There's all kinds of ways God accomplishes His Will. Fire from Heaven has fallen before. Maybe that's what happened tonight."

"But more likely your friends planted some kind of charge—maybe even while I was in there talking."

"Could be. Would it make that much difference?"

"Of course it makes a difference!"

"Think about it, Rory. God sent down fire on Sodom and Gomorrah. Women and children died. God didn't send fire to destroy the Canaanites. He told His people to do the job. He said to kill them all—men, women and children. Equally just. Not pretty. Not nice. But it had to be done."

Rory listened in horror. *This guy is crazy. I'm in a car with a psychopath. So how come he sounds so reasonable?*

"Because what was growing up in Canaan had to be killed," Thumb was saying. "Canaan—the land that became Israel—it's the place where religions are born. Jews, Christians, Moslems, we all look to the God of the Hebrews. But suppose the Canaanites had won. Suppose their gods had been the ones three great religions worship?

"They sacrificed their children, Rory! They were killing their kids long before the Hebrews did. Can you imagine if Mohammed had believed in gods like that? You think the world's in a mess now?

"Stopping it was a brutal business. It hasn't gotten any nicer. And it isn't right that the Lord's church should be mixed up in it. So we—the Hands of God—we carry out the garbage. Prayerfully, humbly, we do the smelly work. That's our calling. We protect the world, and we protect the church.

"So before you make any decisions, Rory, and before you judge us, I want you to think. Because there's a place for you in the Hands of God if you feel the call."

Rory looked at him. "Why me?"

"Let's say the Lord led us to you."

Rory looked out the window. He'd lost his hat—back at the farm he supposed. He wanted to be out of the car, out of the state—the old instincts that had sent him running from Chicago and Los Angeles were still there. *The man was making sense. But he couldn't be right! Say something nutty, Thumb—make this easier!*

"I liked her," Rory said. "We didn't have much in common, but I liked her. I think we could have talked; maybe I could have answered some of her questions. You practically admit you . . . killed her. And you expect me to join you?"

Thumb said, "You think Moses liked it, when they killed the Canaanites? You think Joshua was having a good time? I think it turned their guts. But the Lord commanded it. That's the only excuse in the world for doing it. You know the Lord doesn't command it lightly."

"How do you know He commanded it at all?"

"You're not ready for that knowledge, Rory. You've got to have faith enough to join us before you can understand it. We've saved lives tonight. You've got to believe that. And she felt no pain. It was over before she knew it. What she's feeling where she is now is another matter."

"I could go to the police."

"We wouldn't stop you. What could you tell them? A conspiracy in ski masks? I promise you there won't be a shred of evidence, except maybe somebody's cowboy hat."

Rory jerked in his seat.

"You'd be surprised at the things the Hands of God have done over the years, and nobody the wiser," Thumb continued. "Things you've heard about all your life. Things they told you about in school. If you read our secret chronicles, you'd have to unlearn half your history lessons."

They pulled into the motel parking lot. They could hear the siren of the Volunteer Fire Department's hook and ladder.

"How many of you are there?" Rory asked.

"You wouldn't believe me if I told you."

Rory reached for the door handle, then paused.

"You said the Canaanites had to be destroyed because they were sacrificing children."

"That's right. That's the great Abomination, the thing the Lord will never tolerate."

"I don't think Leslie was going to kill any children."

Thumb looked at his hands, then stared out the windshield.

"It's a good thing we called the Fire Department," he said softly. "A fire like that could have spread. No telling who could have gotten hurt."

Rory looked at the man, unreadable as a mummy in his ski mask. He got out of the car.

"I'll think about it," he said. "But don't hold your breath."

"Think about this, Rory. Where do you think your friend Rowan came from? Everything starts as a baby."

Rory closed the door and walked to his own car.

Chapter IV

The rising north wind whipped the flames, but the firemen drowned them at last. The crowd of neighbors who had gotten out of bed to watch headed home around 3:00 A.M. as the Volunteer Fire Department rolled up its hoses and stowed its gear. By four everybody was gone, and the old barn and sheds, saved only out of principle, stared at the place where the house had been like friends at a surprise wake.

Their rememberings were disturbed after a half an hour, by an intruder.

He was a tall, bearded man dressed in a long black cloak and a wide black hat. He carried a heavy staff.

He walked to the ruins, poked the ash with the staff.

"A good burning," he whispered, not in English.

He gave a short whistle, and the country silence, which is no silence at all, became truly still. He whistled again, a tune now—a minor melody with evergreens and women's eyes in it.

Rabbits, one, two, three, came hesitatingly from the cover of the trees. They hopped and paused, doubtful. But they came.

They crouched, trembling violently, ears back, in a circle around the intruder. Laying his staff aside he knelt and passed a long hand down the back of the largest buck.

Swiftly he caught it up and wrung its head off. As it jerked in his hands, the other rabbits loped away.

He took up a charred board, drew a knife from somewhere, and made a few carvings in the wood. He dipped a finger in the rabbit's blood and stained where he had carved. He set the board down in front of him.

Then he began to sing in deep, rolling tones, turning to the four points of the compass, the dead rabbit held high in both hands. His voice grew louder, but no one who might have heard would have understood the words.

The wind freshened.

He tossed the rabbit into the center of the ruins. It landed in the wet ashes with a slap.

"Come now," he whispered.

And Leslie Prill was there, naked and ashamed among the cinders.

"What's happened?" she cried. "Who are you?"

"You are dead, and I am your master."

"Dead? No. I can't—I was—I was talking to someone and—and—"

"And they burned you, witch, as you feared."

"No! No, I don't remember—anything—"

"That is your final good fortune. You must go soon the way you chose long since. But first you will answer me."

"Answer what?"

"Tell me what shall be! You have the gift. You had it always, in a weak and distracted way; now the distractions are gone. You see plainly. Tell me what you see!"

"It was you! It was you I saw coming! Death and violence and burning, they come with you, like the Wild Hunt, and the wolves and the wind. You've come to meet the comet!"

"Tell me something I don't already know!"

"The comet is the Great Circle—the worm that devours its tail. It passes and returns, and what was may be again."

"Yes! Yes!"

"The Sword is nearby. Even now it is being forged."

"I must have the Sword, but to say it is here tells me nothing. I knew it must be. It's the Spear I must know about! Tell me how I'll get the Spear!"

"Three times you've tried to use the Sword, and three times you have failed. It does not show itself yet, and it can be bent. But if it were easily bent, it would not be the Sword."

There is no man in the world so true as a sword;
And no sword is wholly true.

"What words are those?"

"The words of Sigfod Oski, the poet. I can bend the Sword."

"Bend it, and you will have the Spear. If you cannot, the Spear will have you."

"What more?"

"Nothing more. What I see I've told."

"I know little more than before I called you up!"

"Be grateful you don't know less. I must go."

"Stay, witch! Will I win? Tell me where the road leads!"

"It leads a hundred ways. It leads nowhere. I haven't time to tell the combinations. But this I see:

the Wolf waits at the end. Whatever way you take, it leads at last to the Wolf."

"I knew that as well," the intruder rumbled, but the dead woman was gone, on her own journey—a flight as high as she could rise on her own lifting.

Chapter V

Thor's Day

"The heart of modern poetry is, at least negatively, very like the heart of the barbarian kind. It is an intriguing thought: we have sacked Rome yet again!

Why did the Viking chief revere his poet so? If I may say it—please do not misunderstand—the chief needed his skald as he needed his wife, and for much the same reason.

Listen: when we speak of Siegfried, or Arthur, we speak only tangentially of the heroes themselves. We cannot meet or touch them, can but guess what manner of men they were.

But, being heroes, they shot out tales, and

*tales are a kind of seed. They lodge in the
poet's mind as in a woman's womb, and when
the poet has completed his labor he brings
forth the* saga. *The saga is neither the hero
nor the poet, but their mutual child, a child
who may live forever, or generate eternal
progeny of his own—think how Svipdag's saga
lives on even today in the legend of William
Tell! The saga is all that remains of the hero,
a greater monument than any son. . . .*

Martell closed the cover of *Hrafnsmál*, Sigfod Oski's
best known work. He had picked it up idly and
opened it to the preface while trying to make up his
mind to tackle the student papers on his desk. He
told himself he ought to brush up on his Oski, since
he'd be hearing him read tonight.

His hand hurt, but sleep had helped, and he could
write if he moved carefully. No reason not to work
if he made up his mind to it. But his mind was
elsewhere.

He had dreamed of heroism as a boy, poring over
every book he could find in the school library that
had anything to do with Vikings.

He had fantasized himself born in that age, tall and
strong and grimly brave. He would have been better than the historical Vikings of course. He wouldn't
have robbed, or burned, or taken slaves, or raped;
he wasn't sure at that age what rape was, but he was
sure it was something he wouldn't have done. He
would have fought only for freedom and justice, and
the cargoes of booty he brought home in his sleek
ship would have been taken from evil kings and
oppressors.

He had loved the Viking gods, even for a short
time contemplating praying to them: Thor, strongest
and kindest, though far from the brightest. Tyr, the
swordsman who broke his oath to bind the monster

wolf Fenris, then bravely let the beast bite his hand off in recompense. Frey, the fertility god whose special attributes were not explained in books written for children. And Loki the trickster, father of doom yet blood brother to the greatest of them all— Odin the Allfather. Odin, dark and mysterious, Odin the wanderer, Odin the magician, shape changer, deceiver, doomed to be eaten by the wolf Fenris, Loki's child, on the Last Day; a chieftain who gave great gifts when he pleased but promised nothing. Tragic gods, limited gods, beautiful gods. Gods a man could die for, and with, in a simpler time.

The memories brought that cold regret that haunts every reflective man—the conviction that somehow, somewhere, he has missed the one path that would have led to his proper destiny, a consummation lost now forever. All that remains is the disappointment of friends and the mockery of enemies. *Too late*.

His truth-sickness twisted his gut and bent him over in his chair. *Lie*.

What's happening to me?

When he'd gotten his composure he sat with his elbows on the desktop. He picked his letter opener out of his pencil mug. The opener was a miniature replica of a Viking sword, a souvenir of Oslo. A couple years back he'd snapped its blade prying open a carton. He thought there were two things he could do with it: either locate a miniature anvil and make an Excalibur of it, or find someone to weld it together for him.

A picture from boyhood came to him.

His father had stood in the old tool shed, masked like a knight, lighting a welding torch, the gray rod in its grip burning whiter than white at the end.

"Don't look at it," his father had said.

The welding machine hummed a hair-standing note, and the smell of sulphur filled his nose as he watched the shadows move on the jars and cans of nails and bolts lined up on the shelves over the bench.

Afterwards, while the wagon hitch cooled, he had asked, "How does it work?"

"The welding?"

"Yeah."

"All metals want to weld when they meet," his father had said, pulling off his gloves. "The reason they don't is the impurities on the surface. The welding torch burns the impurities away, melts the metal, and it just runs together. Simple."

The toolshed had been bulldozed and plowed over years ago, and an agribusiness owned the farm. Martell ached for a place and a time lost almost without evidence. How strong his father had been! But then he had had to be, to bear the sadness that had come to stay. . . .

Maybe I should have stayed on the farm, he thought. *Maybe I owed them that—*

His stomach lurched again. It was another lie, self-pity.

What's happening to me?

He thought of last night, of the young man's demand, his own refusal. *I can't lie*, he thought. *Anybody can lie. NOT lying is the problem for normal people.*

Elaine had called him a snob. She said he purposely sought out unpopular positions.

No, he wouldn't think about Elaine.

For distraction he turned to the essays. The first one he opened began, "I think Charlemagne was one of the greatest Frenchmen in history . . ."

Someone knocked at the office door. He put the paper down without regret and said, "Come in."

His visitor was a student, a girl named Cindy Halstrom. Cindy was a good student, an overweight girl with limp dark hair and a weak chin. She was carrying books and wearing a Norwegian sweater.

He asked her to sit down and she said, "I want to talk to you about Scandinavian History."

She was lying.

"Are you all right, Mr. Martell?" Martell made an effort to relax his face.

"It's nothing. What were you saying?"

"I've been having some trouble with Scandinavian History."

"As I recall you've been doing pretty well, Cindy."

"I'm used to doing better. I've almost always been a 4.0 student. After all, I can't depend on my looks." She shifted her small blue eyes and laughed a little false laugh.

Martell looked away too. He would have known what was happening even without the internal lie detector. It was never fun, and sometimes it got nasty. And the timing couldn't have been worse.

His glance fell on the books Cindy had set on his desk. The top one was one of the required texts for Women's Studies 201—*The Myth of Heterosexual Reproduction and Other Feminist Classics*. It seemed so sincere it was soothing. Underneath was another title, this one for a psychology course: *The Psychopathology of Heroism*.

"I've been having trouble concentrating," Cindy said. "There've been things on my mind."

"We all have times like that."

"I've been—something's been bothering me. I guess I'm in love, you know? Only I know I don't have any chance, and it's—it's kind of hard."

His experience in these situations had given him a long list of things not to say. His list of things he ought to say had no items on it.

There was a minute of silence. Rats could be heard scuttering in the walls.

Cindy spoke again. "I've been talking with a lot of my friends—well, not a lot, I don't have a lot of friends—and everybody's glad you didn't get into any trouble over Julie Anderson. Everybody knows she's a slut."

"I suppose she's . . . unhappy, like so many people. But I appreciate your confidence."

"I just want you to know that a lot of people always believed in you. You're—you're very special to us."

"Thank you." *Here it comes.*

"Mr. Martell, what do you do when you're in love—really in love—with somebody you can't get near? When you think about them all day long, and lie awake thinking about them at night, and you can't study or even see straight?"

Martell breathed deeply, avoiding her eyes. "I can tell you some things that are true, but they won't help," he said carefully. "First of all, you *will* get over it."

"I've heard you carried a torch for a woman for more than ten years."

Who had told that story?

"I'm . . . a lot older than you." *What was that supposed to mean?* "But even I got over my first love."

"I know I'm not pretty." Cindy left the sentence hanging between them, suspended eight inches above the desk top.

Martell might have comforted her with a lie.

She tried again. "I've never been able to think of myself as attractive."

Martell said nothing. He notice that his ankles had crossed themselves, and were hurting each other.

"Do you think—would it be possible—could somebody like you, maybe, ever love somebody like me?"

"Cindy—"

"You think I'm ugly, don't you?"

"I wouldn't call you that—"

"But you wouldn't call me pretty?"

Again he had nothing to say.

She broke into tears.

"I can't lie to you, Cindy. I respect you too much to tell you things you know aren't true just to make you feel better."

Stupid thing to say. She went on crying.

"I'd be playing games with you—treating you like a child. I don't think you're a child. I think you're a strong, capable young woman—stronger than you know—strong enough to deal with real life.

"If you feel you've got to be pretty to live, I don't know what to tell you. You don't have to be pretty to be loved. And you don't have to be pretty to me to be pretty to somebody—probably somebody a lot better than me. But you can't escape your own life. You've got to live it and no other."

"It's a lousy life." Cindy's head was bowed, her hands twisted in her lap. "What do they say? 'Blessed are those who expect nothing, for they shall never be disappointed'?"

Martell looked up sharply. "I deny that," he said. "I don't claim to know the meaning of life, but I know it's not that. The universe is not against people who hope and dream. Dreamers sometimes win and they sometimes lose, but the ones who don't dream *never* win. I don't know if you're a Christian or not. I'm not, but that's one thing I buy in Christian theology. No cautious bargaining with life, asking nothing and expecting nothing. It's a matter of giving up everything to win everything, for God and Man both. I can't say I live that way, but I feel the truth of it."

His animation gave her the chance to catch and hold his eye.

"It's easy to talk," she said.

"A lot easier than living. The story you heard was true. There's a woman who walked out of my life, and I think about her every day. I wanted to die at first, and I hated her, and I hated myself. But I lived, Cindy. I chose to live with what I couldn't change, and make the best of the life I had. I found I could live with loneliness, with being different from everybody around me. I learned to put my solitude to use. I think it's worthwhile. I'm not sorry to be alive."

Cindy stood up and collected her books. "I'm sorry I bothered you with something so stupid—"

"I didn't say—"

"Just one thing, Mr. Martell. Would you have turned me down if I looked like Julie Anderson?" She fled, leaving a wake of misery behind.

Martell looked at the door. He felt guilty, but he wasn't worried about her. The Supreme Court's *Mortman v. Main* decision had guaranteed suicide as a constitutional right, and the attrition among teenagers had become frightening, but he didn't think Cindy would go that route. She had brains and courage. She'd survive.

Sure she would.

He called her House Mother to ask her to keep an eye on the girl. He could hear the woman's voice constrict when he said his name, as if she'd smelled something too long in the back of the refrigerator. *Not everybody believes in me*, he thought.

He had no appetite at lunchtime so he walked to the library. On the way he met the Dean of Instruction. He stopped her.

"Oh, hello, Carl." The Dean was a dark-haired, compact woman with thick glasses. "How's the hand?"

"I'll live. Look, I need to know what happened at the meeting last night."

"You were vindicated. What more can I say?"

"Then Julie admitted she was lying? Did she say why?"

The Dean looked away. "That's . . . privileged information, I'm afraid."

"But I'm concerned here! I was accused without warning, now I'm off the hook the same way. I need to make some kind of sense out of the whole thing."

The Dean laughed and laid a hand on Martell's arm. "Carl, you're a romantic. This is the real world. Things never make sense. You're free and clear—don't push it." She walked away.

"You could make money off this," said Roy Corson that afternoon in Martell's office, perched in his usual place on the corner of the desk.

Martell had been explaining why he hadn't let him cover for him; about his inability to lie. "Does it sound pathological to you?" he asked. "Do you think I need professional help?" He didn't say he could detect lies in other people. It was comforting to know he could still withhold information.

Roy said that, in Martell's shoes, he would go directly to a psychiatrist, "Do not pass GO, do not collect two hundred dollars.

"You could make money off this. You could write a book with the shrink as collaborator. You scribble pretty well for a historian. Call it *The George Washington Syndrome*. In six weeks half the country would think they had it." Like most English professors Roy was always on the lookout for a bestseller.

"Does that mean you think I'm crazy or not?"

"*Of course* you're crazy, Carl. Celibacy mixed with religion is a worse combination than booze and pills. Any day now you'll be letting that one-legged preacher dunk you in a swimming pool."

"He's a Lutheran, Roy. They don't do rebaptisms.

You teach at a Lutheran school, you ought to know that."

"Not my department. And don't change the subject. You know what your problem is, and you know Dr. Corson's prescription."

"Yes."

"You need to get laid. Soon and often. Wanton and superficial women, and never the same one twice. Just remember to use protection."

"Crazy sex isn't what I'm looking for, Roy."

"That's because you've crammed your head full of ideals. Believe me—between the sheets, love and crazy sex are all the same thing. Especially if you're plastered, which I also recommend highly."

Martell's usual response was, "I have neither the courage nor the stamina." Today he found himself saying, "I don't think I could treat a woman that way."

Roy looked as if he'd been slapped. Harassment suits and political incorrectness accusations in the departments had made all educators a little paranoid. Trust was carefully given and quick to evaporate.

"I'm sorry," Martell rushed to say. "I didn't mean to preach. It's this George Washington thing—it plays hell with my sense of humor. I'm afraid I won't be invited to many parties."

"I guess not." Martell thought he glimpsed something behind Roy's eyes, some native of a place deeper than a misunderstanding between friends, but he couldn't be sure.

They shared a few moments of silence, listening to the ever-present rats at play.

"You're coming to the Oski shindig tonight, I suppose," Roy said at last.

"Oh sure." Martell was happy to change the subject. "I'm a fan. I wouldn't miss it."

"I wouldn't call myself a fan," said Roy. "All this

Volsungs and Valkyries business leaves me pretty cold. But Oski's hot stuff, especially in a small pond like this. I know I'm mixing my metaphors, you stick to history. Anyway, I'd be a fool to miss the chance to kiss all those important backsides."

"I'll see you there then." Martell looked at his watch. "Almost showtime."

Going out, Roy turned back at the door.

"Are you really falling for this Jesus business?" he asked. "I mean, everybody's got a right to be an idiot in their own way, but some ways are more pleasant than others for your peer group."

"I don't know, Roy. That's the truth. Let's say I'm sure I believe in something. I believe life is good. For all the garbage in the world, I'd say the flowers are worth at least as much as the garbage. And I think the people who look at the flowers are better equipped to survive than the ones who only look at the garbage."

"I could argue that point."

"It seems as if every time I read a book that speaks to me, that's really satisfying and nourishing, it turns out the author has some kind of religious bent. I guess I believe in whatever it is that makes people hope. What do I lose if I'm wrong?"

"My son, you'll find that nine times out of ten the truth will turn out to be whatever turns your stomach worst in this toilet world," said Roy. "And even if you're right, I can't see what it has to do with a Jew on a gallows."

"It gets our attention."

"Flowers and garbage, my friend. In the end they're all the same organic material. All the same." Roy closed the door behind him. Martell wondered what he wasn't saying.

Walking to class he saw Julie Anderson sitting by herself on a bench in front of one of the dorms, wrapped in a long coat. She was wearing stereo head-phones and her eyes were closed.

Martell stood and looked at her. It was important that he go over and speak to her. His class could wait a few minutes.

He went to it anyway.

Chapter VI

When Martell got back to his apartment that afternoon he found his door unlocked. A woman's voice said, "Wipe your feet," as he entered.

He'd forgotten that this was Minna Gunderson's day to clean. He always forgot, though it happened every Thursday.

Minna, the pastor's sister, a large-boned, graying woman, took care of the big house she shared with Harry, and cleaned for others as well. "Just to keep busy," she said. Martell knew they needed the money.

He found her drying a frying pan in the kitchenette. "Dishwashing isn't in your job description," he told her.

"Yes, well it seems like I get started and I don't know where to stop."

Martell wandered into the living room. "I'll never figure out how you manage to get everything clean without moving all these books. You must number them and reassemble them in order, like an archaeologist."

Minna said, "This place is a hog pen," hanging the dish towel up neatly. "You ought to put those books on shelves."

"I don't have shelves enough. I don't have *walls* enough."

"Sometimes I think you enjoy living in a mess."

"Well it's an *intellectual* mess, like Sherlock Holmes' rooms in Baker Street. All my life I've aspired to shabby gentility. And I can honestly say I've read almost all the books."

Minna rubbed a spot on the refrigerator with a washcloth and said, "Maybe if you read less books you'd have more energy to go out and find a nice girl."

"There aren't any girls anymore, Minna, nice or otherwise. They're Femo-American Persons. They're not a sex, they're a political party. If I want politics I can go to Faculty—"

His stomach twisted. *Blast! Can't I even make a joke?*

Minna sighed and shook her cloth out. "You've got an answer for everything, Carl Martell. Maybe you're too smart for your own good. All these books, and you don't know a thing about life."

"You may be right." He was leaning against an armchair, his knees weak.

She hung the cloth beside the dish towel. "Well, I'm done here."

"Hold on a minute—this is my week to pay you, isn't it?"

"I won't say no."

Martell went into his spare bedroom/office and wrote a check.

When he brought it out, Minna was looking around at the walls. "You know, I've always thought there was something missing from this place," she said.

"I know, I know."

"Not *that*. I just noticed. You haven't got a single picture of your family here."

Martell looked at her. "That's right," he said. "Here's your check. Tell Harry I'll pick him up at six."

"The Oski thing, yes."

"We're big fans."

"I've tried to read his poems. They seemed sick to me."

"Few Scandinavian writers have ever been accused of mental health. But Oski's poems are brave and beautiful. Ordinary people can enjoy them, and even the critics don't hold it against him. He's done Christiania a big honor by coming. We'd be ungracious to ignore it."

"I didn't say I didn't understand him. I said I don't like him. You do what you want."

"Thanks for your work, Minna."

"You're welcome, Carl. How's your hand feeling?"

"Cut and stitched. Can I drive you home?"

"No, thanks. I like to walk."

When she was gone he stood before the painting of a Viking on his living room wall, perhaps the most valuable thing he owned. "*Sigfod Oski*. Thank God I'm out of trouble and free to enjoy this."

Minna found her brother in the kitchen, making a turkey sandwich and a mess. "Carl said he'd pick you up at six," she told him as she wiped the counter in front of him.

"I can clean up after myself," Harry said.

"I'm not a young woman, Harry. I can't wait." She rinsed the cloth and hung it in its place.

"Carl is a nice enough young man," she said, sitting in a kitchen chair. "He needs to get out more."

"He's a man with a sorrow, Minna. He's the kind that doesn't give his heart lightly, and once committed

he sticks. Men and women like that sometimes have
a hard time in this world." He took a bite out of his
sandwich and looked at her. She was straightening the
tablecloth. Its pattern had faded, but it was immacu-
late. "He needs our prayers and our friendship."

"He needs a kick in the pants."

Harry started to say something but took another
bite instead. He thought it was a sad world, and
saddest of all for people who understood things.

Martell sat watching the 24-hour news on television. Strangely, he was enjoying the news. There was
very little outright lying in it, which rather surprised
him, but also very little certainty, except for the man
who did the editorial. He had to hit the MUTE button on the remote when the commercials came on.

The announcer said, *"In a controversial decision,
the Supreme Court today refused to consider a challenge to the DRA, the Definition of Religion Act,
which will secure First Amendment rights only to
members of those religious groups which pass certain
legal tests and properly register with the Federal
Government.*

*"President Trang, who fought hard for the DRA,
made this statement at a specially called news con-
ference—"*

The face of the president appeared on the screen.
*"Today is a watershed in American history. This is
a day that will live in posterity as the moment that
America's precious heritage of religious liberty was
secured for all generations.*

*"Every American has suffered through the terrible
conflicts which have torn our society in the past. Con
men, cults and terrorists have used the First Amendment as a shield by which to prey upon their neighbors, upon the ignorant, upon the old and the
gullible.*

"We could not allow this situation to continue. Yet how could we deal with these challenges while still preserving our heritage of freedom of conscience, a freedom which, I might mention, is especially precious to me.

"The Definition of Religion Act untangles this puzzle, and does it in a way which is uniquely American and scrupulously true to our Constitution and our traditions.

"The answer is essentially very simple: We define religion.

"A broad consensus has been growing in our country as to what constitutes a true religion in the American tradition. Through the DRA, the elements of that consensus enable us to protect and preserve true religious faith.

"What is a genuine religion? A genuine religion teaches openmindedness. A genuine religion allows its followers to find their own moral compass, and accepts and affirms all sincere decisions and lifestyles.

"A genuine religion teaches spirituality. It does not concern itself with matters of this world. It does not get involved in political questions or meddle in government. It makes no claim of historical fact.

"A true religion preaches a universal message. It does not claim to have a corner on truth, but recognizes the equal validity of all opinions and beliefs.

"All true believers, those who share the openminded and generous beliefs outlined in the DRA, are protected by this new law. The sectarians, the fanatics, the bigots and the fundamentalists will lose the constitutional weapon by which they have preyed on their neighbors and perpetrated their violence and hate.

"Because of the courage of Congress, which passed this Act, and the Supreme Court, which has upheld it, every American can look forward to a safer, happier and more spiritual America—"

His phone rang. He set down his cup of coffee and turned the volume down.

"*Hello, is this Mr. Carl Martell?*" A woman's voice. He said it was.

"*My name is Victorious Staff. I'm calling from W.O.W.*"

"Wow?"

"*The Way of the Old Wisdom. You must have heard of us.*"

"Yes, of course."

"*Mr. Martell, we've been told that you have some knowledge of the Viking carvings called runes.*"

"I've given them some study. I'm not an expert."

"*We've found a stone on our property which we believe to be carved in runes. We realize that any claims we make about it are going to be suspect. That's why we'd like to have a scholar's opinion before we speak to the press.*"

"I'm sorry, I can't help you. I'm not a runologist, or an archaeologist either. I'm not at all qualified to judge the sort of thing you seem to be describing, and I wouldn't try."

"*I can assure you that we did not forge this stone.*"

"I'm sure you didn't," said Martell, and he was. At least he was sure the girl speaking to him knew nothing of any hoax. "But somebody almost certainly did. Have you ever heard of the Kensington Runestone?"

"*Somebody mentioned something. . . .*"

"The Kensington Runestone was found in western Minnesota back in the 1880s. It raised a stir then, but all the experts today agree that it's a fraud, and it's a fact that there were a lot of Scandinavians with romantic notions around back then who could have carved the thing. You've probably found a copycat."

"*We're not asking for a judgment, Mr. Martell. We can't even tell whether these carvings are runes or*

*not. We'd like you to tell us that, if that's all you can
do. We promise not to use your name."*

"I'm, uh . . . I'm sorry. I can't be associated with
something like this. It would be professional suicide."

*"Please reconsider. We're just asking you to take
a look. Aren't you just a little curious? About us, if
not about the stone?"*

There was a devious edge to her voice, but Martell
found that in many people. He discounted it. He
didn't expect perfect candor any more than perfect
facial symmetry.

"Can I think about it and call you back?" he asked.

*"I'm sorry. We don't have a phone. I'm calling from
a pay phone at a gas station. I apologize for the short
notice, but I need your answer tonight."*

"You should be selling real estate," he said. "All
right, so when do you want me to come out? It can't
be tonight. I have to go listen to Sigfod Oski."

"Sigmund Ostey? Who's that?"

A counseling session with a depressed teenager had
gone longer than expected, and Harry was dressing
for the evening as quickly as he could, praying as his
fingers fumbled. He'd lost two teenagers this year to
the Happy Endings clinic, plus a woman in her twen-
ties who'd left behind a dumbfounded husband and
a new baby. This on top of the sick and the old who'd
simply lost hope. He used to picket the place when
he could find the time, but the clinics were feder-
ally protected now.

When Rory Buchan appeared at the front door
Minna said, "Well, I suppose you can talk to him, but
he's in a hurry."

"That's okay, Miss Gunderson. I just want to ask
a question and maybe borrow a book." Her look in
response told him he'd be held personally responsible
for any unadvertised delays. He followed her back

through the hall to Harry's bedroom, half the parlor partitioned off to save him climbing stairs.

Harry was standing in front of a full-length mirror, struggling with his clerical collar as if it were the iron variety found in dungeons, when Minna knocked.

"Come in, I'm decent."

"I won't keep you," said Rory when Minna had left them. "I wondered if you had any books I could borrow about the Canaanites."

"The Canaanites?" Harry twisted his torso to look at him.

"Yeah. In the Old Testament. Is something wrong?"

Harry turned back to his reflection. "No, I'm just trying to think what books to recommend. It's a subject that gets ignored a great deal. I ignore it myself, whenever I can."

"Why's that?" Rory perched on the arm of an easy chair.

"Because whenever I come to that part of the Bible, it turns my stomach. Why the interest?"

"Just something somebody said. He has a theory. The whole thing seems weird to me, and I wanted to check the facts."

"Well, let's see." Harry left one end of the white collar tab sticking out and limped to a bookcase. "This might help, and there might be something in this one, and I think there's a chapter in this, but be sure to return it, Rory—it's been out of print since before you were born."

Rory accepted the pile of volumes. "Thanks."

"You'll have to hunt down the material you want— none of these has more than a few pages on the subject. But they might help."

"I'm kind of surprised to hear you say that part of the Bible turns your stomach. I thought you believed the Bible."

Harry leaned against the case. "Of course I believe the Bible," he said. "I don't believe it in the nitpicking way the Fundamentalists do, but the Bible is the most realistic book ever written. Just as some things in life turn my stomach, some things in the Bible turn my stomach. I'd be suspicious if they didn't."

Rory thought about it. "Maybe that solves the whole problem."

Harry lowered himself into the desk chair. "No, not really. When men act brutally, I'm not surprised. But when God acts brutally, and tells His people to act brutally, that shakes the very footings of my life. It's something I struggle with.

"If I were one of the young pastors they're turning out today, it'd be no problem. I'd just say, 'This is one of the many instances when the Old Testament writers didn't know what they were talking about. God never commanded anything of the sort.' That's too far for me to go though, and in any case it doesn't really solve the problem. I have to face it again, in a more terrible fashion, every time a child dies. And they die all the time."

Rory shifted the books under one arm. "Well, maybe I can figure something out. Or maybe my friend's right."

"You'll make news if that's so. What does your friend say?"

"I'd rather study up a little before I talk about it. It's kind of weird."

"That doesn't disqualify it. God moves in weird ways, His wonders to perform."

"Yeah. Well. I'll let you get back to dressing. Thanks for the books. I'll bring them back."

"You always do. That makes you almost unique. Good night, Rory."

"Good night, Pastor. Praise the Lord."

"Amen."

Rory left. As he drove to work, he turned on the news on his car radio.

"*The International Olympic Committee today announced it had come to a compromise agreement with the Worldwide Siblinghood of the Physically Challenged, which has been demanding that all Olympic events be made accessible to the disabled. Under the terms of the agreement, physically challenged athletes will be given compensation points—not to be called handicaps—which will qualify them to win medals in all regular events, although their medals will carry a special logo identifying them as special condition awards.*

"*A representative of WSPC said that the compromise was a step in the right direction, but that the fight will go on. He said, 'We will not rest until all vestiges of ableism are removed from the games, and Olympic medals have nothing whatever to do with strength, speed, agility or coordination.'*

"*In California there was fierce debate today over a proposal in the state legislature which would allow convicted criminals to sue their victims. Under the provisions of the proposed law, if a court determines that a victim showed insufficient vigilance and so enticed the criminal to take advantage of them, they would be liable to pay the convicted criminal damages not in excess of . . .*"

Chapter VII

Carl Martell met Rory coming out of the Gunderson house. They nodded but did not speak; they were not acquainted.

Martell found Harry once more in front of the mirror.

"This simple tab collar ought to be the easiest thing in the world," Harry said through clenched teeth. "I'm grateful I haven't had to tie a necktie since my ordination, but somehow I've managed to turn this thing into a kind of Gordian knot."

"It's part of your charm, Harry," said Martell, sitting in the armchair.

"Well, it's lost on the senior pastor, and she'll be with us tonight."

"And what is the gospel according to the Reverend Ms. Hardanger-Hansen this week?"

"Shamanism, I think. Or sha-personism. She says

the worship of the Mother Goddess is the true voice of God's femininity in history, cruelly suppressed by the patriarchal conspiracy. She hasn't announced plans to sacrifice goats in the sanctuary yet, but I'm expecting it."

Martell frowned. "I can understand the bishop thinking you couldn't carry on as senior pastor after the accident. But where did they get the bright idea of yoking you with somebody like Judith?"

"It was for the good of my soul, of course. She was sent here to expand my horizons and lead me out of the ghetto of orthodoxy. But I often think of that awful joke about Heaven where the punch line is, 'She's not my reward—I'm her punishment.'

"What really troubles me is the Extinctionism, though. That's no fad with her. She sincerely buys the argument that we need to work for the end of the human race. Regulated family size, maximum birth control, maximum abortion; easy access to painless death for all who want out. The steady attrition of humanity. The world returns to a state of nature, the balance returns. That's her idea of Paradise. No more human dreams. No more art or poetry. No faith, hope or love, just an environmental laboratory without scientists. If I'd known at twenty what kind of world I'd be living in today, I think I might have looked for a Happy Ending myself."

"And you wonder why I refuse to join up. In my place, Harry—would you be tempted to convert to Judith Hardanger-Hansen's church?"

His collar subdued at last, Harry sank heavily on the bed. His black shirttail had worked its way out of his trousers, but Martell hadn't the heart to mention it.

"It's my church too, Carl; and lest we forget, it's Jesus Christ's. It may be merged with every other attenuated mainline church and reduced to synod status in the NAPC, but I'll stay with it till they force me out bodily. That's a commitment I made a long time ago."

"I respect that. But thank heaven I don't have any such commitment."

"You ought to try a commitment some time, Carl. Any commitment—just for the experience."

Martell stood up and checked his tie in the mirror. His reflection seemed to him plague-pale. "I haven't enough blood in me, Harry. I'm a snowman."

Harry's eyes met him in reflection. "Nobody really knows what they look like, Carl. Our emotions are too wrapped up in our self-images. To me, you look rather like a king. Not Saint Olaf, of course. Wrong hair color and shape. But Olaf Trygvesson, perhaps. Put on a little muscle and you'd be the perfect Viking."

"A truly incongruous idea. But speaking of Vikings, I had an interesting phone call this evening." He explained about the request from W.O.W.

"A runestone?" asked Harry. "As in Kensington?"

"That's the story."

"Incredible. They must think you're an idiot."

"They may be right. I said I'd take a look at it."

"Oh, my friend! Are you sure you want to do that?"

"Absolutely not. But they promised I wouldn't have to make any judgments, and they wouldn't quote me. What can I say? 'These look like runes—these don't look like runes.' Then I say I have serious reservations and I go home."

"I suppose . . . but it bothers me. Are *they* that stupid, or are they playing some kind of game?"

"There you go. Classic Christian bigotry. Just because they worship in secret, and won't discuss their beliefs, and put guards on their gates, and come up with a copy of a noted 19th Century hoax, you just jump to the conclusion that something funny's going on. Want to tag along?"

"I thought you'd never ask. Of course it seems more in the senior pastor's department. . . ."

The drive to the Campus Center was easy, the climb up the stairs to the banquet hall more difficult. Martell had to help Harry, and it took time. There was a service elevator, but it was out of order. Harry's face was red and his hair and clothing all sideways by the time they reached the top. They paused to let him rest for a moment beneath a public health poster that said:

SYPHILLIS? GONORRHEA? CHLAMYDIA?
BE PROUD OF YOUR
SEXUALLY TRANSMITTED DISEASE!

"Oh dear, she sees me," he whispered a few minutes after they had entered the long, low hall. It was crowded and noisy, and blue with cigarette smoke like all public places nowadays.

"Who?"

"The senior pastor. She has that 'weighed and found wanting' look in her eye. I *do* try, Carl. Joanna used to keep me generally landscaped, but since she's been gone . . . Don't look—she's coming this way."

"Make your case on the Rights of the Physically Challenged. Complain about lack of elevator access. She can't argue with that."

"You miss the point, Carl. I'm superannuated. I belong in a condominium in Boca Raton. Purely for my own good, of course."

"Dear God— Sorry, Harry."

Pastor Hardanger-Hansen closed in. "Good evening, Harry," she said. "How nice to see you, Carl. Harry, you look tired. It's wonderful the way you keep your activity up in spite of everything."

Beyond the slight nausea induced by her cattiness, Martell had to admit the woman was attractive. She was blonde, slim and clear-eyed. But as an Extinctionist she tried to neuter herself through baggy clothes, cropped hair and cosmetic STD lesions.

"I've been talking to Arnold Stern," she said, her eyes cold on Harry. "He's a fascinating man. Would you two like to meet him?"

"He's a poet, isn't he?" Martell asked.

"One of the best in the country. He teaches at the University. He's come down specially to meet Oski."

"Sure, let's meet him," said Martell. Any change was welcome—poor Harry was writhing.

"Button your coat, Harry, your shirt is out." She led the way through the crowd.

"I'd think she'd want to keep you away from people," Carl whispered as they walked.

"She wants everyone to see how hopeless I am."

As they moved along the banquet tables and among small clusters of people, many of them wearing the portable breathing systems that had become popular since the passage of the Smokers' Reenfranchisement Act, tags of conversation on the hot issues of the day floated by.

". . . And then she had the nerve to say to me, 'Well, my child is more valuable than your houseplant!' And I said I didn't have to stand there and listen to that kind of speciesism . . ."

". . . Sure it's in the Constitution, but so what? We've already abolished the right to bear arms—the idea that rights are inalienable is one of the fallacies that's brought us to the mess we're in . . ."

". . . What's really exciting is that the younger scientists have liberated themselves from the myth of objectivity. You'll be amazed at what they'll accomplish in the next . . ."

". . . Let's face it, our society is still riddled with oppression. Intelligence is the oppression of the mentally challenged. Virtue is the oppression of the morally creative. Health is the oppression of the differently well. Sanity is the oppression of diversely rational . . ."

Arnold Stern, a stoutish man with a high, freckled forehead and a gentle voice, was the center of a small ring of faculty members. They included a man from the Drama Department who trimmed his beard in open homage to George Bernard Shaw, and the Director of Development, a lean, graying man endowed with the easy geniality that comes of making one's living by lying to people.

"Happy to meet you, Pastor. And you, Carl," said Stern with a smile. "I'm glad we've got you clergymen—sorry, clergypeople—here. We were just getting into your bailiwick. I'm interested in ethnicity, and Scandinavian Lutheran culture intrigues me. But these people tell me you're not a religious school at all."

"No, that's not what we said," said Development.

Stern turned to Pastor Hardanger-Hansen. "Would you call Christiania a Christian institution?" he asked.

"I would say profoundly Christian."

Drama said, "Absolutely."

"And you are church-affiliated?"

"Oh yes," said Pastor Hardanger-Hansen. "I'm not really part of the school myself, of course. I'm pastor of Nidaros Lutheran, but people from the church started the school, and they used to hold Chapel there, so it gives me a sort of unofficial status."

"But they're telling me Christiania no longer holds any kind of religious observances at all. And there are no religious studies—"

"We examine religion in our anthropology and sociology courses," said Development.

"I see. And your policy is to hire non-Christians only as instructors?"

Drama said, "This is a Lutheran institution. You've got to expect paradox."

Pastor Hardanger-Hansen said, "It's part of New Horizons, a sort of affirmative action policy enacted by the North American Protestant Church. We feel we can't speak out against discrimination against racial, sexual, moral and species minorities if we practice religious discrimination in our own institutions."

"But surely you can't have a religious school without a few people who still believe the religion."

"Oh, there are a few fossils left from the old days," said Drama.

"But I'd think you must have some kind of charter or constitution that requires you to propagate the faith?"

"I suppose so," said Development. "But that's like the creeds, you know—nobody expects you to take it seriously."

"Don't the students' parents expect some kind of religious environment for their children?"

Development smiled. "You'd be surprised how little the families notice, if you move it in gradually. They're often old alumni who can't imagine things being any different from their day. Or if they aren't, they probably don't care."

"Well, it goes deeper than that," said Pastor Hardanger-Hansen. "We'd be doing the students a disservice if we created some kind of religious ghetto. We have to prepare them for the real world.

"But even more, I think we're on the cutting edge of a new spiritual understanding. The age of salvationism is past forever, thank God. We're beginning to understand that we're all climbing the same mountain, and we'll come together at the top. Once we've gotten free of the miracle stories—the Virgin Birth and Resurrection, that sort of thing—traditional folk-lore—we touch the true heart of spirituality which all enlightened people share."

"Pardon me," said Stern with a smile, "but I couldn't disagree more. I'm a religious Jew, and my faith is centered on the mighty acts of God. You may be approaching some religious believers when you reject the miraculous, but you're moving away from me."

Pastor Hardanger-Hansen went bright red, which was rather becoming, stammered a few words and excused herself.

"Oh my," said Stern. "I didn't mean to embarrass her."

"She's a woman of great good will," said Harry, "but like most of our young clergy she finds it almost impossible to believe that anyone with an IQ above forty could believe in the God of Scripture. She knows you have a celebrated brain, so the cognitive dissonance must have been considerable."

"Great legs though," said Development.

"Can I assume you don't share her views on religious schools then, ah—Pastor Gunderson wasn't it?" asked Stern.

"Oh, I'm afraid I'm one of those fossils you hear about."

"A conservative? How would you describe the differences between the liberal and conservative wings in your church?"

Drama said, "That's simple. A liberal believes Jesus was a woman. A conservative only thinks he was a hermaphrodite."

While they laughed a murmur began to rise about them, like the wind of Pentecost. Cameras flashed, every head turned, and Sigfod Oski blew in through a side door, followed by the college president and other notables. Nobody noticed the notables.

Sigfod Oski was easily the tallest person in the

room. His iron-gray hair was combed straight back. His jaw was long but squared, his skin tanned and creased like prehistoric leather from a Danish bog. He wore a black eyepatch over his left eye and a miraculously cut suit.

"He looks . . . he looks like Sigfod Oski," Harry whispered to Carl.

Oski came on like a pillar of cloud, his courtiers whirling in his wake, heading for a table set perpendicular to the rest at one end of the room.

"You want someone who looks like a king, Harry, there's one for you," said Martell.

"At least that."

"I'd love to meet him. I don't suppose I will."

"Why not? He'll be here some time, won't he?"

"Will he? I haven't been able to get any clear word on that. Some say he'll be here a couple days, others say half a year. Administration won't say a thing."

"Maybe we'll find out tonight."

Everyone was moving to the tables. Hampered by the leg in the narrow aisles between tables, Harry and Martell ended up near the corner furthest from the head table.

Harry sighed. "I *am* sorry, Carl. Of course the Lord said to seek out this kind of spot, so the host can exalt you. At least we won't have to worry about craning our necks to see. It wouldn't help."

Martell said it was all right. It wasn't precisely how he felt, but his stomach didn't object.

A figure moved up behind them. They twisted around to see Dr. Saemund Lygre, President of Christiania.

People always had trouble describing Dr. Lygre beyond saying he was middle-aged and roundish. He usually left a vague but pleasant impression with new acquaintances; the impression he left on colleagues and underlings was just as vague but less pleasant.

"What are you doing down here?" he whispered to Martell.

"I was invited," said Martell, alarmed. He was sure he'd gotten an invitation. Hadn't he?

"You're supposed to be at the head table with us."

"The head table? I don't understand—"

"Didn't you get my note?"

"I don't think so."

"Carl, you're impossible! The invitation was for you and a guest to sit at the Table of Honor. Oski asked for you especially. Now come along. You're holding us up."

"Oski—Oski asked for me?"

"Yes! Come on!"

Martell tried to push his chair back, but Dr. Lygre was in the way. "Wait," he said. "If it's for me and a guest, can Pastor Gunderson come?"

Dr. Lygre glanced at Harry, who had just spilled water in his lap while a paper napkin had attached itself to his left coatsleeve. "Yes, all right. Just hurry."

"See, I told you what the Lord said," Harry whispered as they worked their way forward.

"Sometimes you scare me, Harry. I'm sure I never got a note. Why would Oski ask for me? Are people staring at us?"

"Only in envy. You for your honor and me for my beauty." Then he tripped over a microphone cable.

At the Table of Honor, Dr. Lygre said, "Mr. Oski, this is Professor Carl Martell, of our History Department."

"Delighted to meet you," said Oski, shaking Martell's hand firmly and fixing him with one bright gray eye. Like most educated Norwegians, he spoke with something like an English accent. "I read your paper on Erling Skjalgsson. Excellent."

Martell said, "This is a very great honor, Mr.—you read *my* paper?"

"I try to read all the serious work in the field."

"You flatter me."

"Not at all. Your approach was extremely sound, especially when you compare it with most of the twaddle they're writing about the Vikings these days. You have a good instinct for when to ignore the experts. One can never go far wrong by ignoring the experts."

Martell stood dumbfounded. Harry poked him in the ribs.

"Oh yes—may I present my good friend, Pastor Harald Gunderson? He's also a great fan of yours."

Harry moved in closer. His hair was a bird's nest, his collar was working loose again, and there was now an adhesion of what looked like cotton candy on his chin. *"Det gleder meg å treffe dem,"* he said.

"I like måte," said Oski stiffly. "Well, shall we seat ourselves and begin?"

Oski sat facing the room. The Lygres were on his right and Martell and Harry on his left, with Arnold Stern on Harry's left. Across from them were Mayor Sorenson and his wife, who was looking shy, a state representative and her husband, and the chairman of the Board of Regents and his wife.

A small bottle of akvavit sat in front of each place, and Dr. Lygre stood and proposed a toast. Then he gave a general greeting and they all addressed their salads, except for Oski, who showed no interest in his.

"We seem to have an empty place at the table," observed Ruth Lygre. She was a tallish woman with curling gray hair and very blue eyes.

"Yes," said Oski. "I chose not to bring my mistress. I thought she might be out of place at a religious institution."

The British call it "dropping a brick." Everyone got very quiet for a moment.

Oski seemed to enjoy the reaction. "Perhaps I should have referred to her as my secretary. My apologies, Herr Pastor."

"Don't mind me," said Harry. His shirt was coming unbuttoned around the breastbone, exposing a ribbed undergarment.

"Well, of course we are a little provincial here," said Ruth Lygre. "This *is* a small town. Lake Woebegon, and *Main Street*, and all that."

"There's nothing wrong with a small town," said Oski, "as long as you remember that there is a wider world."

"My wife grew up in Japan," said Dr. Lygre.

"Indeed."

She explained, "My parents were missionaries."

"Well, we'll pass that over," said Oski, smiling.

"Are you a Lutheran?" Dr. Lygre asked.

"To the extent that a Norwegian can avoid the state church, I endeavor to do so. What offends me most about the church in Norway today is its broadmindedness. They even throw an official sop to pagans like me, but the kind of paganism they encourage is so sentimental it makes me want to convert to Islam."

"What do you mean by that?" asked the representative. "I'd like to hear more—if you don't mind, Pastor." She turned to Harry.

"You're very kind to worry about my feelings," Harry answered, "but I've met unbelievers before and survived the experience."

"Perhaps you could tell us about your home in Norway," said Ruth Lygre. "It's such a beautiful country."

"Beautiful indeed," said Oski. "So beautiful as to be nearly uninhabitable. It was made for looking at, not living on. But returning to Christianity—I hold it to be, simply, an unacceptably weak religion for a man with any dignity."

"That's funny," said the representative. "Speaking from experience with lobbyists and PAC groups, I'd say it's sometimes unacceptably strong."

"I do not speak of politics. Of course the hierarchy has always had the sense to keep Christ's idiotic ethics out of their real business."

"Very true," said the representative's husband. "Look at the Crusades. Look at the Inquisition. Look at the conversion of Norway, for God's sake—those two Olafs sailing around killing anybody who wouldn't be baptized."

"You miss my point, sir," said Oski. "I think the Olafs were wise in their generation. If they had tried to do the job by turning the other cheek and walking the extra mile, then I would fault them. They were hypocrites, of course, but that is another matter."

Oski stroked his chin as he spoke. He looked, Martell thought, like a man remembering a newly shaved beard, only there was no tan line on his rust-colored cheek.

"Jesus Christ," said Oski, "made a haven of the soul for cowards. There may be such a thing as a strong man turning the other cheek to an enemy he could crush, but I can't recall ever seeing such a thing. But a man—"

"Or woman," said the representative.

"A man," said Oski, turning his eye on her. "I do not play games of moralistic one-upmanship, madam. If you dislike masculine imagery you'd best stay away from tonight's reading. A man who is weak, and fears the responsibilities of manhood, can run like a puppy and tell himself he is being *charitable*. The apostle was right—love *does* cover a multitude of sins. Sins of cowardice, of sloth, of irresponsibility and worse."

Harry said, "There *have* been those who died forgiving their killers. Are you saying they did nothing remarkable?"

"Anything unnatural is remarkable. A three-legged calf is remarkable. But it is not therefore desirable."

Arnold Stern asked, "Do you prefer the sort of thing we're seeing in the Middle East? Vengeance, vendetta—the ever-widening circle of violence?"

"I say that such problems will never be solved by the meek. In a sense the meek have already inherited the earth, and we can thank them for most of its troubles. Christ called them sheep—that was appropriate. Professor Martell"—he turned—"you strike me as a circumspect man. Tell me what you have observed at this Christian institution. Would you call its administration courageous?"

Martell felt the tip of Oski's gaze in his soul. *I can't lie, and my boss is listening.*

"I—I'd say they're as courageous as any," he managed to say, forming the words with difficulty. It was misleading enough to twist his stomach.

"Ah," said Oski, not taking his eye away. "I did not ask for comparisons. Do the administrators of this Christian institution not scramble to embrace each new fashion of thought on the one hand, while on the other piously assuring their financial supporters that all the old values are carved in stone? Do they not dance about, promising everything to everyone, struggling to offend no one, kissing most especially the feet and other parts of anyone with money to donate?"

Martell felt Dr. Lygre watching him, along with everybody at the table. *Why is he doing this?* he wondered, tasting acid in his throat. *Is it a game? Can he read the sickness inside me?*

Harry said, "There are some who suggest that the administration of Lutheran colleges has very little to do with Christianity."

A few people laughed, Oski included. Martell silently blessed the pastor. Dr. Lygre did not look amused. Martell had a feeling he'd pay for his hesitation.

Oski turned to Harry. "In the car park I noticed that you reserve the choicest spots for the weak and disabled. I call that symptomatic. Encourage weakness, and it will rule in the end like a dog in a manger."

Harry said nothing, but his face went red. Disheveled as he was, he looked like a man who'd been in an accident. Which, of course, he was.

"That," said Stern mildly, "sounds dangerously close to the Nazi line."

Oski turned quickly on him. He pointed to his eyepatch with a finger like an autumn twig. "I gave this eye fighting the Nazis," he said. "I can say what I like, and no one has the right to make that accusation."

"I made no accusation," said Stern. "I was talking about ideas. And since I make no claim to be a Christian, I have no intention of letting you bully me as you have these people."

Oski burst into laughter and hit the table with a fist, making the silverware ring and causing the room to go silent for a moment.

Martell did a little math in his head, trying to estimate how old Oski must be. Not impossibly old of course, but very, very old. Much older even than he appeared.

A waiter arrived with the entrée. While he served them, Ruth Lygre said, "That's a beautiful suit you're wearing, Mr. Oski. Wherever did you get it?"

"This? I have a London tailor, just off Savile Row. Actually I found him through T.S. Eliot—many years ago, of course. There's an amusing story behind that . . ."

That story led to others, all of them excellent, and everybody relaxed. They made it to dessert, but

Martell wasn't able to eat much. Oski touched nothing at all, though he asked the waiter for more akvavit. Martell wondered if the man was an alcoholic.

After they had consumed their portions of lime or orange sherbet, Dr. Lygre spoke up. He had been quiet since the discussion of courage.

"I think you misunderstood the religious nature of our school, Mr. Oski," he said. "We are not a 'Christian' school in the old, salvationist sense. We see Christianity in a broad, embracing posture, listening with open mind to all religious wisdom. I think you'll find us eager to listen to your wisdom as well."

Oski replied without looking at him. "I am not myself a broad-minded man," he said. "It is a prejudice to assume that all apostates are gentle, genial souls. I am nothing of the sort.

"Some years back I watched with interest as the Danes carried out an experiment in what is called 'Living History.' The young volunteers moved into a reconstructed Bronze Age farmstead. They spent an extended period there, wearing the clothes, eating the food, doing the work of their ancestors.

"These were highly educated people; young scholars and their families, raised with books and television and cradle-to-grave socialism.

"But after a time a change came over them. They became what you would probably call superstitious. When the weather went foul, or disease attacked the stock, they began to blame the spirits. They took to saying little prayers to the elves and trolls—'If you let me graze my cows in your meadow you can have some of the milk.' They left out bowls of porridge for the house spirits. They knew, of course, in their civilized brains, that all this was absurd, *but they could not help it*. Because, for the first time in their lives, they were living a *real* life in a *real* world.

"Confronted with real life—with soil and wind and

water and fire—they reverted to their true religion. The one true religion of mankind."

Harry said, "That's assuming that people will naturally find their true religion. Christianity assumes no such thing."

"There are but two choices," said Oski. "The western world has only two faiths. Both have their roots in the Middle East.

"One is the religion that founded this school. It began when a Sumerian named Abram climbed a mountain with his son, intending to cut the boy's throat and give him to his peculiar god. Instead he brought the boy back down with him, along with a story that his god had only been testing his faith. This was a watershed in history—the first heresy if you like.

"Abram and his descendants insisted ever after that the true God was only one, and that He is a great prig, and that He does not wish the blood of our children, except when He sheds it Himself.

"The other, older religion—my religion—recognizes in the chaos around us a chaos of powers. These powers are neither infinite nor moral, and they are incredibly dangerous. They may bless us in return for gifts, or at their whim, but it is risky to let them see us too blessed."

"The Greeks spoke of *hubris*," said Martell.

"The Greeks were of my creed. The names changed but the powers remained, shifting, battling among themselves, growing or diminishing in strength as Abram's God drove them northward. But always they echoed the great denial—the heroic cry that the world is cruel, and that all must die and rot; yet a man can laugh in death's face and, falling in flame, bring down his enemy with him. We know that life is a tragedy, calling for the most terrible sacrifices; that by placating the gods we not only turn away their wrath but share in the agony of the great mysteries. Better to slay what you love yourself than wail while it is torn from you."

"They also knew a tale about a god who dies and comes to life again," Harry said quietly.

"A nature myth. A great mystery," said Oski with a frown.

"I'm sure . . . I'm sure there's much we can learn from your faith," said Dr. Lygre.

"Ah, but you have! I've read the meditations of your newer theologians, and I am much moved. You have grasped that truth has nothing to do with *ideas*"—he glanced at Stern—"with moral taboos, or promises, or prohibitions or doctrines—but with the inner, unspeakable truth of the spirit."

"Yes," said Dr. Lygre. "The essential subjectivity of truth. That's very important. Kierkegaard's leap of faith—"

"The leap of faith!" Oski's eye flashed. He smiled, showing unusually long teeth. "Yes, I have felt it—the utter freedom that soars far above judgments and categories and petty rationality! I experienced it first during the war, and what it did for me!"

"What did it do for you?" asked Dr. Lygre.

"It enabled me to kill six men one night on a glacier!"

Dr. Lygre dropped his spoon. The representative's husband coughed.

Oski beamed around him. "The splendid thing about a leap of faith is you never know what you're leaping into."

No one spoke for a minute.

"Well," said Dr. Lygre. "I guess it's time for the formalities." He rose and tapped his glass with his knife.

Conversations trailed off, and Dr. Lygre said, "I'm very happy to see such a fine turnout tonight, to share in what is unquestionably a high-water mark in the history of Christiania." Cameramen from five Twin Cities television stations crouched forward along the aisles, their lenses focused on the head table.

"When Sigfod Oski announced that he proposed to spend two years in the United States, a number of academic institutions clamored to offer him their hospitality. Invitations came from some of the most prestigious schools in the country. To be frank, Christiania did not make such an offer. We felt we had little to offer a man of Oski's stature—a man who has become something of a legend both in his native land and internationally.

"Think of our astonishment then, when Sigfod Oski informed us that it was here he wished to come. We hastened to extend an invitation, of course. We found it difficult to believe our good fortune, and frankly we weren't quite sure what to do with it. For that reason there has been some confusion as to Mr. Oski's business here and the length of his visit.

"I am happy to announce, therefore, that Sigfod Oski has come to Christiania in the capacity of Poet in Residence, and that he intends to make us his research base for the entire two years of his stay."

There was loud applause, then a standing ovation. The cameras panned the crowd.

When the room was quiet again Dr. Lygre continued. "Before he shares a few words and we all retire to the auditorium for tonight's reading, I think it appropriate to say a few words of a biographical nature.

"Sigfod Oski was born in Avaldsnes, an island village in western Norway. He was only a boy when the Nazis sailed in, but he soon became an active and valued member of the Resistance, serving at first mainly as a courier. By the age of sixteen he was part of a demolitions unit, doing dark and dangerous work, often in killing weather.

"In the last year of the war, he and his comrades were betrayed by a quisling and arrested. They were all tortured. Mr. Oski lost an eye. Of the six men in his unit, only he survived to the end of the war, a prisoner in Grini Concentration Camp.

"It was in the camp that he began to compose poetry. He had no paper or pencil—he composed in his head, committing his poems to memory and reciting them to the other prisoners like the Viking skalds of old. We have the testimony of many of them that it was those poems that gave them the courage to endure.

"After the liberation Oski's reputation grew steadily. He took his degree from the University of Oslo, where he became a lecturer and later a professor. And of course his reputation as a poet grew, culminating in the award of a Nobel Prize for Literature eight years ago.

"If you read Oski in English translation, and I guess most of us do, you aren't missing anything. Mr. Oski does his own translations, new compositions in effect, equal to the originals in every respect.

"And now, just so you can find out for yourselves how well he uses English, if I might prevail on Mr. Oski to say a few words . . ."

He turned to Oski's place. Oski was not in it.

Carl Martell stood, looking uncomfortable. "I'm sorry," he said. "Mr. Oski said for me to tell you that he . . . he said he disliked after-dinner speeches, and that he'll be happy to see all of you in the auditorium in forty-five minutes."

Dr. Lygre glared at Martell. Martell whispered, "It's not my fault."

Minna Gunderson was praying in her bedroom.

Every night at 7:30, except when it had to be postponed for other people's convenience, she lowered herself by her bed, knees on a cushion—she was not an ascetic.

She opened her Bible, the one she'd been given at her confirmation. Its leather was crumbling, the binding loose, the typeface too small, but she was accustomed to it.

It opened naturally to the single passage she'd fed on in these sessions from the beginning, Isaiah 40:28-31.

> *"Hast thou not known? hast thou not heard, that the everlasting God, the LORD, the Creator of the ends of the earth, fainteth not, neither is weary? there is no searching of his understanding.*
>
> *He giveth power to the faint; and to them that have no might he increaseth strength.*
>
> *Even youths shall faint and be weary, and the young men shall utterly fall:*
>
> *But they that wait upon the LORD shall renew their strength; they shall mount up with wings as eagles; they shall run, and not be weary; and they shall walk, and not faint."*

There were people who knew more about the Bible than Minna Gunderson. There were probably people who led more spiritual lives. But she was the world's foremost authority on that passage. She had gone through her brother's commentaries and Hebrew lexicons to analyze each word, in isolation and in context. She had read volumes on running, and everything she could find on eagles. She had studied the historical setting and the various theories on authorship—about which she had definite opinions.

Shortly after her fiancé had died, so many years ago now, she had gone on an obligatory visit to her grandfather. The old man lay in his last bed, nursed by two unmarried daughters, inexorable women who disapproved of everything in order to save time and effort.

Her grandfather had been a fiery preacher of the gospel. Minna could remember squirming long hours in the pew beside her parents while he consigned thieves, liars, card players and ballroom dancers to the eternal pit, all in a thick Norwegian brogue. Now he was shrunken and fragile as bone china among the linen, staring out at her with bruised, 19th Century eyes.

With a word he dismissed the Terrible Sisters. They left with bad grace, outraged at Minna's youth, perhaps afraid she'd infect their father with it.

"Don't let them scare you," the old man said, his voice barely above a whisper. "They're yust frightened old vomen. Try not to be like them. They'll go to Heaven, but vhat vill they do there?"

Minna said nothing. She feared her grandfather.

"They tell me you have lost your young man. He vas in the Air Force?"

Minna nodded. "His plane crashed," she breathed.

The old man closed his eyes, the lids so thin one wondered if they kept any light out. "So sad. He vas so young. And he vas a good fellow, even if he vas a Methodist. Vhat vill you do now, Minna?"

She had prepared her speech. She knew the words a good Christian girl should say.

"I'll get over it, *Bestefar*. And someday I'll find a good man to marry."

He shocked her when he said, "No, I don't think so, Minna."

She stared at him. His head was shaking, slowly. *He must have gone childish*, she thought.

"You're not a good liar, Minna," he said. "None of the Gundersons ever vere. I hope it's true, girlie. I hope you find a good man, and the Lord blesses you vith many good years and happy children. But you don't believe it, do you? In your eyes I see no hope. You loved your fellow vith all your heart, and you're not the kind to go from vun love to another like changing hats. You're true and faithful, Minna. I've alvays seen that in you."

She cried then, great racking sobs that brought up all the clotted misery she'd clenched under her heart. The old man reached out and took her hand and held it with a baby's strength.

When she was cried out, he said, "Minna, it's not true that there's somevun for everyvun. Ve Lutherans like marriage because Martin Luther got married and sang its praises, and he vas right. I thank the Lord for the years I had vith your *bestemor*. But the Bible says that some people aren't meant for it. You should know that life can be blessed and good even vithout marriage."

"I don't know, *Bestefar*. I just don't know."

"Of course you don't, Minna. How could you? You're young, you're not supposed to know. The trick is to learn to be happy even vhen you can't get vhat you vant. I forgot to teach that to those two out in the hall, and God forgive me. Maybe I can help you.

"I can't show you how to understand. Everyvun has to start at the beginning for themselves. But if I had things to do over again, I vould have started earlier to meditate on vun Bible passage. Do you know Isaiah 40:28-31?"

She shook her head.

"If I could start again, I'd take a few minutes a day and think about that vun. It's taught me a lot in these months since I been sick. Maybe it can help you too. Telling you this and praying for you are all I can do to help, Minna. But you are in God's hands. It's enough."

She had looked up the passage and marked it when she got home. But it wasn't until the old man's death three months later that she had started meditating. She'd been doing it ever since.

They tell of jars of flour and oil that once kept people alive beyond all hope. A few bread and fish fed thousands one day.

The Isaiah passage had fed Minna most of her adult life.

It had changed her spirit, drawing out the bitterness. It had changed her soul, which moderns call personality, so that acquaintances often took her for a widow. Finally, just recently, it had begun to change her body. She felt her strength renewed. She rose up on wings as of eagles.

It was not a metaphorical rising.

Somewhere between twenty and twenty-five minutes into her meditation, she would often find herself lifted into the air, suspended about four inches above her kneeling cushion.

The levitation did not frighten her. She was curious, though, about God's purpose in it.

As with most miracles in this world, the rule was, "Tell no man." "I'd look pretty silly," she told herself, "doing this on television. I wonder what it's *good* for?"

Chapter VIII

"All right, Carl, how did he do it?"

Martell and Harry were sitting in Martell's car, ready to leave for the reading.

"He just whispered to me and walked out during the standing ovation. He was so calm about it I didn't realize anything strange had happened until everybody started staring at the empty place beside me. You really mean nobody noticed until then?"

"I was sitting on your left, and I missed it completely. Remarkable. I suppose it all goes to show what a man can do with poise."

"Poise? The man's plain arrogant." Martell started the car and pulled out of the lot. The headlights briefly illuminated a bumper sticker that read, "LOVE THE EARTH—SPAY OR NEUTER YOUR CHILD." It wasn't far to the Andrew Volstead Memorial Auditorium, but they wanted to get good seats.

"Well," said Harry, "some people say genius is above common courtesy."

"Bull."

"The man has paid his moral dues, Carl. At least for this world. Maybe you've got the nerve to criticize a man who's been tortured by Nazis. I'm not sure I do."

"Arnold Stern did okay. You seemed to get on well with him."

"We had a good conversation. We agree on very little, but we understood each other perfectly. It was refreshing."

"I envied him his nerve in throwing Oski's trash back in his face. I wish I were more like him. I don't care if Sigfod Oski is Raoul Wallenberg in an eye-patch, he has no right to talk about—well, the handicapped—the way he did."

"You're not supposed to say 'handicapped' anymore, you know, Carl. For a while it was 'disabled' and now it's 'physically challenged.' I'm not sure why. When I was handicapped I felt like a racehorse. When I became disabled I felt a little like Cain. Now that I'm physically challenged I feel like somebody wants to fight a duel with me." He was fiddling with his collar but it wasn't helping.

"Well, forgiveness is your business, Harry. You're a Christian and the injured party. I'm neither, so I'm free to hate the—"

"Joanna liked Oski," Harry said softly. "Or rather, she liked his poetry. Odd when you think of it—she was the gentlest of God's creatures. What could she have seen in those grim sagas? Maybe she only enjoyed the way *I* loved them. I used to read them to her in the evenings sometimes, and I'd get carried away to an extent—well, to an extent I don't get much chance to anymore. I'd be waving my arms and shouting the words, my shirt coming apart in three places, and she'd smile and her eyes would shine. And then . . ." He sighed. "I can't hate him. Not while I remember those evenings."

Inside the auditorium a line of folding chairs had been arranged on one side of the stage. Facing the stage, in front of the bleachers, hundreds more folding chairs had been set up in rows on the basketball court. Martell and Harry found the place nearly filled already, but they got seats near the middle of the right-hand section, close to the main entrance, not too far back.

"You're sure you want to stay for this?" Martell asked as they sat.

"Absolutely. Why suffer the man's worst and miss his best?"

"Well, his best had better be good."

"Stay put, Carl. Unless you have the heart to leave a poor, physically challenged cleric to walk home by hand."

Martell slumped in his folding chair, arms crossed.

The auditorium filled quickly and through the cigarette smoke they watched as Dr. Lygre, various VIPs and Sigfod Oski paraded onto the stage. The others sat while Dr. Lygre went to the podium.

Listening to his introductory remarks—the same speech he'd test-driven at the banquet—and staring at Oski, Martell didn't notice the blonde woman until she had nearly reached the stage.

But the moment she stepped into his right-eye peripheral vision she had his complete attention. His belly knew her before his mind did.

His mouth formed her name.

The woman stopped at the edge of the stage and gestured to Oski. He went down to the apron, knelt, and spoke to her. As they spoke he passed a long hand possessively down her shoulder and arm. Then he straightened and returned to his chair, and she started back toward the door.

"What did you say, Carl?" asked Harry.

Martell got up and excused himself down to the end of the row, head craning to watch her as she went out. If people stared at him, leaving before things had gotten started, he didn't notice.

Outside in the darkness he looked from side to side. The woman was nowhere in sight.

He set out down the sidewalk and followed it clockwise around the block. He didn't see her.

He was running when he got back to the auditorium. There he stopped, turning around and around.

"Elaine!"

He went into the parking lot and looked in all the cars. She wasn't there.

He sat on the concrete step of the building, under the bronze plaque dedicated to the author of the Prohibition Amendment. He hadn't had a cigarette in years, but he wanted one now. His hand hurt. The wind was cold.

Elaine.

Confound her for walking back into his life.

He could hear Oski's muffled voice from inside. His voice was rich and sonorous, with boulders and saltwater in it. He couldn't make out any of the words.

Confound Sigfod Oski. No question now of not hating him.

Elaine, what's become of you?

For two hours he sat on the cool concrete step. He hadn't been so miserable in a very long time. To be alone and rejected, alone and sitting in the cold and dark while all the rest were inside in the warmth and light and human fellowship—he knew the feeling from boyhood, when he had envied happier boys even while scorning them. He thought, *It was always like this—you were born for this*.

His stomach clenched, and for a moment he couldn't breathe. The old self-pity was another lie, and there was no comfort in lies anymore for Carl Martell.

He felt robbed. He felt judged and shamed. He wanted to say, "A man ought to have the right to a little bitterness!" but he couldn't say that either.

He stood up, clutching his head. He felt as if he were vomiting with his mouth taped shut.

He thought he'd go mad.

Instead he cried. He sat again and cradled his head in his arms, arms on his knees, and wept honest tears for a long time, and the pain eased. At the end he was limp and a little numb. He sat shivering in a sort of suspended state, for how long he wasn't sure.

Finally the doors opened and people began to come out. He got up quickly and worked his way in, against the flow.

He found Harry in conversation with a small group of parishioners, all competing for better ways of saying how wonderful the evening had been, although parts of it were hard to follow. They left after a while, and Harry looked at Martell.

"I'm sorry," Martell said.

"You look terrible, Carl. What happened? No, wait—not here. Let's go out and talk in the car."

"Do I really look that bad?"

"You should see yourself."

The slow walk gave Martell time to decide how much to tell. In the car he sat with his keys in his hand. "I'm not sure how to explain this," he said, "without sounding like somebody out of a bad Victorian poem. Probably there isn't any way."

"It has to do with that woman?"

"You noticed her?"

"I think everyone noticed her. A remarkable beauty. She's someone you know?"

"Her name is Elaine."

"Elaine . . . of course."

"How do you know about Elaine?"

"You told me. Not much, but I could tell it was important to you."

Martell shook his head. "I was under the delusion I'd kept her a secret. Which just goes to show something or other. You've seen how it is, Harry. I don't date. I avoid every offer to set me up with some nice girl. Partly it's cowardice, fear of commitment, whatever the fashionable analysis is these days. But I have a hole in my soul, and it's shaped like Elaine. Nobody else can fill it."

"Well, if you have to have a hole in your soul, I'd say hers is a pretty nice shape for it. . . ."

"I'm feeding you straight lines. Now *that's* appropriate . . . It's been fifteen years. But when I saw Elaine tonight it was as if the time hadn't happened. I got the same jolt. It's not normal, Harry. I'm supposed to be saying that she's no longer the woman I remember, that the old flame has died. It *should* have died by now."

"Who says? Am I supposed to scold you for fidelity?"

"This isn't fidelity, it's neurosis. I'm not keeping any marriage vow. I'm hanging onto a fantasy."

Harry clapped his hands twice. "Bravo. 'I know I'm a fool, but at least I despise myself.' You're looking for an absolute within yourself, Carl. You won't find it there.

"Besides, who's to say you're neurotic? Or if you are, what's wrong with a little neurosis? Mental health is largely a matter of fashion. St. Augustine would tell you your celibacy makes you one of the few healthy people in town, though he'd say you came by it in a pretty poor way. Every generation writes new specs for the healthy personality, and each one in turn turns out to be a new kind of monster. Our monster is different from the Victorian monster, but he's no less a monster.

"For all either of us knows, your passion might be exactly what God wants for you. You should talk to Him about it."

Martell sat silent for a moment. "I have to see her."

When Rory Buchan left the radio station after midnight, he found Thumb's Chevy waiting for him in the parking area. Thumb rolled the window down, and Rory saw that he had his ski mask on again.

"Want to talk?" Thumb asked.

Rory said, "I'm not sure."

"Let's take a ride. Nothing interesting will happen, I promise."

Rory shrugged and got in. Thumb drove to a quiet residential street, stopped and turned the engine off. There was dim light from a street lamp further down the block. Papery leaves blew from the elm trees and scraped along the roof.

"Been thinking about our talk?" Thumb asked.

"Haven't thought about anything else."

"Decided anything?"

"The more I think, the more confused I get."

"I know just how you feel. When you were a kid, they told you to be nice to people and to leave justice to the cops and the courts. And here I come, telling you that there's some people you just can't be nice to, and that there's times when you've got to take the law into your own hands. God's ways aren't our ways, you know."

"That's just it," said Rory. "Maybe God's ways aren't my ways, but why should I believe they're *your* ways either? I mean—Hitler said pretty much the same thing." Rory felt frightened to say it. He had seen Thumb kill. Probably.

"Hitler was an evil man," Thumb said. "Let's make no mistake about it. And if I'm like him, then I deserve what he got and more, and the sooner the better.

"But you know, nobody gets as far as he did without telling a piece of the truth. And if you believed the things he believed, well, then what he said made sense. Of course what he believed was wrong and evil. But if he'd had his facts straight, he'd have been justified. You follow me?

"Look. The Jews aren't an inferior breed—they're God's Chosen People, for Heaven's sake. And they don't run some secret world-wide conspiracy.

"But suppose there *were* a conspiracy like that. Suppose there were people out there, people with great power, manipulating things to oppress people and pervert everything good. Then you'd be right to do something about it, even if you broke the law—in fact you'd *have* to break the law.

"Everybody believes this, you know. No matter what they say, everybody's got somebody they'd like to see go into the ovens. Conservatives want to execute murderers and rapists. And no matter what the liberals say, you won't hear them weeping over the terrible injustices done to Himmler and Eichmann. If an abused wife burns her husband alive, the feminists make her a folk heroine.

"We all know deep down that there are some things just so awful that anybody who does them ought to be killed, and if it's slow and painful that's all right too.

"There's human sacrificers out there, Rory. I know it for a fact. I believe you can't live in peace with people who do that. You've got to root the thing out, and sow the place with salt."

"I don't think Leslie Prill was sacrificing anybody."

"She was a carrier. Maybe other ways would have been better if we had more time, but we don't have time. It's all coming to a head. Soon. We know that."

"*How* do you know that? How in—how do you know all these things you're so blasted sure about?"

Thumb said, "I'm a prophet."

Rory said, "I've heard a lot of people claim to be prophets. Most of the time they don't tell me anything the Bible doesn't already say a lot better. Or if they do, it turns out to be wrong."

"Test me, Rory. I'll tell you something, and you see whether it doesn't happen. Deuteronomy 18:22— *'When a prophet speaketh in the name of the LORD, if the thing follow not, nor come to pass, that is the thing which the LORD hath not spoken, but the prophet hath spoken it presumptuously: thou shalt not be afraid of him.'*

"This is the word of the Lord to you, Rory: This morning, before you sleep, you'll meet a friend. Somebody you haven't thought of in years. I'll give you a call tomorrow, and you tell me if I'm wrong."

"What do you want from me if I decide to join you?"

"You have a voice that reaches all over this county. We need you to give a signal, to let people know when it's started."

"When *what's* started?"

"The battle. Armageddon, maybe. No, not Armageddon. But an early skirmish. Important enough. Important enough for our lives, if it comes to that."

Rory stood on the sidewalk, watching the tail lights fade, shivering. He wondered what old friend could come forward at this hour, in this place, and what it would prove if one did. He wanted to think and pray, but he thought that going home would make things too easy for Thumb.

Suddenly he knew where he should go.

He drove his Golf out toward the farm where Leslie Prill had died. On the way he tuned in WEEP. The network news feed was on.

"WEEP News, brought to you by Hinderaker's Grocery World. A spokesman for the Coalition for Rational Government today announced that the group

*will change its slogan, 'Abolish the Constitution now—
if it saves one life it will be worth it,' which has drawn
fire from Extinctionists and animal rights' groups for
its alleged anthropism. A spokesperson told report-
ers that the new slogan will be, 'The Founding Fathers
are dead—get over it.'"*

Rory switched the radio off when he reached the
farm. The police had chained off the driveway so he
pulled over by the mailbox and cut the engine.

He hadn't slept the night before, and he felt it.

"I liked her, Lord," he prayed. "I don't think she
deserved to die." Why didn't he just go to the cops?
Thumb had said they couldn't prove anything, but how
did he know? And so what? He knew he was supposed
to do what was right, not what was smart. If he was
an accessory he should take the consequences.

He knew the answer. It was Rowan. As long as he
remembered Rowan, and what he did to Heather, he
needed a way to fight back. He *wanted* Thumb to
be right. He wanted to stop running scared.

"Will you show me, Lord?" he prayed. "Will you
show me who's right and who's wrong, and what I
ought to do about it?"

The crunch of feet on gravel took his attention,
faint through the car windows.

Oh boy. Don't get excited. It's probably nothing.

Fast footsteps. Running. Who'd be running at this
hour on a country road?

The sound was approaching from behind. Rory
craned his head to look over his shoulder.

A slender shadow appeared at last. A jogger. It
looked like a girl.

The shadow stopped and tapped on his window.
He was afraid to roll it down, but he did.

A girl's voice panted, "You got the time, friend?"

Rory switched on the dome light to see his watch.
"1:07," he read.

"Hamster! I can't believe it!"

The name jolted him. Nobody had called him that since—

He looked up at the face in the dim light. She was round-faced, dimpled, red-haired and freckled. Pretty. Not familiar.

"I'm sorry—" he said.

The girl laughed. "I'm not surprised you don't recognize me, Hamster. I was a lot younger and skinnier back then. They used to call me Zippy on the street. You remember?"

Rory gaped. "Zippy! My—gee! The last time I saw you, I didn't figure you to make it through the winter! Hey, get in—we've got to talk!"

The girl went around and got in on the passenger side. She sighed as she sat.

"Old Hamster," she said. "Small world. Yeah, I almost didn't make it, back there. Of all the old gang, I thought I was the only survivor, except for Snorkel, and he's in a county hospital now, sucking paint chips. Whatever happened to you? Let's see—you dropped out just about the time Heather did. Everybody thought you'd bought it together."

"I ran up against something I couldn't handle, so I got out. I'm a born-again Christian now, Zippy. I work at the radio station here in town. You look like you've straightened out too—did you find Jesus?"

The girl smiled. "Sort of. I found the Way of the Old Wisdom. We believe Jesus was really one of us, only the disciples misunderstood. They turned me around, Rory. Turned me from a burned-out street junkie to a whole human being. Look at me. Clean five years. I run three miles a day. I eat healthy food and get lots of sunshine, or at least I did before I moved back to Minnesota, and I hardly ever black out anymore."

"I'm glad to hear you got clean." Rory's hands

tightened on the steering wheel. "But I'm sorry to hear you're a witch."

"'Witch' is just a word, Rory. It means a way of relating to nature. It isn't true, what they say about witches. We don't hurt anybody—we help people. We heal. We protect. You should come and visit us sometime and see."

"I'd like to do that," said Rory, thinking of Leslie Prill.

"Come out anytime. We're doing exciting things. We've been watching Cerafsky's Comet. It's very important, the comet. Something's going to happen soon. Just tell the guys at the gate you're my guest. Say Young Goat Star invited you."

"Young Goat what?"

"Young Goat Star. It's my new name."

"I never knew your old name."

"Laura Tysness. My grandfather used to own the farm we're living on."

"Oh, then you're the girl who gave her inheritance to her religion."

"I hear Jesus recommended it. I did it out of gratitude, Rory. W.O.W. was there for me when I needed them. They saved my life. Our High Priest is really a fine man. I've never met anybody as totally loving and giving."

Rory smiled. "We've got a lot to talk about."

"Come and see us." She smiled back.

With a jerk, the wolf woke. It shivered; not from the cold, though it was cold; and not from hunger, though it was hungry. A wolf's dreams are often terrible, but they are not remembered. This wolf remembered.

A monstrous sight—a man had reached out his hand toward it. And the wolf, bound and held by some awful force, had been unable to flee. So it had snapped at the hand. Its jaws had clenched on the fist. They had stood face to face for a long minute, the man and the wolf, each reading in the alien eyes of the other the message without words: *Between your house and mine there has been no peace since the world began.*

The wolf had strained at its bonds, but they would not yield. Maddened with fear, it had closed its jaws and bitten through flesh and bone, tasting the salt, forbidden blood under the sour man-smell. And the man had stood watching, as if unhurt, with those, mad, white human eyes.

The wolf scrambled unsteadily to its feet. It felt the need of movement. The beckoning smell was on the wind, and the itching wriggled in its brain, and there could be no rest until the prey had been found.

Chapter IX

Freya's Day

Martell's telephone rang at 6:00 A.M., a few moments before his alarm clock was set to sound. By the time he'd untangled his bedclothes the clock was buzzing too, and he had trouble sorting them out.

He turned the alarm off and minced across the cool linoleum to the living room, with its carpet, and the phone. It was still dark and the dial light hurt his eyes. His hand burned and itched.

"Hello?"

"Professor Martell. This is Sigfod Oski."

Martell nearly dropped the receiver. The voice was cheery and robust, as if Oski knew nothing of mornings. *"I hope I didn't wake you."*

"I—I was just getting up anyway."

*"That's all right then. I understand you're going
out to the Way of the Old Wisdom farm this morning to look at their stone."*

"Well, yes, I said I'd look. I doubt if I'll be much
use to them though."

*"You're not a runologist, of course. Small call for
them on this side of the pond. I suppose that's why
they invited me."*

"They asked you? You're not going, are you?"

*"I thought we might motor together. If you have
no objection."*

"I—well, I'm surprised—"

"You're surprised I'm interested?"

"I'm surprised a man of your stature would want
to be mixed up with it. I mean, it's a pretty obvious
fraud. Isn't it?"

*"Why, Professor Martell—you have a prejudiced
mind."*

"Yes, yes I do, now you mention it."

*"How refreshing. Well, I can be at your apartment
in about forty-five minutes, I would think. We'll take
my car—it's quite comfortable."*

"I promised to bring Pastor Gunderson along."

*"I see. Well, I'm sure it can't be far out of the way.
Expect me a bit earlier then. Now tell me exactly
where you live."*

Martell told him, then dressed and shaved. In front
of the bathroom mirror, he touched the injured place
on his head gingerly, then decided he could do without the dressing. He drank a cup of instant coffee
standing up in the kitchenette. He hadn't eaten much
in the last couple days, but this didn't seem the time
to start. He wasn't looking forward to a morning with
Oski.

"Elaine, Elaine," he whispered. "You were many
things, but you were always independent. What have
you been through, to bring you to this?"

He washed the melodrama out of his mouth with the dregs of the coffee.

At the time appointed, a silver-gray Cadillac limousine appeared like a Cunard liner at the curb. A very large, very black driver got out to open the door for Martell. He wore no uniform but his dignity, and it was enough.

"Good morning, Professor," said Oski as Martell slid in beside him. The car's interior smelled like a shoe store.

"I'm just an assistant professor," Martell said. "We Americans are a little informal with our titles."

"I'll call you Martell then, in the Norwegian fashion. And you shall call me Oski."

Martell coughed. "I'm not sure I'm up to that."

"As you wish. There is much to be said for formality. In Norwegian we have the formal and familiar pronouns, *de* and *du*, so we always know where we stand."

Martell said, "Sometimes it's better not to know."

"Hm? Perhaps."

"I'm familiar with Norwegian, by the way. I studied two years in Oslo. *Jeg snakker norsk*, but I read it better than I speak it."

"Then let us by all means speak English. If I have to listen to another Norwegian-American practice his grandfather's dialect on me I think I'll strangle someone." Oski tapped on the glass partition and the driver hummed it partway down.

"Matthew," Oski said, "please follow Professor Martell's instructions. We are picking up a passenger."

Martell gave directions to the Gunderson house. Matthew drove with small, economical movements. The limousine moved quietly as ectoplasm through the streets.

"I'm fortunate to have Matthew's services for a few weeks," said Oski. "He generally drives visiting celebrities in Minneapolis. I fear he'll be bored in Epsom."

Matthew said nothing.

Oski reached into his breast pocket. "I hope you don't mind if I smoke," he said, producing a cigar. "Do you care for one?"

"No, thank you," said Carl.

"I was delighted to find you Americans had abolished those ridiculous antismoking ordinances you were so mad for a few years back."

"It happened when they passed the Smokers' Reenfranchisement Act. The smokers' and industry groups used evidence that there's a gene that makes it hard to quit smoking to argue that they were an oppressed people. The Supreme Court declared the antismoking laws unconstitutional, and now it's politically incorrect to suggest smokers should quit for their health. The official line is that it's the government's responsibility to find cures for cancer and heart disease."

"What a wonderful country," said Oski, blowing a ring. "The comedy never ends."

At the house Martell said, "I'd better get out and fetch Harry. He's expecting to hear a car pull up."

He met the pastor coming onto the porch in hat and overcoat, the overcoat buttoned wrong, a puzzled look on his face.

"I'm sorry, Harry. I should have called to warn you. Sigfod Oski called me and asked to drive me out. I was so surprised I didn't think."

"It's perfectly all right, Carl. I don't often get to ride in a comfortable car." They walked to the comfortable car and Harry had to clutch his hat to keep the wind from taking it.

Matthew held the rear door open for them and they got in, Martell in the middle beside Oski.

"Good morning, *Herr Pastor*," Oski said.

"Actually it's *Pastor Harry.*"

"Your wit, at least, is not lame," said Oski.

Harry opened his mouth, then looked thoughtful and closed it. He settled in the seat and said, "Well, it's a beautiful morning, except for the wind. And this is a splendid car to see it from."

"I decided to lease while I was in this country," said Oski, as Matthew pulled out. "I've always wanted to travel in one of these huge American automobiles. I was disappointed at first to see how many of you drive the small ones now; but I've found that standing out this way gives me a satisfying sense of ostentation. I always suspected that wealth would be more pleasant in America, even aside from the tax structure. It was a Norwegian-American, I think, who coined the term, 'conspicuous consumption.'"

"Thorstein Veblen in *The Theory of the Leisure Class,*" said Harry. "He grew up not far from here."

"He knew whereof he spoke."

"Yes, I think you'll find that as long as you have wealth and influence you can get away with being almost any kind of beast."

Oski smiled wider, uncovering his indecently long teeth. "Exactly! Why else do we pursue wealth? In order to live like beasts. It's the deepest human need, to reverse evolution."

"That's rather good Lutheran theology."

"Yes, but Luther disapproved of it. He called it the Bondage of the Will. I call it the Freedom of the Spirit. Let a man lose his reason and run the hills as a wolf for a few nights—he'll never need theology again."

"Until he dies. An animal can die in peace, but not an animal that was once a man."

Oski's eye glinted. He was enjoying this. "And why should a man die in peace?" he asked. "There is no peace in the world. A man should die in frenzy. A man should die berserk."

"A man should die with courage. A berserker isn't a hero—he's just a short-circuited nervous system. Even the Vikings understood that."

"You'd have people expiring politely in hospital beds, I suppose, giving their lives up by inches to cancer or Alzheimer's."

"I've seen greater courage in hospital beds than any Viking skald ever saw on a battlefield. I only pray I face my own death as well, when the time comes."

Oski bent towards him, wafting smoke in Martell's nostrils. His breath smelled of alcohol as well. "That's the great question, is it not, Pastor Harry? Tell me, how did you lose your leg?"

Harry closed his eyes and said, "It was an auto accident."

"You came near death."

"Yes."

"And how did she appear to you? Lights and music and flowers as the out-of-body-experience people tell it?"

"No. It was a nightmare."

"I thought so." Oski settled back in his place. "You have the look of a man who's been tortured. I knew many such, in the war. Once a man loses the illusion of invulnerability—ah well, he may learn to function, but his spiritual balance is bad. He falls over at odd moments, like a stroke victim."

"Harry's the best balanced man I know," said Martell, looking straight ahead at the asphalt road that took them out of town. The wind was scudding leaves like tiny, thrill-seeking animals in front of the tires.

"Loyalty!" said Oski. "I like that. I like that very much." He turned his long smile on Martell.

Harry said, "Fortunately I have a faith that doesn't depend on my own courage."

"Quite so," said Oski.

Harry said, "Last night you spoke of an old European religion. Do you really believe in that?"

"Yes, in a broad sense. I serve the hard gods. My faith is a venerable one, though long underground."

"You're referring to what they call Witchcraft?"

"Yes. The Old Wisdom, if you like."

"Then we're on our way to your church?"

"Perhaps. I've never visited this farm, so I couldn't say whether it's my sort of place or not. We have schisms of our own, you know."

"Do you practice the Sabbat—the Black Mass?"

"*Langt derifra, Herr Pastor!* The Black Mass is a fantasy of the witch hunters. It became a reality in time, in the court of Louis XIV, but that was the Church's script, acted by degenerate Christians.

"A man with your education ought to be aware that the confessions of the witch trials were extracted from people both ignorant and innocent. They confessed to make the pain stop, and embellished the stories to please the torturers. This produced wonders of fantasy, but little hard information.

"Consider an accused witch, perhaps a child, closed up in a stinking hole, stripped and raped by jailers, beaten, branded, stretched, hoisted up by arms tied behind the back, flesh torn by pincers, forced to sit on a red-hot iron chair, or to kneel on spikes—"

"For the love of Heaven!" cried Harry. "I know about the witch trials. It was a shameful business. There's no excuse."

"But honestly, Herr Pastor, if you had been there—in that time, that place—would you have had the courage to oppose it? If you had lived in Salem, or Spain of the Inquisition—"

"Not Salem and the Inquisition, please," said Harry. "*You* ought to be aware that they were both small potatoes as witch hunts go—although any is too many—and both of them stopped voluntarily and confessed that they'd been wrong.

"Meanwhile two hundred thousand people were tortured and killed in Europe over a period of a couple centuries, mostly in France and Germany. Witch hunting was a growth industry there, run on the profits from confiscated property. Those witch hunters never recanted. And now everybody's forgotten them."

"I commend you, Herr Pastor," said Oski. "You have done your homework. Most Christians deflate like used airbags when I mention witch trials. But the fact remains, it was a Christian crime."

"Too true," said Harry.

"What's more, you miss the irony: how all the time you Christians were earnestly broiling your own, the true witches—my people—were going about their business almost unmolested, although in secret."

"Thank God for that," said the pastor. "In a sense."

"Do not misunderstand me. I don't consider Christianity a cruel religion. Quite the contrary. I could wish you more violent. Burn all the false witches you like." Oski smiled. "I bait you, Herr Pastor. Forgive me."

He turned to Martell. "You've been quiet. Did you sleep poorly?"

"Since you mention it, yes."

"Do you live alone?"

"Yes."

"Well there you are. I've never met a man living by himself who slept decently. Find yourself a strong, lusty woman to keep your house and warm your bed. But—and this is the secret—don't marry her. It gives them an exaggerated sense of their importance. I myself sleep like a stone." He showed his teeth again. Martell wanted to push them down his throat.

They rolled up to the farm driveway. The gate was

opened by two husky young men in flannel shirts, and
the tires rumbled on the gravel to stop where an
ancient barn on the left and an equally old house on
the right flanked the open side of an uneven square
of farm buildings—sheds, granaries, a chicken coop.
Beyond the house and a neglected apple orchard, the
dark, bare trees of Troll Valley fell away northward.
Junk was everywhere—discarded rusting iron wheels,
empty oil drums, a single deflated rubber dinghy.

They stepped out into the wind and a thousand
smells—chicken manure, hogs, cattle, alfalfa hay and
gravel dust—took Martell for one moment back
twenty years, to a place very much like this, and a
panicky sense of work undone. . . .

A group of young people in overalls and shabby
jackets came out of the barn to greet them. Their
leader was easily recognized, both by his carriage and
the way the young people's gazes kept swinging back
to him. He was a tall, strong-looking middle-aged
man, with salt-and-pepper hair and a black beard, and
striking black eyes. His green hooded sweatshirt had
brown stains on it which Martell knew for manure.
The moment he spoke, Martell knew he was a liar.

"Good morning, gentlemen," the liar said, shaking
their hands in turn. His hand was strong, but not yet
callused like a farmer's. "I'm Solar Bull, the priest
here. You must be Professor Martell, and of course
you're Sigfod Oski. We appreciate your coming out.
Uh—who's this?" His eyes fell on Harry's collar.

"I took the liberty of bringing my friend, Pastor
Gunderson of Nidaros Church," said Martell. "He's
interested in this sort of thing. I hope it's all right."

"I trust you're an open-minded sort of minister,"
said Solar Bull.

"I'm relatively harmless anyway," said Harry. "Solar Bull, you say? Any relation to Ole Bull?"

"Ole Bull? I'm afraid I don't understand."

"A 19th Century Norwegian violinist," said Oski. "The pastor is having a little joke."

Solar Bull smiled bleakly.

He said, "I've got to apologize for the way things look around here. We'll make this farm a showplace in time, but there's lots of work to do yet. Jack Tysness was a good farmer—he used very few chemicals on his soil for one thing—but he was a lousy house-keeper. A pack rat. We're still cleaning out the house. And we're modifying some of the buildings for new purposes."

"I see you've lopped the top off the silo," said Harry.

Solar Bull ignored him. "The stone we called you about is right this way. Down here in the granary." He led them towards the far side of the farmyard.

Oski walked beside him. Martell and Harry followed.

"I knew Jack a little," said Harry. "He never came to church. I didn't know he lived this badly. I don't think that house has been painted in twenty years, although I see they're painting it now. And look at the junk everywhere. Jack was one of Keillor's Nor-wegian Bachelor Farmers if anyone ever was. He had a bad reputation, you know. He kept sheep."

Martell said, "My father used to warn me that if I didn't straighten out I'd end up a dirty old bach-elor in a place like this. I suppose Minna would say he was a prophet."

Harry laughed, and they followed Solar Bull and Oski into the granary, a white two-story building with a concrete floor and a big sliding door half open. An old hammer mill hulked in one corner. The grain bins were on both sides and on the floor above.

A gray, rectangular stone, about a yard long, had been set on a pair of sawhorses in the middle of the floor. It was broken, almost exactly halved by a frac-ture across its width.

"Here she is," said Solar Bull. "I think you'll agree that it's not something we could have whipped up ourselves."

Someone switched on a bare light hanging on a cord from the ceiling. They stepped in closer, Martell and Harry circling, hanging back a bit like visitors in a museum. But Oski approached like a lover, or a wrestler, laying his hands on the slab, running them over its surface, probing the chiseled, twiglike letters with a long finger. Martell and Harry had to lean in to see.

After several minutes Oski tilted up his face. "Well, Martell, what do you make of it?"

"They *are* runes."

"No question about that."

"It's hard to say more. I'm not qualified to judge age. I could probably translate it if I had a few days and some reference books."

"Ah, well, that's no problem," said Oski. He straightened, set his finger on the top row of symbols and moved it, reading:

*Dead are Erik and Johan and Ommund.
AVM and Blessed Holy Trinity grant us . . .
er . . . rest. Hard it is to die in a heathen land.
Remember to our account how we slew the
wicked and bound the . . . the gelding with
this sign—*

"The last figure has been obliterated by the fracture." He took his hand away. "That's all."

"I suppose 'the wicked' would be their description of Indians," Harry hazarded.

"Not necessarily," said Oski. "If you've read Hjalmar Holand on the Kensington stone—I grant he was no scholar—you'll remember he pointed to an expedition to Greenland contemplated by the king of Sweden and Norway in the mid-14th Century. There were rumors that the Greenlanders were coming back to my side, taking up the old religion, and he suddenly saw his Christian duty to chastise them, although he'd never given them a thought before.

"Supposing the expedition did sail—its leader was to have been a noble named Paul Knutsson—Holand thought it would have found those particular Greenlanders fled to America. The colony was declining by then."

"You think there were Greenlanders—this far inland?" asked Martell.

"It's possible. A few refugees in a hostile land. Easily slaughtered by the Church's picked thugs."

"Let me get this straight," said Martell. "Are you suggesting the Kensington Runestone is genuine? I thought all the experts agreed that it's a fraud, and not even a good fraud."

"The story of historical research," said Oski, "is the story of experts with egg on their faces. I have examined the matter to my own satisfaction and am convinced of the authenticity of the Kensington inscription."

"What's this business about a gelding?" asked Harry.

"I confess I am at a loss about that," said Oski. Martell's stomach jumped. *Lie!* Breathing deeply, Oski said, "It rings a bell, but . . ."

"Excuse me," Solar Bull put in. "What's this Kensington stone?"

Martell looked sharply at him. The man was a liar, but he wasn't lying about his ignorance.

Oski said, "Go ahead, Martell. It *is* an American artifact."

Martell said, "Kensington's in the western part of the state, near Alexandria. Just before the turn of the century, a Swedish farmer claimed he had found a carved stone caught in the roots of a tree. When it was finally deciphered, it told the story of a party of Swedes and Norwegians who had been exploring and had lost men in a fight with Indians. The date given was 1362. Almost nobody took it seriously then, and almost nobody takes it seriously now. But its defenders have always been pretty passionate."

"You think this stone's connected with that one?" Solar Bull's nostrils were flaring.

"It almost certainly is, one way or another," Martell answered.

Solar Bull looked at Martell with cold eyes. "You mean you think they're both frauds?"

"I'm not qualified to say, as I keep telling people. Mr. Oski here is an expert. Ask him."

Oski was smiling. "A bit early to say. But this stone is very interesting—very interesting indeed."

Watching him, Martell sensed only sincerity, and it troubled him more than a lie would have.

"What the hell is that?" asked Solar Bull, turning towards the driveway. They all looked up to see a van pulling in, followed by a car. Both vehicles had insignia on their sides and the van sported a satellite dish like a jaunty cap. The guards stopped them and voices were raised.

"That will be the television news," said Oski. "I rang a station in Minneapolis. I hope that's not inconvenient, Mr. Bull."

Solar Bull said, "No! It's not time for television yet!"

Oski said, "It is precisely the time."

They glared at each other. Martell and Harry looked on, a little alarmed.

It was Solar Bull who broke eye contact at last, and when he did he seemed to Martell somehow smaller than before. He turned stiffly and waved to the young men at the gate. The gate was opened and the van and car rolled in.

Quickly the crew emerged from the van, bringing out cameras, microphones, coils of cable and various black boxes, which they assembled rapidly. A young man in a Civil War forage cap took a light meter reading on the stone and asked if it could be moved out into the sunshine. Solar Bull nodded, frowning, and four strong young men from W.O.W. carried it and the sawhorses out onto the gravel. They set it back carefully, lining up the two halves along the fracture.

A beautifully groomed young man in a handsome suit emerged from the car. His face was strong, his blue eyes clear, his teeth perfect. He carried a small notebook in one hand. He went directly to Oski and shook his hand. "I'm Ben Goss," he said. "Very pleased to meet you, Mr. Oski. Perhaps you could give me an interview later, since everything's set up."

Oski introduced the others. "Mr. Martell, Pastor Gunderson, Mr. Bull," Goss said, flashing his teeth and looking each of them straight in the eye. "Glad to meet you." Martell read that as a lie, without surprise. Goss opened his notebook.

"So what's the story here?" he asked. "First the stone. Afterwards, I want to hear about W.O.W. too. You don't mind a little free publicity, do you, Mr. Bull?"

Solar Bull glanced at Oski and said, "No," shortly.

Goss asked deft questions and took shorthand notes. When he had the story, he turned to the crew and asked, "Okay, you guys ready to roll? Let's do it."

Somebody ran a comb through Goss's hair, a little tangled by the wind, and it fell miraculously into place. Harry, whose hat was on sideways, watched in wonder. The cameraman focused on Goss and he looked into the glass eye, saying, "This is the American heartland, a typical dairy farm near a typical Minnesota small town. But then maybe not so typical. You wouldn't expect to find an unorthodox religious commune here, or a controversial archaeological find. But that's exactly what we've discovered, at the Way of the Old Wisdom, just outside Epsom.

"A few months ago this farm was acquired by the W.O.W. group, formerly headquartered in California. Its leader is a man who calls himself Roller Ball. Mr. Ball says the stone was discovered under somewhat sinister circumstances."

He pointed his microphone at Solar Bull, who scowled but spoke. "We found the stone a few weeks ago, in the roots of a tree stump, near the place where Mr. Tysness—that was the farm's last owner—the spot where he died last spring. But we never noticed the carvings until just yesterday."

"How old was the tree it was found in?"

Martell wanted to kick himself for not asking this question himself. The tree that had, or had not, been growing around the Kensington stone had been lost, and its size had always been a point of contention.

"I'm afraid we chopped it up for firewood," said Solar Bull. "We use a lot of wood for heating. But it was a big tree—an oak." *He's not lying*, Martell thought.

"Mr. Tysness died mysteriously, didn't he?"

"So I understand. We were in California at the time—I don't know much about it."

The camera followed as Goss turned to Oski. "This is Sigfod Oski, the Nobel-prize-winning Norwegian poet who has caused considerable stir by coming to Christiania College in Epsom. Mr. Oski, you are an expert on this kind of carvings, aren't you?"

Oski said, "Yes. They are called runes."

"Would you say these ruins are genuine? By that I mean, were they actually carved by Vikings?"

Oski smiled at the lens. "Let me clarify, please. Vikings could not have carved this stone. You must realize that the Viking Age ended, for all practical purposes, during the 11th century. We Scandinavians have been respectable, some would say dull, Europeans ever since. But we continued to use the runes here and there up into the 16th century. The runes on this stone indicate a date sometime in the 14th century. The men who carved them were not Vikings, and probably would have been offended if you had called them Vikings. But they were well ahead of Columbus, which is, I think, the point."

"And you would call this stone genuine—not a forgery or a practical joke of some kind?"

"Absolute certainty is impossible so early in the day. But I am inclined to judge it authentic. I know I wouldn't question it for a second had it been found in Norway." *Lie.* What part was a lie Martell could not tell.

Goss turned back to the camera. "Also here to view the stone is Professor Charles Marcell of Christiania College. You are an expert on the ruins also, Professor Marcell?"

Martell took a nervous step toward the microphone, and as he moved he touched the stone.

The wave ran up his arm, swift as pain. Pain, not nausea.

"Professor Marcell? Professor?"

Martell came to himself again. For a moment he looked blankly at Goss and his equipment.

"Professor Marcell?"

"Martell. It's Martell. Carl Martell."

Goss said, "Cut," irritation on his face. "Look, Professor, if there's any corrections to be made we can fix them in production. For now just go with the program, okay?"

The camera was cued again and Goss pointed his microphone. "Professor Martell. You *are* an expert on ruins?"

"Not an expert. I'm familiar with runes. I'm the

closest thing Christiania had to an expert before Mr. Oski came."

"But what's your opinion? Is it a fake or not?"

Martell took a breath. "I—I'd say it's genuine."

From the corner of his eye he saw Harry turn to goggle at him.

"How sure are you?" Goss seemed to crowd in, his microphone's head as big as a cannon's mouth.

"I'm morally certain of it."

Goss turned back to the camera. "So," he said, "the mystery begins. You can be sure this isn't the last we'll hear of the Epsom Ruinstone.

"I'm Ben Goss for Viewpoint News." He stared into the camera until somebody said "Cut," then relaxed. He shook hands all around and told them they'd been just great. Then he went to Solar Bull and Oski. "We'd love to do a feature on the operation here," Martell heard him saying, "and then I'd like to set aside some time to talk to you, Mr. Oski."

Harry limped to Martell and said, "Didn't you say—?" But in a moment everyone was following the newspeople on a guided tour of the farm.

It proved unremarkable. The young people—there seemed to be about twenty-five—were all working very hard at painting and fixing up, and there were a lot of livestock about: cattle, sheep, pigs and goats. Also chickens. Martell sneezed and stayed out of the chicken house. Even as a boy, he remembered, he had hated the smell of chickens. If bizarre sexual acts or dark and bloody rites were practiced here, they were not going on that morning.

After a half an hour, Harry told Oski he had to get back to his office for a premarital counseling session.

"We certainly can't have you missing that," said Oski with a smile. "Let people lose the habit of marrying in church and they'll forget what the places look like."

"And what will they do when they're looking for a hypocrite?" said Harry blandly.

"Here's what we'll do then, if you're agreeable. I'll send you home in my car now and have Matthew return for me later tonight. I'd like to see more of the establishment here, and I imagine I'll have to give Mr. Goss a few minutes."

Martell and Harry thanked him and walked back to the car. They found Matthew waiting inside, reading the *Wall Street Journal*.

When they were seated, Matthew asked over his shoulder, "You two want some privacy?"

"How did you guess?" Harry asked.

"You spent the morning with Oski." The glass panel rolled silently up.

"He's quite a man, Sigfod Oski," said Harry, leaning his head back against the upholstery.

They were turning out of the driveway when a pickup truck roared up out of Troll Valley and shot past them. Matthew handled the limousine skillfully, braking and steering, avoiding a collision and keeping them out of the ditch as the gravel slipped under the tires. He was saying something as he steered, but the men in back couldn't hear.

Martell turned to Harry and found him white-faced, open-mouthed, clutching handfuls of soft leather in each fist.

Martell put a hand on his arm. "Are you all right, Harry?"

Harry looked at him without recognition for a moment, then shook his head and relaxed a bit. "I'm sorry," he said. "It's a thing I have about auto accidents. You understand."

"Of course."

"Oski had me pegged perfectly. I'm terrified of dying. Especially in a car . . . and fire."

Martell nodded. Harry had been pulled from the

wreck badly burned, but the burns, like the fears, were in hidden places.

Harry was still breathing hard. "He pushed all my buttons, Carl. It must be some kind of predator's instinct. Death, and then all that business about the witch trials. The shameful places in Church history. There are a lot of people out there who think I must be a closet inquisitor because I'm an orthodox Christian. They assume that if I were a man of good will I'd be broad-minded like them. It's a hard argument to refute, like all arguments from emotion."

"I think I know what you mean," said Martell, remembering Professor Forsythe.

"What do I answer when somebody says, 'Well, how about all those good Lutherans who shoveled Jews into the ovens for Hitler?' And to make it worse—let's face it—Luther said some inexcusable things about the Jews."

Harry seemed calmer now. Martell said, "I've never bought the argument that Luther was a proto-Nazi. Nazism was a heresy of 19th century Romanticism and Darwinism, not Lutheranism."

Harry said, "Can you imagine a meeting between Luther and, say, Goebbels?"

Martell laughed. "I don't think they'd have gotten along."

"They'd have been rolling on the floor trying to gouge each other's eyes out. But then we go on to the Crusades, the Inquisition, the Witch Trials—I'm always vulnerable in a way. I am, after all, what those men were—a conservative in my time. And everyone seems to agree that it's only conservative Christianity that's evil.

"Of course how could the liberal brand be evil? You've got to *be* something to fall to the level of the demonic. Whoever heard of an evil sentimentality?"

"You were pretty impressive with your statistics on

the witch hunts," said Martell. "I'm a historian, and I'd forgotten a lot of that."

"Self-defense, Carl. A good, hard fact is the best defense there is—against everything except tears. There's a whole generation of debators in the church who've learned that you don't have to refute an argument if you can only burst into tears and make your opponent look like a cad. And not all of them are women."

"I know," said Martell. Then he opened his mouth and found himself telling it.

"I lost my nerve about eleven years ago. I had a master's and an instructorship at the University, and I thought I had the Philosopher's Stone. I published some of my deathless thoughts in one of the smaller journals. To make my point I attacked a book written some years earlier by one of the heavyweights in the department, a man named Riley Forsythe."

"I think I've heard of him. He wrote that biography of Mother Teresa, didn't he?"

"That's the one. An analysis of the kind of psychological dysfunction that would drive a person to waste her life in service to others, rather than in normal healthy self-interest."

"Appalling book."

"He was an appalling man, take it from one who knows. Anyway, I tore an earlier book of his apart. I was brilliant. I dismantled him point by point. My logic was elegant, seasoned with a dash of wiseacrey.

"You know what I think about history. I see a pattern—it isn't a mindless process. It's a work of art. And individuals—remarkable, serendipitous individuals—shape and define the pattern. I don't deny that there are other forces at work, but individuals create those forces too. Anyway, some of my arguments were very good. Some of them were codswallop. Very few were as original as I thought.

"Forsythe didn't even confront me at first. He just sent a note inviting me to debate. I should have expected the rest. People started avoiding me in the halls.

"My God, Harry, he was beautiful. He didn't waste time addressing my arguments. He beat me on poise. He beat me on wit. He beat me on sarcasm and good tailoring. He opened up my belly and displayed the color of my guts to the assembly of my peers. If it had happened to somebody else I would have carried away a lot of very useful information on how the real world works. But being the victim I just had to crawl away and lick my wounds, and my broken legs."

Martell felt clammy at the armpits as he remembered Dr. Forsythe, with his long, pale face, at the podium across the stage, a half-smile on his lips, the light gleaming on his bald skull. *"Mr. Martell has done us all a service,"* he had said. *"He has brought us a new historical tool—or is it an old one?—Revealed Truth. Revealed to him alone, of course. But not to worry—we can always come to him and sit at his feet, and listen to the divine syllables that drip from his lips. OR WE CAN LEARN TO USE OUR REASON. WE CAN LEARN TO REJECT NONSENSE.*

"I do not say that Mr. Martell is a burner of heretics, or a gasser of Jews. But his thought—all the myths of our barbarous and vicious past—lead certainly to the stake and the death camp. We have had enough of Romance, of Heroism and Idealism. They promise much, but end in vicious parody. We shall not again be taken in by such demagoguery . . ."

Harry said, "It's not a unique experience, Carl."

"I had a responsibility. To the truth. I failed in my defense of it. I made the truth look as foolish as I was. And, like Oski's tortured man, I never got my balance back.

"There's an epilogue to the story too. Properly

farcical." He saw in a snapshot of memory Elaine standing in a sunny room, holding a yellow dress in her hands. "The next day Elaine moved out on me. It seemed to make sense. I guess the logic of the story demanded it."

"You think your life is governed by the logic of the story?"

"I suppose I do."

"And what does the logic of the story demand of you now?"

"That's easy. I have to redeem myself by a noble death."

"*Kyrie eleison.*"

Matthew pulled the car up to the curb in front of the church, as instructed. He helped the pastor out, was thanked for the ride.

Before walking away, Harry tapped on Martell's window. When it opened he said, "I was going to ask you—I almost forgot—I thought you were going to be cautious about that stone."

Martell looked back, smiling crookedly. The skin around his eyes was almost blue.

"Can you believe six impossible things before breakfast?"

"I've had my breakfast. I'm probably good for a dozen."

"Something's happening to me, Harry. I've become a kind of human polygraph. God knows how or why, but when somebody lies to me, I know it. If I try to tell a lie myself, my gut cramps up. And it's been getting worse. Lately I've been able to tell when people are lying on paper. And, apparently, on stone.

"When I touched that stone, I knew it was no lie. I felt—I felt pain, and fear and faith. But no lie. Nobody lied carving that stone. I'm sure of it.

"Of course I'm probably just losing my mind."

"It's a strange world, Carl. '*Turn but a stone and*

start a wing.' Is there any evidence this sense of yours has ever deceived you?"

"Actually, no."

"Then keep an open mind. You might even pray about it, if it wouldn't offend your sensibilities."

"I'd be pretending. I believe in God in some sense, but I'm not sure He or It answers prayer. It would hurt." That wasn't quite how he wanted to put it, but he had trouble saying what he meant about God.

"I'll pray for you then," said Harry.

Martell smiled again. "Yes, you will."

Harry turned away and steeled himself for the walk to his office. It had been a tiring morning, and the stump hurt more than usual.

In the car Matthew rolled down the divider and said to Martell, "So, did you gentlemen have a nice morning?"

"I wouldn't call it that exactly." Martell smiled.

"That Oski's a piece of work, isn't he?"

"How is he to work for?"

"When you've driven drunken movie stars and stoned politicians, brother, you learn not to let anything get to you. You'd be surprised how many of those friends of humanity call me 'boy' when they get a snootful. At least Oski's no hypocrite."

"You enjoy doing this?"

"Beats teaching school."

"You were a teacher?"

"High school. Teacher of the Year runner-up in Illinois once."

"Why'd you quit?"

"It got worse and worse; you know how it is. One day in a class I stood up for a white student who was trying to make a point. Just trying to make a point. Freedom of speech, right? 'I may not agree with what you say, but I'll defend to the death your right to say it'?

"Some of the students complained, and I got called up before a union disciplinary board.

"I said, 'The kid had some points. I was just trying to keep the discussion fair and open to everybody.'

"They said fair play was a dead white male concept designed to oppress women and minorities.

"I said, 'You mean I have to give up fair play because I'm black? You're saying because I'm black I have to cheat and lie and bully, to be true to my people?'

"Then they got really mad. It ended up with me losing my accreditation. I could have appealed it, I suppose. But I thought, 'Hell, if teaching is just propaganda, if nobody cares about finding the truth or living decently, what's the point?' Maybe if I'd stayed on I could have made a difference. I don't know. Driving this boat around's a lot easier on the nerves."

Martell said, "You need another driver?"

"I'm really gonna do it this time," said the young woman's voice over the phone.

"I'm not questioning your seriousness, Cassie," said Harry, hunched over his church office desk. "I'm just asking you to think it over. Think about your family—think about—"

"I just want the pain to go away," she said.

"I know—believe me, I know something about pain—but the Happy Endings Clinic is no answer. You don't get another try at this, you know—you go inside there and you don't come out again."

"All I care about is ending the pain."

"Will you at least come in here and talk to me about it?"

"What can you tell me I haven't heard before?"

"I love you, Cassie. I love you as Christ loves you. You know it will hurt me very much if you choose

to end your life. Not to mention your mother and
father."

"I can't let other people run my life, Pastor."

"Will you come talk to me?"

The voice murmured.

"What was that?"

"I'll come in."

"Thanks, Cassie. I appreciate it. I owe you one."

"You sure do." She hung up.

Harry bowed his head in prayer for a moment. The
phone rang again.

He listened to a distraught voice for several minutes, then promised to get over to the hospital right
away, hung up, rose and stumped down the hall to
Pastor Hardanger-Hansen's office. He found the senior
pastor at her computer, working on statistical reports.

"What do you want, Harry?"

"I've got a situation here—I need you to help me
if you can."

"What's the problem? I'm pretty busy here. The dis-
trict gets nasty if we get behind on our demographics."

"Jerry Mathre just called. Amelia's passed away."

"Oh, I'm sorry."

"He's pretty broken up—you know how long they've
been fighting it—and he says he needs me over there
right now. The thing is, I've got Cassie Jensen coming in in a few minutes."

"Suicidal again?"

"Yes. It's one of her bad days."

"How old is she again?"

"Seventeen."

"Poor kid."

"Indeed. Can you fill in for me? This'll take a
couple hours, and then I have my Bible Study to lead.
Cassie'll probably be upset that I'm not here—she'll
take it as a rejection. Make it clear that it was a
sudden death that took me away. Do the 'just between

us women' thing. Maybe she'll open up to you. She needs desperately to feel loved and important to someone."

"Yeah, okay—of course this takes precedence. I'll handle it. It's what I'm here for."

"Thanks. I owe you one."

"Yesterday we talked about Harald Finehair and the beginnings of the Norwegian monarchy," Martell told his Scandinavian History class. He looked out over the students and experienced a bizarre mental fugue. It seemed for just a second that the thirty desks were filled by neat rows of sharply dressed young people in dark suits and long dresses. The class of 1912. Then his vision cleared and the twelve strangely barbered heads he knew were back. Only a few of the class members were paying attention, and even more weren't present and never would be (they knew they'd pass on VQ points), yet he was determined as the sower who goes forth to sow. These young people, while he had them here, were *his* students. He felt a fierce responsibility for them.

"In spite of all Harald's exertions, you still could have asked the reasonable question, 'What *is* Norway?' Look at it on the map—a ribbon of land along the coast of the Scandinavian peninsula. Incredibly rugged terrain. The easiest route between almost any two points is by sea. And populated by people who, even into the 19th century, often couldn't understand each other's language from one valley to the next. How do you build a political entity out of what is essentially a trade route? Today we answer that question, and we answer it with an epic—a saga Norway would never forget—the story of the two Olafs."

"Aren't we a little overbooked with Olafs here?" asked Jason Scaretti, the designated class cynic. He had enrolled for obscure reasons but did well. Martell relished the friction Jason generated. "How do you tell them apart? All you squareheads look alike to me."

"Good point," said Martell. "Few people even realize that there were two Olafs, and most who do think they were father and son. Let me illustrate." He drew a tall stick figure with a helmet and a sword on the board, and drew a beard on him with yellow chalk. "This is a reasonable facsimile of Olaf Trygvesson. Tall, blonde, athletic, handsome. If he were alive today he'd be an Olympic skier."

"He's a lot more interesting than St. Olaf," said Cindy Hallstrom, who seemed to be recovered from her heartbreak.

"Most people would agree, Cindy. Olaf Trygvesson is the *beau ideal* of the Viking Age. He climbed mountains and juggled swords and ran around the outside of his ship on the oars like Kirk Douglas in the movie. And Snorri Sturlusson, in his great saga of the kings, the *Heimskringla*, gives him a ripsnorter of a childhood, full of chases and escapes and slavery and vengeance. Yes, Kimberly?"

Kimberly Benson-Odegaard-Martinez-Braun, the class chronological snob, a thinnish young woman with very long fingernails, asked, "Hasn't modern psychology proved that all this macho sword swinging and heroism is just an outlet for repressed sexuality?"

Martell said, "No, it has not. If there's one thing I'm reasonably sure about, it's that very few Vikings were sexually repressed.

"Where was I? Oh yes, Olaf Trygvesson converted to Christianity in Britain, then sailed home to conquer Norway. He picked the best possible moment. Everybody was sick to death of Jarl Haakon, the Trondheim earl. Haakon was killed, Olaf took over. His main domestic program was to convert the land to Christianity, and he used the direct method—baptism or death."

"But isn't it true," asked Gary Qualle, a fat young man who sat in the back, did well in tests, and only spoke when he thought he'd caught the instructor in a mistake, "that Adam of Bremen said Olaf Trygvesson wasn't a Christian at all? And Adam wrote a lot earlier than Snorri."

"Good point. You're right . . . as usual. Adam accused Olaf of subsidizing witches and practicing divination with birds, so that he got the nickname 'Crowbone.'

"This brings up an important point in the theory of history." There were groans from the students. "Who do you believe? Adam, because he was closer in time? Perhaps, but he had a political axe to grind related to ecclesiastical jurisdictions. Snorri, because he passes on what seems to be genuine Norwegian tradition? Again, perhaps, but we can never lose sight of the fact that Snorri was primarily an artist, a storyteller.

"You can take your own choice, but the truth probably lies somewhere in between. There are plenty of historical precedents for half-savage chieftains who practice the best Christianity they can cobble together, mixing in a lot of the old— Yes, Jason?"

"Does the truth always lie somewhere in between?"

"Gotcha! I have tricked you into asking a Meaningful Question. Does the truth always lie somewhere in between? Historians like to think in formulas, just like real people. We assume the truth lies between two extremes, but it may not. It may be crouching in ambush at one end or the other. But the extremes tend to be romantic and exciting, while the middle is nice and dull, so we bet on the middle for fear history will become too interesting and get overrun with riffraff. Yes, Jason?"

"What it comes down to is that we don't know anything for sure, right? Didn't somebody say that history is a lie that's been agreed on?"

"Voltaire, yes. And he had a point. History books are usually written by the winning side. One obvious exception is the Bible, which was mainly written by the losers, and is more dependable because of it. But when we go to an archaeological dig and look for physical evidence, it generally supports most of what the books say. It's a little like physics, I suppose. If you take physics too seriously, you discover that this desk I'm leaning on is really a pattern of electrical fields consisting mostly of empty space. It disappears, in theory. But in fact I remain supported by it. Too much precision can be the greatest falsehood of all for finite minds. Don't ask me what that means."

"You mean we don't see the forest for the trees," said Gary Qualle in a bored voice.

"Yes. Well put. I'll tell you this though—if there were such a thing as selling your soul to the devil, I'd be awfully tempted to sell mine for the chance to watch a day in the life of somebody like Olaf Trygvesson."

"Maybe you could get into that new program at Berkeley," said Kimberly. "They say using psychic evidence in the study of history is a very promising discipline."

"If you consider wishful thinking a discipline," said Martell.

"That's pretty judgmental, isn't it? Who are you to decide what another person's truth should be?"

"If the truth is something each of us makes up for himself, then there's no reason for us to be doing this. I'm here to help you develop skills to evaluate hard evidence for real events."

"Are you saying you believe in Absolute Truth?" Kimberly had her pencil poised over the red notebook she always carried.

"I plead the Fifth Amendment."

"How would you know absolute truth if you found it? How can you judge absolutes in a relative world?"

Martell thought a moment. "The time-honored principle of Occam's razor," he said. "Both the principle and the razor. The principle says that you should always opt for the simplest adequate explanation. The razor says you should always opt for the answer that cuts you, because people are not essentially good, and therefore the truth always hurts us a little. That's how I judge truth—simplicity and discomfort."

Silence fell on the room. It was the first moment of real silence Martell could remember in this class.

"Well, Olaf must have been a Christian," said Cindy at last, "because it was his missionary work that got him in trouble, right?"

"Not necessarily," said Gary, not bothering to be called on. "Central monarchy was a new idea in Norway. Jarl Haakon's family thought they had every bit as much right to rule as Olaf, only they didn't call themselves kings. And you've got to give them credit for that."

"Absolutely," said Martell. "Also, there were probably a lot of Christians in Norway already, and they weren't all friends of Olaf's. Norway was just a very bad place to king in those days, as a long line of kings who died with their boots on testifies.

"Anyway, Haakon's son Erik joined forces with Svein Forkbeard of Denmark and Olaf Skottkonung of Sweden, and they caught Olaf at sea—God knows where, but we call it the battle of Svold. Olaf jumped overboard in full armor, an act of dubious orthodoxy, and ceased to be a political force."

He drew a fat figure on the board, giving him a red chalk beard. "This was around 1000 A.D. Olaf Haraldsson here was about five years old at the time—"

"He wasn't Olaf Trygvesson's son?" asked Cindy.

"No. He was some kind of cousin."

"Didn't Olaf Haraldsson have brown hair?" asked Gary.

"According to Snorri, yes. But I didn't have any brown chalk, and some sources say his beard was kind of red, like Thor's."

"And this one's the saint, right?" asked Jason.

"Officially at least. He was canonized, although he never got much of a following outside of Scandinavia. That must have left him in a pretty awkward spot in Heaven when the Scandinavians went Lutheran."

Jason said, "He should have been glad to get into Heaven at all."

"Very true. Nowadays, and all through history really, most people have preferred their saints more along the lines of Francis of Assissi. And of course they're perfectly right. Kimberly?"

"Hasn't modern sociology proved that the medieval craze for sainthood was just a misplaced manifestation of earlier polytheism?"

"I suppose you could say that if you believe that Thor is somehow more real than Francis of Assissi. Is that what you mean?"

"I'm . . . not sure."

"All right. Olaf Haraldsson started his career in the approved manner, raising bloody hell all over the Baltic and England, also possibly France and Spain. In France he was baptized, then he went to England to fight against Ethelred—or for him as a mercenary, we're not quite sure.

"Now you all remember who kicked Ethelred out of England, don't you?" He looked expectantly at the class.

"Knut, the King of Denmark," said Gary after a sportsmanlike pause.

"That's right. Knut the Great. And apparently it

occurred to Olaf that with Knut busy in England trying to turn the tide back and learn to spell his name with a *C*, now was the time to kiss babies in Norway. His timing was as good as the first Olaf's—everybody was sick of the new generation of Trondheim jarls—and Olaf got one look at the jarl's heels and found himself on the throne."

"And he made himself holy by breaking legs for God," said Jason.

"That's one way to put it. Christianity was a political program for him, and he enforced it by police methods. But try an experiment with me—try to look at it from Olaf's point of view. Your Sociology courses are supposed to teach you to do this with people from every possible different culture, and if 11th century Norway isn't a different culture, I don't know what is. *Why* was Christianizing Norway so important to Olaf?"

"Because he wanted to bring it the blessings of civilization," said Jason drily.

"You are groping towards the point," said Martell, "but sarcasm won't get you there. You've learned how to do this with Papuans and Eskimos—try for once to be fair to your own ancestors. Yes, Jason, your ancestors too. What did civilization mean for a country in those days?"

"Equality with other countries?" asked Cindy.

"Yes! As long as Norway served the old gods, and got its moral and social ideas from the old gods, Norwegians would see the rest of mankind as a sort of cattle, to be hunted for sport or sold for profit. And the rest of Europe would see them as subhuman barbarians. Olaf knew that the robbing, the killing, the raping, the slavetaking—that all had to end. And the sooner the better for all concerned."

"Still, it was a lot to give up," said Jason with a smile.

Somebody whispered something, and Martell let it pass, but Kimberly made a note in her book with a frown.

Gary Qualle said, "Most modern historians disagree with you about that, you know. They say the Vikings were no different than anybody else, but they got a bad press from the monks because they weren't Christians."

"That's true," said Martell. "All I can say is that, from my study of the documents and the scholarship, I can't agree. Nobody loves Vikings more than I do. I study them because, for me, it's the most fun I can make a living at. But it's only a pleasure from a safe distance. I would not want a Viking in my neighborhood. The high god Odin is a magical, very moving presence in my imagination, but I have to remind myself that he also stood for death, and scavenger birds, and madness and hanged men."

"All right," said Jason. "So Olaf was a progressive politician. That doesn't make him a saint."

"Ah!" said Martell. "Here comes the intriguing part. This is where I do something really heretical. I'm going to talk to you about Providence. I apologize for using an unfashionable word, but for the life of me I can't find a better one. Never let on that I've mentioned it, because I'd be blackballed from all the historians' clubs.

"I contend that the explanation for the beatification of Olaf Haraldsson can only satisfactorily be found through the artistry of Snorri Sturlusson. By which I do not mean that Snorri made Olaf a saint. That had been done long before. But Snorri's poetic approach gives us a perspective on what happened that ordinary history can't provide. Because Snorri gives us a peek into Olaf's heart, and it's Olaf's heart that explains what happened to him, and to all Norway after him. Yes, Kimberly?"

"Doesn't modern historical theory prove that individuals cannot influence history? That everything would have been the same regardless of who was king?"

"If you persist in that kind of thinking, Kimberly, you will probably end up a respected historian in some prestigious university, long after I've starved to death in a gutter somewhere. Yes, that's more or less what they say. I happen to think they're wrong, but I'm outnumbered and you all should know that.

"As I was saying, here's what we know without Snorri's help: Olaf was a good king. He established law. He ruled with total integrity and utter ruthlessness.

"His first big mistake was to join the Swedish king Onund Jakob in an expedition to chastise Skåne, the part of Sweden that used to be part of Denmark. Knut the Great showed up in time to cut them off at the pass—or the Kattegat anyway—and Olaf had to leave his ships in Sweden and go home overland. Once there he found that most of his richest subjects had gone over to Knut. Snorri says they were bribed—that's probably uncharitable. The nobles were accustomed to revolting every few years, and Norwegians are creatures of habit."

"Erling Skjalgsson was one of them, wasn't he?" asked a student named Howard, an earnest, well-groomed young man who cultivated his instructors and understood *nothing*.

"Yes, Howard, Erling Skjalgsson was one of them, and as you all know I have published a paper on him. You're not going to get me going on Erling today, except to mention that he was probably the most appealing Viking in Snorri's book—the kind of man who operated self-help programs for his slaves. Also a Christian—one of many opposed to Olaf. Olaf's second, and biggest, mistake was to cause Erling's murder. Apparently by misunderstanding."

"Or so he said," said Gary Qualle.

"So he said. As he pointed out to the killer, it was a disastrous political move. He fought a few battles, sniffed the wind, and hightailed it for Russia. So now, who's in charge of Norway?"

"Denmark?" asked Cindy.

"Right. The first British Empire—England, Denmark and Norway. But Knut the Great made a mistake. When his Norwegian regent died, he tried to replace him with his own son Svein. The Norwegians started sharpening their axes again. Olaf thought this was his chance. It was, but not for the kind of crown he had in mind.

"Most of the nobles and farmers didn't want Olaf any more than Knut, so they gathered an army and marched to meet Olaf at a place called Stiklestad, northeast of Trondheim, or Nidaros. It was a Norwegian army, with a lot of Christians in it. Olaf's army was much smaller, composed of anybody he was able to scrape up, including a lot of heathens, although Snorri swears it wasn't so."

"I get it now," said Jason. "The reason they made him a saint was because he was too stupid to run away."

"You're not far off. The old Vikings believed that there were times when a man started acting in self-destructive ways, when no one could persuade him to be sensible; and that meant he was doomed to die. Snorri's Olaf seems 'fey' in this way. He claims he has seen a vision of all of Norway, and all the world beyond, and he's acting in response to that vision, not strategy. The morning before the battle he puts money in escrow to pay for prayers for the souls of his enemies. This is not like him.

"Critics will tell you that Snorri made Olaf get more spiritual at the end of the story as a literary device. Maybe. But I think the men who marched

with Olaf to Stiklestad saw things that made them
marvel, that made them rethink their world, things
that set a slow poison at the roots of the Viking ethos.
The men who followed Olaf saw the logic of the story.
They saw saga turn into tragedy, and a king turn into
a saint, and they found that tragedy and sainthood
have their own kinds of glory.

"I contend—and you may be sure that nobody
agrees with me—that there never was a Norway
before Stiklestad, and after it, Norway was almost
impossible to kill. What kept the Norwegians Norwegian during four hundred years of Danish rule, and
one hundred years of Swedish? It was a memory. It
went like this: 'We are the people who killed Olaf.
We are the people Olaf died for.'"

"Of course that's nonsense if you reject the myth
of the Great Man," said Kimberly.

"That's true. I myself reject the myth of the Myth."

"So do we follow you or the experts when we
answer essay questions?" asked Jason.

"Follow your own best reasoning, and back up what
you say. That's all I ask."

Jason held one fist up in a Black Power salute and
said, "*Fram!*"

Martell looked at him. "Very good. Jason has just
quoted Olaf's battle cry, 'Forward, forward, Christ-
men, Cross-men, King's men!' Also the motto of St.
Olaf College in Northfield, where some of you are
rumored to party on weekends. Speaking of weekends, your reading assignment will be—" He gave
them a chapter in the textbook and dismissed the
class.

Howard and a few apple polishers came forward
to stroke the instructor, and between their heads
Martell saw Cindy walking out in earnest conversation with Jason. It struck him that they might make
an excellent couple.

The following hour he lectured a European Civilization class on the decline of Rome and the Ostrogoths. As usual he related a quotation from General Belisarius to the bromide, "Rome wasn't built in a day," and as usual no one thanked him for the insight.

He was in his office just after 11:00, when the phone rang.

"Carl? This is Elaine. Please don't hang up."

Martell's hand tightened painfully on the receiver.

"Carl? Carl? Please."

"Hello," he said. "What's on your mind?" He thought, *I ought to get the Nobel Prize for Banality.*

"I've got no right asking you for favors, Carl, I know that. But I do need to see you—if you can spare the time—"

"I'm in my office. Free till one."

"I can't come to your office. Someone might see me. It's got to be someplace neutral. And not public."

Martell couldn't think of a reply.

"I know it sounds melodramatic, Carl. I'm sorry. I'll explain when we talk. Can you think of a place?"

"Well . . . how about the church? Nidaros Lutheran on Third Street. I can get a key from the assistant pastor."

"A church? No. Or . . . all right. Maybe it's a good idea. All right. I can be there in half an hour. Is that all right?"

"Fine. I'll . . . see you."

He sat for several minutes, his heart pounding. He had only imagined a reunion like this a few thousand times, lying awake in bed at night, woolgathering over piles of student essays, driving in his car. None of the things he'd imagined saying seemed any good now. He wasn't at all surprised.

"All right, we are alone. What do you want?" Sigfod Oski asked Ben Goss. They stood in the dim granary room, on either side of the gray stone, which had been returned to its place. The big sliding door had been pulled closed except for a space wide enough for a man to walk through. Goss had flipped a switch, activating the bare light bulb.

"I want to talk to you about that exclusive interview," he said, smiling.

"I made myself clear when I telephoned you. The stone merits publicity in its own right. I plan no exclusive interviews at the present time. When and if I choose to grant one, you will have first consideration."

Goss shook his head. "Not good enough. I'm here. You're here. I did you a favor by showing up. I need this interview. It could be a career maker for me. You're the biggest story in Minnesota since our last presidential also-ran. National exposure—I need it and I'll do what I have to to get it."

"Are you threatening me, Mr. Goss? What could you possibly do that would inconvenience me in the least?"

"It's all on videotape, Mr. Oski. Television is a wonderful tool. With a little creative editing I can make you look like Jesus Christ or some guy naked under a raincoat. So you have a choice. Cooperate and I'll see we both look good. Hold out and I'll make you look like the front page of a supermarket tabloid. Either way, I make my name."

Oski smiled. "You can't frighten a man who's been tortured by the SS."

"Don't give me that! This isn't 1945. There's no old boys' code anymore. I do what I can, what I have to do, to get what I need."

"Even if it comes to stealing a man's honor?"

"Honor? What language are you talking?"

"What about courage? Do you despise courage? I thought journalists were supposed to possess courage, and a certain integrity. What is that but honor?"

Goss smiled. "That was before the camera. That was when it was about writing, putting words on paper. That's all gone now—even in the newspapers.

"It's a visual world. You know what they say—'A picture's worth a thousand words'! That's a conservative estimate. Because people always mistrust what they're told just a little, but they *never* mistrust a picture. They *can't* distrust a picture—seeing's believing. So the guy who takes the picture *owns* the truth, you see? And only he knows the secret the public never guesses—that a picture's just another point of view. One point of view at one point of time. You pick one out, you print it—behold the truth!

"During your war, remember that little film clip of Adolf Hitler dancing when he heard Paris was captured? Only Hitler didn't dance—that was just a glitch in the film. But it doesn't matter. The *event* only happened once. But the *film's* been run thousands of times. The film cancels the event. Hitler *did* dance. We made him dance, us guys with the cameras.

"And that was only the beginning. Newsmen were naive then. They still had that patriotism bug. They thought they had a duty to help defeat tyranny.

"Never again. We may end war forever—us guys with the cameras. At least we can make it impossible for our own country to win one again.

"Look at Vietnam. Everybody knows Vietnam was a criminal mistake, and why do they know it? Because they saw a cop execute a prisoner with a revolver, and a naked kid burned by napalm. A different set of pictures and the war could have had a different end. But we decided. Not the politicians. Not the generals."

"I begin to see," said Oski. "In my war, we endured the unendurable sometimes, because we'd been told we could. But you told the soldiers they could not endure, and they didn't. If courageous or noble deeds were done, you undid them by ignoring them. You took their honor away."

Goss laughed. "That word again. Haven't you heard? Honor's a myth."

"A myth that protects civilians from soldiers in wartime, and soldiers from themselves when they carry their memories home."

"Well, it was all before my time. Look, don't get me wrong. I'm sorry we have to bury America—it has its good points. But we're talking survival now. This is the nuclear age, the killer virus age, the age of terrorism. As long as we can defend ourselves there's no chance for survival. I'm not an Extinctionist. I want to live, and I want my children to live, if I ever decide to have any. In a world like this we can't afford honor. My honor, if you want to call it that, is to persuade people, any way I can, that nothing—nothing in the world—is worth dying for. And I think people are getting the message. You know why we've only fought little wars since Vietnam? Because Americans don't have any stomach for long-term sacrifice anymore. I like to think we had something to do with that. It's an incredible power we have."

Oski stroked his chin. "Incredible indeed," he said. "And not really a new one, for all your pretensions. Think what you could accomplish if, instead of being an adversary, you made common cause with your betters. There are places where that is well understood. And suppose one wanted to bring in a new order . . ."

Goss leaned over the stone, staring at Oski. "What are you getting at?"

"A new kind of skald, the glory of kings," Oski almost sang. "I will need someone like you, Mr. Goss.

"But not you personally. You personally offend me very much."

The room seemed suddenly darker, and Ben Goss turned pale, like a man seeing a thing he knows does not exist.

Chapter X

Martell walked to Harry's house and got a key to the church from Minna, who said her brother was out and looked at him strangely. But Minna always looked at him strangely.

The church was only a few houses down, a big gothic building in yellow stone. He was turning the key in the lock of a side door, the wind in his ears, when Elaine's heels tapped up behind him.

"Please, let's get inside," she said.

He let her in.

They stood in the dim narthex, facing one another. Martell's instinct, shooting unbidden from long-dormant ganglia, was to take her in his arms. Instead he looked at her as she looked at him, each shifting balance like a wrestler.

The old pictures rose in his mind—Elaine standing in a sunny room, a yellow dress in her hands.

She was folding the dress to pack in the suitcase which lay open on the bed.

He had stood in the bedroom doorway, poleaxed by the incarnation of his fears.

She's my student, he thought, my responsibility. I shouldn't be living with her. So it had to happen one day. And what better day than today?

He had turned and left the apartment without a word spoken. When he returned she was gone.

Today she wore a pale trenchcoat over a warm-looking knitted dress in blue. Blue went with her eyes. She untied a scarf and released her long, heavy golden hair. He caught his breath. Her face, a perfect oval, had been lovely in a girl. Now it was wondrous. But there remained a softness, almost a supplication, in the slightly formless mouth that spoke of a hurt and lonely child. Only the hardest of men could have looked at that face without warming a little.

"You look beautiful," he said.

She smiled.

"My God, don't do that!" he said, turning his head away.

She touched his shoulder with a slim hand. "I'm sorry, Carl. Some people say my smile's a deadly weapon. I didn't mean to take advantage of it. I guess nowadays men are so scared of women, a nice smile's the sexiest thing a girl can wear. You look pretty good yourself, you know. You look—well, more distinguished. Character lines. And you haven't gotten fat or bald. I'm impressed."

Martell had trouble meeting her eyes again. He'd always found it hard to take compliments. Now, able to sense that she meant what she said, he felt like a voyeur. And what if she started lying? He didn't want to know if Elaine lied.

"I thought we'd use Harry Gunderson's office," he

said. "He's the assistant pastor. He's a friend of mine, and he's out."

"Okay, lead the way." Her nervous smile dissolved him.

He led her down a side aisle of the sanctuary, toward the office addition behind the chancel. The light shone faintly from an overcast sky through the looming stained glass. He glanced back and thought Elaine looked cold and uneasy.

In the dim office hallway, two doors down on the left, he stopped in front of Harry's door, unlocked it and held it open for her.

The office was like the man—wildly unkempt and comfortable. Martell always felt at home there. He cleared some books off an upholstered chair for Elaine and sat behind the desk.

"Full circle," Elaine said. "You teacher, me pupil."

"I suppose I get formal when I'm feeling awkward. I'm sorry."

"Do you feel awkward, Carl? After all this time?"

She took off her coat and he saw that her figure had not visibly changed. Shapes and textures he knew in his bones clamored for recall. She sat erect but graceful, her long legs crossed at the ankles.

He looked out the window. It had books stacked in it, and an obsolete brass candlestick and, oddly, a harmonica. A shadow flapped down and blocked the light from the outside. It looked crowlike, huge, like a raven. Strange to see a raven this far south.

"You know who I think about every now and then?" he asked. "Mrs. Corcoran."

"The landlady."

"I wonder if she's still alive."

"She was the last I heard, but that was a while back."

"I suppose she'll outlive us all, drinking and smoking and coughing and falling down through the centuries, sustained by the purity of her vices."

"I remember her peering up the stairway as we climbed it," said Elaine. "She'd be hanging onto the railing for support, vibrating like she did all the time. You knew she had a word for me. I suppose people still do. Do you have a word for me, Carl?"

He was still looking out the window. The raven, if that was what it was, hadn't moved. "It's a problem," he said.

"Would it be a problem if one of your men friends *kept* a mistress?" Her eyes fixed him with the same intensity as once upon a time. Sometimes, when she had loved him, that intensity had frightened him. Even when he didn't face her, as he didn't now.

"As a matter of fact it would. More to the point, I'm not in love with any of my men friends."

She looked down. "All right. It's a problem for me too. You know it's not what I planned."

"I know."

She looked around the office. "God, I hate churches. It brings back all those hellfire-and-brimstone sermons in chapel at the academy. That school. A boarding school. It was like my parents said, 'You're not good enough to live at home and go to public school like normal kids. We've got to spend our hard-earned money'—they always made sure we knew how much it was costing them—'to send you to a Christian prison, because otherwise we know you'll grow up to be a degenerate or a welfare case.' Boy did I show them. I think this is the first time I've set foot in a church since I was seventeen."

Martell glanced at her, looked away.

"What I mean to say is, when I say I'm embarrassed about how I live, it's got nothing to do with middle-class morals. But I live with a man who treats me like a thing. He uses me, he shows me off, he despises me. I'm ashamed of that. You've met Oski."

"Why do you stay with him?"

She thought. "Did you ever face a bull, Carl?"

"A bull?"

"One summer when I was a girl, the first day of vacation, I went into one of my Dad's cattle pens—mainly because I wasn't supposed to, I suppose. I didn't know Dad had put his new bull in there.

"I remember standing, frozen, looking into the bull's eyes—you know how they look, blue all around, not like human eyes at all—and realizing I couldn't do anything about that animal. I was crushable, breakable, no more able to protect myself than a piece of Kleenex. I suppose that was my first feeling of—what do you call it? Mortality. Oski makes me feel the same way."

"He seems to have that effect on a lot of people."

"I stay because I'm scared of him, Carl. Do you know what it's like to be scared? Really terrified?"

"You know I do."

She looked down. "I guess I had that coming."

"I'm a man who relishes petty revenges."

"You're a sweet, kind man. That wasn't enough for me once."

"I don't blame you for leaving, Elaine."

"It had nothing to do with Forsythe. I didn't even know what had happened until later. You must have thought—"

"You were very young. If you hadn't left then you would have later. Forget it. Go on with what you were saying."

"Do you believe in magic, Carl?"

"How do you mean?"

"Charms, spells, enchantments, raising the dead?"

"I'm . . . open to persuasion."

She smiled. "You used to say things like that in the old days."

"And you used to laugh at me."

"I'm not laughing now. What if I were to tell you

that Sigfod Oski can raise a storm on a clear day?
Or disappear in one place and appear someplace else,
miles and miles away, a moment later? Or bring up
a ghost to scare someone into a heart attack? Or
make—or make a woman love him—or something that
seems like love, and is just as strong?"

Martell closed his eyes. She wasn't lying, and that
troubled him. He couldn't lie, and that troubled him
too.

"You used to say," she continued, "that there was
no reason except prejudice for rejecting the possibility
of the supernatural."

"I was making a theoretical point. Forsythe said
that he'd read my work and he wasn't surprised that
a man who delighted in the illogical should embrace
the irrational as well. The crowd enjoyed that."

"I've come around to your side."

"It doesn't matter anymore."

"It matters to me. I need a friend, Carl. A friend
who has some idea how to deal with powers like
Oski's. More than that, a friend who knows something
about this Old Norse business. It's perfect that I've
run into you just now—but it's scary too."

"I don't follow."

"With Oski, you get used to nothing being coincidental. I can't help thinking our coming back together is something he engineered, for his own reasons.
He's always miles ahead of everybody else. God knows
what he's planning here."

"You mean he could rain on me, or make me fall
in love with him?"

"Look, Carl, if you think I'm crazy just say so!
Don't make little jokes. I always hated your little
jokes."

She's gone mad, he thought. *That would explain
it. Or maybe it's Oski who's mad. Maybe he just convinced her.*

"What do you want from me?" he asked. A simple question. No need for awkward truths.

Elaine dug in her purse for a cigarette and lit it. Her hands shook a little.

"Like I said," she sighed, "it may be this is just what Oski wants me to do. But it's the only thing I can figure out. I've got to try.

"I've seen him kill, Carl. Did you ever hear of Oskar Berglund?"

"There was a runologist—"

"That's the one. He died a couple years ago. Oski told me about it. He told me about it *before* it happened. Berglund was up for a committee chairmanship that Oski wanted. He was in the way."

"You're saying Oski killed him?"

"Not with his hands. Heart attack. Very sudden."

Martell grimaced.

"Do you think I'm crazy?"

He looked at her, unable to answer. As he met her eyes—he hadn't allowed that to happen before—he saw the desperate fear and loneliness at their bottom, blue as a pilot light. And he knew that his love was hopeless as ever. He was caught now, and all the pain to endure again.

Her eyes said she felt it too.

He bowed to it. He could see the noble death, the logic of the story, as a man looks at his hand in the split second after he burns it, knowing the pain is coming.

"What do you want me to do?" he asked.

"I need to run. I need to disappear. Go somewhere where nobody can ever find me. I can't do it alone. I don't even have a car. He only gives me a small allowance. I've got maybe fifteen dollars in my purse. Money is freedom, and he doesn't let me have much."

"You need money?"

"I need you to drop everything, and get in your

car with me and drive away. Leave your job, leave
your friends, leave everything you own. Run with me."

"That's a lot to ask."

"You love me, Carl. I was afraid you wouldn't, but
you do. I'm a bitch to ask it, but I'm desperate, so
I'll take advantage. I'll try to make it up to you in
other ways."

"How will we live?"

"Any way we can. I'll hook if I have to."

"What a charming picture you paint."

"I'm not offering you a vine-covered cottage, Carl.
I'm offering you me. I'm no prize, but you seem to
want me. What am I worth to you?"

He shook his head. "There's a problem."

"You think I'm crazy."

"I—I don't know. Maybe you are. More likely Oski
is. The point is, I *definitely* am."

"You're talking crap."

"To hide, to live underground, you've got to be able
to tell lies. I can't."

"Not even for me?"

"I mean I *can't*. See this bandage? A young man
cut my hand the other night because I refused to say
something that wasn't true. He threatened to cut my
face. The point is, I *couldn't* tell the lie. Not to save
my life. I've got a serious psychological block."

She frowned. "I've never heard of anything like that
before."

"How could I run with you? I couldn't even sign
a false name on a motel registration."

Her mouth tightened. Her eyes glistened. The offer
had been a kind of insult, but it had cost her to make
it.

"I'll do what I can for you," he said.

"What can you do if you can't help me get away?"

"I'll . . . I'll talk to Oski."

"You *are* crazy."

"I'll talk to him. I'll threaten to go to the college administration. To the press."

"You think that'll mean anything to him? And let's face it, Carl—you're not exactly an intimidating guy."

"I know, running away is more my style. But I can't do that. So I'll talk to Oski. You're right about this much—I'll do things for you I wouldn't do for anybody else."

"I don't want you dead."

"I'm not afraid of magic. If you are, maybe you should talk to the fellow who belongs behind this desk."

"A preacher?"

"He's an actual Christian. I'm not. He believes in the other world and he has . . . authority, I suppose."

"No. Maybe I believe in the devil, but that doesn't make me ready to tie up with Jesus and his daddy. Besides, after all this time it would be kind of lousy to come running to him for help."

"You came running to me."

She covered her face with her hands for a moment. "I suppose it's good for me to be turned down once in awhile. When you grow up with everybody telling you how beautiful you are, you get to thinking it'll buy you anything. It's bad for the character. Being beautiful is such a fraud. I want to apologize for it sometimes. 'I'm sorry I have a nice face. I wanted a nice brain but I got stiffed.' "

"That's not true and you know it. You have an excellent brain. And what's wrong with beauty?"

She looked around and spotted an ashtray on a bookshelf. She got up to take it, then sat again. "It's only skin deep, haven't you heard? It was in all the papers. All my life people have been expecting me to do as pretty is, but let's face it. I'm a bitch."

"Maybe so," said Martell thoughtlessly. "That has nothing to do with your beauty. A great intellect or

a great athlete or a talented artist can be a complete
pig, but that doesn't make brains or strength or talent frauds."

She crushed her cigarette out. "Also it doesn't last.
One of these days I'll look in the mirror and Edna
Mae Oliver'll look back at me."

"The same thing can happen with brains, strength
or talent. None of them is enough by itself. None of
them is nothing either.

"My friend the pastor would say that everything
except Good Itself—he means God—is a Second
Thing. Second Things are good in their place. You
can't compare them with one another any more than
you can compare apples and oranges, or apples and
sunsets."

He sighed and shook his head. "I'm sorry. I slipped
into my classroom mode. I forgot about your problems for a second."

She smiled and the room brightened. "It sounds
good. Like old times. Good times."

They walked back to the narthex together. At the
door she said, "Please don't get hurt."

"I'll try not to."

"I wish you'd run with me."

"I really wish I could." For one moment he felt
a bull-powerful impulse to take this woman in his
arms and to be a man, just once again. He shuddered,
fighting it down.

"I'll go first," she said. "You wait a few minutes
before you leave. I know it's melodramatic, but you
never know who's watching." She opened the door
and went out.

Martell stood shivering and studied the twin portraits of Frette and Bendikson on the wall. Those
redoubtable immigrant faces in their stand-up collars
had taught five generations the meaning of the Law.
Martell lowered his eyes, appropriately chastened, and

browsed through a copy of a denominational magazine. The cover story was entitled, "The New Establishmentarianism—Beyond the Wall of Separation." His blood screamed to him, full of wonder at the smoothness of Elaine's skin, the scent of her hair.

It was only a feeling in his stomach, as if he'd stepped down an elevator shaft, that reminded him he'd promised to defy Sigfod Oski.

Ghost farmsteads are a common sight in the countryside. Consolidation has left many of the old family farms abandoned, the windows of the empty houses staring like madmen's eyes from unpainted faces. More often the buildings are gone altogether, efficiently bulldozed, buried, plowed and planted over.

The windows of one old farm watched four cars pull into their driveway that evening, arriving singly at five-minute intervals. Each switched its lights off before turning.

Three men got out of each car. The wind was cold enough to warrant their heavy jackets, but not the ski masks they wore.

"I must be getting old," one of them whispered. "This wind hurts my ears. Kind of gets down inside 'em and whistles like a trapped fly."

"Some kind of wind," said the man beside him.

Another masked man came out of the barn and walked towards them.

"Is it ready, brother?" the one called Thumb asked him.

"Yeah. Right inside."

"Bring it out."

The man went back in and came out with a half-grown Holstein heifer. Her black and white head came to about the level of his shoulder.

"Over here by the tree," said Thumb. He led them to a big cottonwood.

"This ain't getting any easier," one of them grumbled.

"It's got to be done," said Thumb. "Evil must be shown to be evil."

"I'm just saying it ain't getting easier. I didn't say I wouldn't hold up my end."

"I used to work in the Chicago stockyards," said another. "Same kind of thing. Hundreds of 'em a day. You get used to it."

"We got the tools?" Thumb asked. "Knives, rope? You sure that knife's sharp?"

"Sharp enough to cut a fart."

They all laughed, but they stopped when Thumb pointed at the joker. "This isn't funny, brother. This is a serious, tragic matter. We're not here for fun, and none of us is going to enjoy this. Remember who we are. We're God's garbage men. You want to have fun, go sing in a quartet."

"I didn't mean nothing."

"That's right, you didn't. St. Paul says, '*Neither filthiness, nor foolish talking, nor jesting, which are not convenient . . .*' should be named among you. Ephesians 5:4. This is just the sort of thing he was talking about.

"Now before we stain our hands, I think we should bow our heads and say a silent prayer."

They stood for a minute in a circle, eyes down, shivering in the wind.

"All right," said Thumb. "Hold her still. Throw that rope over the branch. I'll cut."

Mrs. Maxine Ohlrogge was telling Harry Gunderson about her latest visit to the doctor.

"So I got to the parking lot," she said, "and there wasn't a single spot left, except one of those handicapped ones, and you know me, I'm not the kind of person who'd park in a handicapped spot. I just think that's the lowest thing in the world, well, not as bad as child molesting, but very bad anyway. What can these child molesters be thinking of? It's beyond me. Of course that's the sort of thing that's happening all the time now, it's part of the breakdown of the family, I mean that sort of thing never happened back in my day, and if they'd caught somebody at it they'd have known what to do with him, I can tell you. All they do nowadays is send them to doctors and spend the taxpayers' money on fancy treatments, when we all know what they really need is—well, I mean we didn't talk about those things when I was a girl, but you *knew* that the police knew how to handle that sort of thing. Nowadays nobody knows how to handle anything. And the Extinctionists say that any kind of sex that doesn't make babies is a good thing, and how can they say something like that?

"And now they're talking about Extinctionists neutering their children, and some people cripple them so they'll have more VQ points, and the courts say that's their constitutional right, and I just don't understand. I think I've lived too long. I said that to an Extinctionist once, and she said I was right."

"And what did the doctor tell you, Maxie?" Harry asked.

"He said I was as healthy as a woman half my age. I mean I know I don't *look* like a woman half my age—I know I'm an old fool, Pastor, but I'm not so much of a fool as that, but he said my heart was as good as a woman of thirty, and I think that's something to take pride in, don't you? And it's a relief, too, because I'd hate to be in my friend Maddie's shoes, with her family pressuring her to go to the Happy Endings Clinic because her heart treatments cost so much. I mean I weigh a little more than I used to, but I've always tried to watch what I eat, except for ice cream, I'm afraid I just couldn't live without ice cream—well, I suppose I could if I really had to, but I'd hate to have to make the choice, because at my age, Pastor, you have to cherish the little pleasures you have left."

"I like ice cream too, very much."

"Well, I mean it's awful when you think of it, people are starving in the world, and here we are eating precious food when we really don't need it, and wasting it on treats when it could be filling empty stomachs, but my Rudy used to say when he was alive, I can hear him now, he'd say, 'You can't help people by living in a cave, you just have to be thankful to the Lord for what you've got, and try to do all you can to help others.' And that's what I've always tried to do. I'm sure I don't do as much as a lot of people do, but you know how fixed my income is, Pastor, and you know I do try."

"You're one of the most generous people in our congregation," Harry said sincerely.

"Well I try, I mean I know it's never enough, but I do try to share as the Lord prospers me. I mean there have been things I wanted—or would have liked to—that I couldn't—I mean I'm sure lots of people do more, of course."

"We never can know, Maxie. I think it's time to start the Bible Study. Here comes Stoney."

Livingston Berge entered the church's Fireside Room and rolled along toward them like Popeye the Sailor. The only sign of his hospital visit was a gauze bandage on his right hand. He gave the pastor a silent look that said he did not wish to discuss it.

"Well, I guess we're all here," said Harry. "We might as well sit down and get started." Most of the weekly regulars were there—Minna, Stoney, Mrs. Ohlrogge and a retired farm couple, he stout, she fat, who carried matching Bibles and never spoke.

They sat in a circle of folding chairs in front of

the unlit fireplace, and after a brief prayer Harry began.

"As I recall, we got up to 1 Corinthians 1:21 last week. Would someone read verses 22-29, please?"

Stoney read:

"For the Jews require a sign, and the Greeks seek after wisdom: But we preach Christ crucified, unto the Jews a stumbling block, and unto the Greeks foolishness; But unto them which are called, both Jews and Greeks, Christ the power of God, and the wisdom of God. Because the foolishness of God is wiser than man; and the weakness of God is stronger than men. For ye see your calling, brethren, how that not many wise after the flesh, not many mighty, not many noble, are called: But God hath chosen the foolish things of the world to confound the wise; and God hath chosen the weak things of the world to confound the things which are mighty; And base things of the world, and things which are despised, hath God chosen, yea, and things which are not, to bring to nought things that are: That no flesh should glory in his presence."

"Thank you, Stoney," said Harry. "Now—"

"Excuse me," said Mrs. Ohlrogge, "I'm having trouble following. I'm used to the Revised, you know, but I got this new Bible this week, and it seems to run a lot different from Stoney's King James and—"

Harry asked, "What translation have you got?"

"It's—uh—I'm not sure. The—the salesman said it was the very best, the latest translation available, and I thought, well, it may be a long time before I buy another one, so I'd better get a good one—one I can use a long time, you know—here it is—it's the Winnowed Bible."

"The W.B.!" snorted Stoney. "Hoo boy, you got yourself a dandy there, Maxie."

Maxie's face went slack, like a soufflé scorned. "I don't understand."

"You've got the new translation there's been so much fuss over, Maxie," said Harry.

"I'm afraid I don't pay much attention to those things. . . ."

"Yah," said Stoney. "That what everybody says. Next thing you know, they got a pitcher of Groucho Marx hangin' above the altar."

"I think you mean Karl Marx," said Harry.

"Him too?"

Maxie stared at them. "What's the matter with my Bible?" she asked. "I wasn't trying to do anything controversial—I just wanted a good Bible. I don't have a lot of money to spend, you know, and if I have to go out and buy another one—I mean, I don't know how I'd be able to do it, what with groceries and doctors' bills, and—"

"It's up to you, Maxie," said Harry. He knew that interrupting her wasn't rude. It was silence she feared, and she didn't care who filled it. "I don't think the Winnowed Bible will hurt you, but I wouldn't use it myself. What it is, is a sort of condensed Bible. Shortly after the last merger, the church had to come out flatly and admit that if what it was saying was right, then Scripture had to be simply wrong in some places, and must be ignored. The Winnowed Bible is the first attempt to separate out the portions they've repudiated. They also made some textual changes, mainly in calling God 'She' exactly half the time. It's scheduled to be revised every ten years.

"And of course they cut the 'hard passages.' And a lot of the miracles are gone. So are the bloody parts of the Old Testament and the vengeful Psalms. They cut a lot of Paul's words, and even more of Christ's."

"I told you it was comin'," said Stoney. "When they

took 'Onward, Christian Soldiers' out of the hymn-book, I told you it would come to this."

"What you're saying," said Maxie, "is that our church says that the Bible isn't God's Word anymore. Just parts of it are. And only they know which parts?"

"That's about it," said Harry.

"And they're going to revise it again in a few years?"

"They'll be revising it regularly."

"So I've got a Bible with planned—what do they call it?"

"Planned obsolescence. What the bishop would tell you, if he were here now, is that you shouldn't depend too much on this Bible or any other, because only trained theologians can interpret Scripture properly."

"That's not what I was taught when I was a girl."

"They won't kick you out for being behind the times. As a matter of fact, they won't kick *anyone* out. We've got seminary professors who don't believe in God at all."

"But when did all this happen? How did they change my religion without my knowing about it?"

Stoney raised a bandaged hand. "All you gotta do is to look at the signs of the times. I told you when they made the Corn Ceremony a sacrament that we were on the road to ruin. But did anybody listen?"

Harry said, "Maxie, there are still lots of faithful people in the Church. And even the ones I disagree with most are sincere, loving people for the most part. We've got to remember that the Church belongs to Christ. He'll look after it."

Stoney said, "Somebody shoulda told that to Martin Luther."

Harry shook his head. "Luther was driven out, against his will. There's still freedom to preach ortho-dox Christianity in the NAPC."

"Well yes," said Minna with a smile, "but mainly

in western North Dakota. There's a saying among the pastors: 'Whosoever believeth in Him shall not get a parish.' "

"Minna!"

"Nobody listens!" said Stoney. "The whole world is going to Helena in a handbag and nobody will admit it! You know what's happening in our town? We got devil worshipers out on the old Tysness place, doin' God knows what kind of heathen ceremonies and sacrifices. Farmers been missin' their animals, and they've found some of 'em all cut up—what do you say—mutilated. Who knows what'll be disappearing next? Little kids?"

"That's alarmist talk," said Harry.

"Everybody knows about it! You ask anybody on the street downtown. They're all scared."

"I've been to the W.O.W. farm, Stoney. There's no evidence those kids have anything to do with those things."

"Evidence? You wait for evidence, they'll shut down the country on us! Sometimes you just gotta act on what you know!"

"That's a dangerous way to think. You could end up doing things you'll regret."

"I'm not gonna sit by and watch my town go— pardon me, Pastor, but I mean this—to the Devil," Stoney said. He got up and walked out.

Harry stared at his back as he left.

The couple who never spoke stood up together and the husband said, "I don't like to make a fuss, Pastor, but Stoney's right for once. You don't know what's going on. But the town knows. We all know, and we're scared. We'll be going now."

They left.

"What I want to know," said Maxie, "is what I'll do for a Bible now. I mean, I'm sure I don't want this one, but my old one is just falling to pieces, and

the money only goes so far. When Rudy was alive
there was a little more coming—he used to do odd
jobs, you know—but now I just barely make it from
week to week, and I hardly ever drive the car, and
I mean, it's been so hard since he died, and I thought
I could at least depend on my church, and now I just
don't know—"

"I've got a good Study Bible I never use," said
Minna. "You can have it."

Carl Martell watched himself, taped at the farm,
on the six o'clock news that evening. He thought he
looked like a whitewashed sepulchre.

Sigfod Oski looked like a monument to Victory.

Afterwards Martell tried to eat a sandwich but gave
it up. He sat on his sofa, ignoring the television,
looking at the telephone. He had to call Oski.

He'd promised.

He wondered what would happen if he broke a
promise. If lying hurt, what would promise-breaking
do?

*Just do it, Martell. Don't think about it. Get it over
with.*

He lifted the receiver. He pushed the buttons.

Ring. Ring. Ring. Ring. Ring. Ring. Ring. Ring.

No answer.

Oski must still be out at the farm.

Thank God.

The face of a well-known movie critic appeared on
the TV screen. He said, "The self-appointed guard-
ians of public decency have made themselves heard
once again this week in connection with the Cannes
Festival award-winning film, 'Nap Time.' As is so often
the case, these people, who have not even viewed the
film themselves, feel free to condemn what they do
not understand. They've particularly made noises
about a single scene in the film, where the antihero

sodomizes and strangles six screaming children, one
at a time, to the music of 'Let Me Call You Sweet-
heart.' Okay, I'll grant it's not a pleasant subject, but
you've got to look at it in the context of the director's
technical mastery. . . ."

"You see those crazies out at the old Tysness place
on the news?" a seed corn salesman asked his friend
at the Home-Maid Cafe that evening.

His friend across the booth swirled a french fry
in ketchup and said, "Pretty weird. Vikings right here
in Epsom, five hundred years ago. Sounds crazy to
me."

"What's crazy," the salesman said, fishing a pack
of Marlboros out of a pocket of his lumberjack shirt,
"is that we let those nutbags stay in this county. Henry
Olson told me—and he saw it himself—that they
found a dead cow on his brother's place. Somebody'd
strangled it and stabbed it maybe a hundred times.
And I'll bet—"

"You know that's funny, 'cause Myron Skalholt told
me the same thing happened on Sievert Borson's
place. And somebody else—I forget who it was—he
told me the same sort of thing a few weeks back, only
I forget all the circumstances. You know they reported
a couple of those things on the news a few weeks
back, and then you didn't hear a thing anymore.
Somebody's covering up, you betcha."

"Well, I'll tell you this—there isn't a soul in this
town doesn't know about it happening someplace. And
if it's cows now, who's to say it won't be people next?
But who's gonna do anything about it? You can bet
your life the cops won't get off their cans."

"You know what I heard?" the salesman's friend
asked. "I happen to know this is true, because I got
it from Ron Sogge at the elevator, who heard it from
his brother-in-law. This brother-in-law has a friend

who was driving along around midnight one night, out near Sogn, a couple weeks back. Well, he picks up this hitchhiker. Young guy. Beard, long hair. He sits in the back 'cause there's a sack of chicken feed in the passenger seat. At first he won't hardly say a word, won't say where he's going, where he comes from, nothing, so the guy starts worrying—'Who is this guy? Some kind of psycho I picked up?' Then, after ten, fifteen minutes, the hitchhiker speaks up and he says, 'The Antichrist is coming.' And the guy looks in the back seat, and what do you know? The hitchhiker's gone. Disappeared, like he'd never been there. What do you think about that?"

The salesman shook his head. "Tell that to some folks, they wouldn't believe you."

The friend chewed another french fry meditatively.

"How about that wind tonight?" he asked. "Brrr."

"Well, that's one thing about Minnesota. If you don't like the weather, wait a minute."

The friend laughed, as he always did. Especially when the other fellow was picking up the check.

"No ma'am," said Deputy Sheriff Clarence Stokke to the telephone, "we don't know anything about anything like that. You can be sure that we'll tell the radio and TV people if anything develops. There's no reason for alarm. Yes, ma'am, I'm sure. Thank you for calling. I'm sure you'll be perfectly safe in your bed."

"What the hell is going on?" he growled when he'd hung up. He turned to Deputy McAfee, who was eating a turkey-baloney sandwich. "Sixteen calls! In two hours! From all over the county! Over two dead calves, a couple weeks back!"

"Well, they were cut up pretty bad," said McAfee, wiping his mouth.

"Yeah, but it's been two weeks! Now all of a

sudden, people think there's been whole herds cut up in Moland, Skyberg, Sogn, Aspelund. Somebody out there's spreading rumors."

"Maybe it's Solar Bull's Lunar Tunes out at the old Tysness place. One of these nights somebody's gonna burn those kids out of there and, buddy, I don't want to be around."

Stokke shook his head. He picked up his copy of the *Draft Horse Journal*. Police work was not his life's dream. What he really wanted was a little farm of his own where he could raise Norwegian Fjord Horses.

"You read the memo on the DSL yet?" McAfee asked.

Stokke put his magazine down. "Yeah, I read it. Can't say I like it much. What does DSL stand for again?"

"Dangerous Sectarians List. You think you'll have a problem with it?"

"I don't know. We sure wouldn't get away with it if we were keeping records on Vegetarians or Extinctionists."

"But you know things have gotten out of hand. Terrorism, cults, all that crap. We've gotta keep tabs on these people."

"I can see that, but I'm supposed to write up people for publishing unlicensed newspapers, or holding Bible studies in their homes. My grandma used to hold Bible studies."

"The law's real clear. Everybody's got the right to think whatever they like. But talk about it in public, or publish it or hold meetings, and it's our business."

"Yeah, but still—"

The phone rang again and he picked it up. He said, "Yes . . . Yes . . . *What*?"

When he'd made a few notes he hung up. "Let's take a ride," he said to McAfee.

"What happened?"

"Somebody just found another calf."

McAfee threw his brown bag into the recycling container. "Maybe it's that comet," he said. "You seen it yet?"

"Sure. Lot better show than Halley's was. Better even than Hale-Bopp. And you know what happened with Hale-Bopp."

"Could be the comet, maybe. Or the wind. You feel that wind tonight? Feels like January."

Bart Swanson had finished carrying Julie Anderson's boxes of belongings down to his car from her dormitory room. He climbed the stairs again, feeling a little dizzy. His head still hurt from the knock he'd taken the other night, and the cold wind outside seemed to aggravate it, making cave noises in his head. He walked down the hall to her room and stood in the door, nearly filling it, looking at her. She was sitting, smiling at him, cross-legged on the stripped mattress. The empty dorm room with its cinder-block walls reminded him of a jail cell.

"I think it sucks," he said. "You having to quit school, and your folks making you leave town and go to this hospital, as if you were some kind of crazy. And all because of Whitey Martell. And he gets off free."

Julie giggled. She was small and slender, with dimples and light brown hair. His instinct was always to be gentle with her, though she didn't much care for gentleness.

Bart frowned. "Julie, get serious! You've been laughing at me all night! I'm not gonna see you for months maybe, and it's making me crazy, and all you can do is laugh! It's like everything's a joke to you. Even me." He closed his eyes. The noise in his skull was almost pain.

Julie giggled again. "Poor Bart. You don't get it, do you? It's such a scream!"

"What the hell are you talking about?" He moved toward her, angry and confused.

She sing-songed, "I know something you don't know!"

He took her wrist in one big hand and squeezed. "Talk sense!" he said. "Don't play games!"

She whimpered, and tears welled in her eyes. "Don't, Bart! All I mean is, it was a joke. Just a joke!"

"What was?"

"The whole thing! I tried to come on to Mr. Martell, I thought maybe he'd give me a break on midterms. But he said no, and he gave me a D on the next quiz, so I thought, 'I'll get even with you, you bastard,' so I complained to the Dean. He had it coming. He made me feel cheap."

"You—you were lying?"

"It was only to get back at him!"

"You tried to screw him for a grade, then you tried to get him fired for turning you down? You lied to me! You know what I did? I coulda killed the guy!"

"That was the best part!"

Bart hit her then.

He hit her many, many times, and the noise in his head drowned her screams.

Harry stood in Pastor Hardanger-Hansen's office, across the desk from her, white-faced and trembling.

"*You took her to the Happy Endings Clinic?*" he shouted.

"Sit down, Harry, before you have a stroke."

Harry collapsed into a chair like a sack of laundry.

"Surely you understood that self-termination was always an option."

"You could have talked her out of it. I have, many times."

"Didn't it tell you something that she kept coming back to it?"

"Of course it told me something! It told me she was desperately looking for attention and love and a reason to live."

"And you thought you could provide that? I'd say that's pretty arrogant, Harry. Do you really think a life that depends on your powers of persuasion is really worth living?"

Harry stared at her. "I was trying to help her open her heart to the love of God. How is that out of line for a pastor?"

"You tried to force your personal values on her. You have this taboo against suicide. It clearly didn't relate to her personal needs. I'm glad I was able to intervene before you wasted more of the church's time trying to interfere with an intensely personal decision."

"Wasted time? Saving the life of a child?"

"What does it profit a person if she saves her life and forfeits her soul? Cassie was trying to follow her heart, the true way of the Spirit. You were trying to keep her off the path of God."

"The path of God? Since when is the path of God the way of death?"

"We must die to live again."

"You know as well as I do that has nothing to do with a child putting poison in her veins."

"I know nothing of the sort, and it offends me deeply to hear you questioning my compassion. God is calling us to cleanse this earth by phasing out human corruption. Every person who's called to further that goal by removing themselves ought to be encouraged."

Harry shook his head. "I heard you talking Extinctionism," he said. "I never knew you'd take it to this length."

"I'm no hypocrite."

"Well, you call Cassie's parents, then. Explain to them why it was good for the earth for their daughter to die."

"I'm prepared to do that."

Harry got up to go. His face was wet. As he walked out the door he said, "I'm going to talk to the bishop, too."

"Be my guest."

MEMORANDUM

FROM: A. Carnegie Hall, Station Mgr.
TO: WEEP announcers.
RE: Studio Doors, Earephones.

Once again I must reutterate again station policey on entering and exciting out of the studio. All anouncers WILL enter the studio at the beginning of his shift from the west door (by the utilty room) and exite from the North door, (by the transmitter.) Thus insuring a free flow of traffic flow in the building. And remember, do not hang around in the studio if your not on shift.

ALSO, from now on WEEP will not be responcible for keeping earphones in the studio. If employees wish to use earphones, they may purchase there own. Otherwise, make do with the moniters.

Thank you.

A.C.H./cak

Rory's listeners could tell he was in a good mood, and several called to mention it.

He'd found peace. He knew what he was going to do.

Thumb was smart, but not as smart as he thought. Rory didn't know how he'd predicted the meeting with Zippy (or Laura—he'd have to start thinking of her as Laura now), but the result had been just the opposite of what he'd wanted.

He'd always liked Zippy. And now that she was a pretty girl instead of a skinny kid, he liked her even better. No way he'd do anything to hurt her.

No. He'd talk to her. He felt sure in his heart he could bring her to Jesus if he just had the chance to spend some time with her.

He'd drive out there tonight, after his shift. Let Thumb sit on his name.

"Weather forecast for WEEP Country—colder and windier, folks, and there's a chance of some snow sneaking up on our blind side. Nasty weather for October, but praise the Lord, when He's in our vessel we can smile at the storm. . . ."

Chapter XI

Two thick-necked young men in north woods jackets stopped Rory at the gate of the W.O.W. farm. When he mentioned Young Goat Star, they sent someone to get her. Rory pulled a stocking cap down over his ears and shivered in the wind until she came to vouch for him.

"This isn't the best night, Rory," said Laura as they walked down the driveway.

"I tried to call first, but the operator said you aren't listed."

"We don't have a phone. We're holding a ceremony tonight, and outsiders aren't allowed to watch. It's not like we've got anything to hide, you understand, but you wouldn't get anything out of it unless you believe. You know what I mean."

"I guess so."

"You can come to the preliminary lecture though.

Then we can go someplace and talk. It'll be a good night for that. The comet watching will be good, and I know I won't sleep."

"Something important happening?" asked Rory. They walked down the driveway, crunching gravel underfoot, the lights of the farmhouse glowing on their right, Troll Valley black beyond it. The stars were precise as watchmakers' tools, and the moon was a little gibbous, like a kicked cheese. The cold wind raised goosebumps and expectations.

"Like I told you, Hamster—Rory—something special's happening here. Now. Like a birth, only it'll be everybody's baby. And we'll be ready. Very soon."

They swung around the yardlight pole, past a windmill, a pump house and a chicken house, into an old grove of willow and pine, planted in wide rows long ago.

They followed a path through a gate under the shadow of the Troll Valley trees. Laura pulled a small flashlight from her jacket pocket to light the way. The path took them gradually down until, rounding a bend, they saw a crowd of young people gathered around a bonfire near the foot of a tall ash in a wide place by the riverbank. A tall man in a turtleneck and a leather coat stood by the fire, speaking to them. He wore an eyepatch.

"Isn't that Sigfod Oski?" asked Rory.

"Shh. Of course it is. He's the speaker tonight. He's an incredible man."

Oski was saying, ". . . and Loki looked about him, and all the gods were laughing at him, and pointing at him where he lay on the ground, pinned by the giant's belt. And none laughed louder than the fair Freya. And Heimdal took off his sealskin and resumed his own form. He said to Loki, 'Now the Brisinga necklace is mine, and I shall enjoy Freya tonight. And you must pay the forfeit of both your eyes.'

"And two dwarfs came and ripped out Loki's eyes, and Heimdal threw them into the sky, so they became the stars you see—just there."

Everyone craned their necks and looked at the stars he pointed out.

"And Heimdal went into Freya's house and gave her the necklace, and they had great sport that night. And Loki found a boy to lead him deep into Giant's Wood, and there he found a witch. She took two hot coals from the hearth and gave them to him for eyes, so that ever after no man could look Loki in the eye unblinded. And he found the dwarfs who had ripped his eyes out, and he changed them into ravens, and since that time ravens have always picked out the eyes of the dead.

"Ah! The tales are many! So few of them found homes in books. It's a mercy that even a few were saved, when the cold hand of the Church stretched to clutch the heart of Europe.

"You cannot know—you cannot guess—how it was in those days. And yet you shall know, and soon. For the great Truth—the truth which has been lost, but cannot be forgotten—is that Time is a wheel. Birth, death, spring, winter, good fortune and bad—they come and come again, in small circles or large, like the comet above us.

"The Christians say not so. The Christians say Time is a straight road, starting here and ending there. They speak thus because they see nothing, they feel nothing. The world they have built is a narrow, walled place, full of signs that say, 'Keep Off,' 'Don't Touch,' 'Don't Look.' You know nothing of life. You see nothing born, you see nothing die. You plant not and harvest nothing.

"But that circle too turns over. Soon all of you here will learn the true wisdom born of earth—Earth, our common Mother. She is a mighty goddess, wiser and kinder and crueller than you can conceive. She teaches in rhythms and cycles, with no law but the law of life and death and rebirth. Harmony is all.

"But I stand and look at your faces, and I ask, Are you all equal to the quest? Are you ready to take the cold plunge into the world of the spirit? Can you turn your backs on the little rules they've taught you? Can you be strong to defy the thousand niggling voices?"

"We have to go now," Laura whispered. "The ceremony will start soon." Rory felt her hand on his arm, and he roused as if from a pleasant dream.

"What?" he said.

"We have to go."

"I'd like to listen some more."

"I'm sorry, it isn't allowed." She glanced at two big young men in plaid moving toward them. "Not now. But come with me and I'll show you something you'll like."

He followed her back up the path to the farm. They went into the barn, which stood a little tilted, like a mugging victim. Laura switched lights on as they went, revealing cobwebby posts and rafters, as they passed through the main barn with its gutters and dangling iron stanchions and into the little shed that connected with the silo, sweet with the smell of remembered alfalfa silage.

Unlike the more common old brick silos, and most new silos, made of a glass material, this one was built of galvanized steel panels bolted together. The curved wall faced them like the hull of an upended submarine. A row of square steel doors with rungs on the outside provided a ladder up, sheltered by a vertical steel half-cylinder.

"Follow me," said Laura, skipping up the rungs and twisting to look down at him.

"I'm not much good at heights."

"You're not *scared*, are you?" She grinned, and he melted a little.

He followed her up. He enjoyed the view of her blue jeans bottom, and that kept his mind off the height. And other things that were troubling him.

He was surprised to come out onto a platform, in the icy wind under the stars.

"We took the whole top off last week," Laura said, whirling with her arms spread. "Isn't it an awesome observatory? You feel so close to the stars!"

Rory shivered, feeling much too close to the stars. He got as near the center of the platform as he could, and still felt insecure. It was clearly a recent construction, and he wouldn't have sworn to its strength.

"We've got our telescope here—" Laura went to the edge, where there was a short parapet, and took a tarpaulin cover off a very expensive piece of astronomical equipment. "You'd be amazed at the view you get of Cerafsky."

"It—it seems like a lot of work just to watch the stars. Putting all this up here, I mean."

"It's part of our faith. We've got a working astrologer on staff. But the big thing is Cerafsky. Cerafsky is the key."

"You waiting for a flying saucer, like the Heaven's Gate thing?"

"No, of course not. Cerafsky is the key to the new age. Our astrologer figured it out, and Solar Bull saw it in a vision. Something passed out of the earth on Cerafsky's last pass, hundreds of years ago. She's coming close again, and we have the chance to get it back."

"And what'll you be getting?"

Laura smiled. "It's hard to say. But it's beginning to look like it has something to do with Sigfod Oski. There's real power in that one. You felt it. I know you did."

Someone had nailed a vinyl-covered cushion to the platform, and Rory sat down on it. "Yeah, I felt it. To tell the truth, it scares me a little." Rory felt like a man trying to nail a piece of plastic over a window in a hurricane—he kept losing control of corners of his thoughts and feelings. The wind seemed to have gotten inside his ears, whistling, making it hard to think.

"You've got to be brave, Rory. I know you are. If you could just see what I've seen—feel what I've felt—I know you'd join us."

He wanted to tell her what *he'd* seen, what he'd felt when he gave his heart to Jesus. But somehow, with the wind in his head and Oski's words looping in his memory, he couldn't get his thoughts in a row.

She sat beside him and pointed upward. "Look at the comet, Rory!"

Instead he put his arms around her and kissed her.

They made love on the cold cushion, in the singing wind. When it was over, Rory pulled his clothes together, suddenly freezing. He said, "Oh God, I'm sorry."

"Why, Rory? I'm happy."

"I wanted to show you there's—there's another kind of love than—"

"Who needs another kind of love?"

"I wanted to show you that a guy can love a girl without just using her body." He spat a word he hadn't used in years. "I haven't done anything like this since I left L.A.!"

"Then it's high time. Don't look so mad."

"I'm not mad. I'm sorry. I apologize—even if you don't know what I mean. I've got to go."

She caught his arm. "You'll come back, won't you, Rory?"

"No! Yes. Maybe. I don't know. Maybe it's not a good idea."

"You've got to come back, Rory. You've got to meet our High Priest. He's somebody from the old days— maybe you met him, back on the streets."

"Who?"

"We call him Solar Bull, and he's the most wonderful, giving man I ever met. He's got so much to share. Back in California, they used to call him Rowan."

The Reverend Judith Hardanger-Hansen sat in the front row of the crowd, firelight in her eyes, the wind in her ears, watching Sigfod Oski. Solar Bull's arm was around her waist, and she felt more exalted than she had since her wedding day, long ago. This was greater than a wedding, and certain to be more permanent.

She'd never met a man like Solar Bull before: one who respected—no, venerated—her womanhood. He saw her as a True Soul, a Person, a Priestess.

Which, of course, she was.

In the wind, she heard again the Call that had led her into the ministry. Ever since that day when, as a child, she had told her preacher daddy, "I want to be a pastor like you when I grow up," and he had patted her on the head and explained that little girls shouldn't grow up to be pastors, she had known her Call. Justice. Equality. The struggle that never ends, for the sake of all the weak, all the poor, all who are exploited and deprived and stunted by power. For the sake of every hungry belly, every tortured prisoner, every child without hope, every soul in chains in all the world, she must follow that Call anywhere. Anywhere at all.

So, at Solar Bull's invitation, here she was, ready to be initiated, ready to take the next step in the eternal pilgrimage of the Spirit.

"How I envy you," Solar Bull had said to her that

first night when they had talked and talked in the parsonage. "Just being a woman gives you a primal knowledge—a wisdom I can never aspire to. Your body is tuned to the cycles of the moon goddess. You carry the miracle of life—you bring forth children. You—any woman—you're like a flower, like an altar, like an ocean. A man can't know a woman any more than he can swim to the ocean's floor."

She felt the truth of it in her bones, in her woman's heart, felt her priesthood like a bud in the belly.

And now she would see greater mysteries still, in the eye of Sigfod Oski.

"And what of women?" Oski cried. "What of the crime done to them? Thrown down from their high places, made bond-slaves to their husbands, saddled with the blame for what they call Original Sin! Was any rape ever so cruel?

"There are men, you know, who fear women. They won't admit it, but if you search you can see it in their eyes. When a man looks at a woman—any man, any woman—he sees the Goddess. And small men, men who fear life itself—for Life Itself is in the woman—such men fear the Goddess and wish to dethrone her. Such men make religions where the Male is supreme. They turn their backs on the wisdom of their mothers and try to remake a world where they need not kneel to Woman, need not pay the price Earth demands.

"And growing up under their fist, we are all made little. Lost is the beauty, lost is the terror, of the true earth, of life.

"Come back with me, children! Do not fear the night, do not fear the fire, do not fear the blood. All these are Woman, all these are the Goddess—your mother and your lover."

He stretched wide his arms and cried, "Will you follow me?"

"Yes," the crowd murmured.

"Can you touch the Night?"

Louder: "Yes."

"Can you embrace the Fire?"

"Yes!"

"Can you drink the Blood?"

"YES!" they shouted, and Judith shouted with them.

"THEN BRING THE GOAT!"

"Wait! Wait!" somebody called.

Judith turned her head to see a tall young man and a thin young woman pushing forward through the crowd. What could be wrong with them?

Once near the fire the young man said, "Nobody said anything about sacrifices when we joined up!"

"It is time," said Oski, frowning.

"That's not what W.O.W. is about! This is just what the witch hunters are watching for, so they can start the burnings again! We'll never beat the prejudice this way!"

"The time for overcoming prejudice is past. Our victory will come by other means."

The young woman yelled, "Get away from here, old man! You're poison! You're not one of us!"

Oski laughed. "Look at them!" he cried, swinging a long arm toward the crowd. He shouted, "The goat!" and the crowd began to chant, "The goat! The goat!" clapping their hands, weaving in a reggae beat.

Oski took a step and seized the young man by the front of his flannel jacket. "It is you who do not belong!" he shouted. "Courage is demanded! You fail!" He lifted the young man with one hand and threw him against a tree.

The young man lay stunned for a moment. The young woman went to him, looked at Oski, looked back at the young man.

"EVIL!" she screamed.

Oski laughed again. He laughed as they stumbled away together, was still laughing as he turned back to the crowd.

"THE GOAT! THE GOAT!"

A girl led a billy into the firelight. She had a rope over one arm. She handed the rope to Oski.

He made a noose with practiced hands, then tossed one end up over a hanging branch of the ash. He pointed to a young man, who came forward. He gave the young man the end to hold while he fixed the noose about the goat's neck.

"Pull up the slack," he said to the young man. "But not so tight as to strangle it yet." It was done. The goat bleated and leaped short leaps on its back legs.

Oski kneeled and took up a length of pole, which someone had converted to a spear with a survival knife.

"The offering must be stabbed and hanged," he said. "That is the ancient law."

"You!" He pointed at Judith. "Come here! You are a priestess!"

With joy she said, "Yes!"

"When I have stabbed the offering, you must put your hand inside the wound. I want you to feel the life in the heart!"

Carl Martell felt a weight of guilt as he sat in his office and gazed at a pile of uncorrected tests.

"If I'm going to be a teacher, I'm going to have to start working at it now and then," he said. But if he read the tests, he'd know who'd cheated. It seemed unsportsmanlike.

Besides, he had other things on his mind. A few hours back he had turned down the offer of Elaine's body. It was morning now and, as he'd expected, he hated himself in it.

"Welcome to the Prig's Hall of Fame," he told

himself. "Someday they'll display you in a glass case, with a card that reads, 'The Common Victorian, Extinct.'"

But he laughed, because there had been other reasons than moral ones, and because he knew bathos when he heard it.

I'll never make a Byronic Hero, he thought. *Possibly an Ironic Hero. This is important to understand. If I'm moving toward a Noble Death, I'll want to know what kind of an exit to make.* But that was more self-pity, and he couldn't take it seriously.

Blast! A man should have a bottle in his bottom desk drawer, like a hard-boiled detective, for times like this.

He should call Sigfod Oski. He'd tried to reach the man off and on all night, more frightened each time. He'd promised.

He dialed the number, his hand trembling.

The phone rang. He let it ring ten times. Nothing.

He hung up, missing the cradle the first time. His palms sweated. *Thank God.*

Something crashed out in the hall.

He rushed out of his office in time to see a fist sticking out through a hole in Roy Corson's door.

He went closer to investigate.

The fist was withdrawn, and Carl bent to peer through the hole, keeping well back. Corson was looking out from the other side.

"Hi there," said Corson, smiling lopsidedly.

"Hello."

"Terrible workmanship in these doors. I'm barely hurt."

"Glad to hear that."

Corson pursed his lips and wrinkled his forehead. "I suppose you're curious why I did this."

"I don't want to pry."

"But *I* want to puncture! Ha! Come in, Carl." He opened the door and waved Martell in.

Corson settled behind his desk, and Martell noticed a small semiautomatic pistol sitting on it.

"You notice the firearm," said Corson. "That, like the broken door, is what they call a subtle cry for help."

"What's the matter, Roy?"

"I've got a garbage bag here," said Corson, fumbling in a desk drawer. "My idea was to put it over my head before I blew my brains out.

"See, I knew a fellow once who shot himself in his living room, and his wife had to clean up the mess. Brains all over the wall, blood soaked into the carpet—I mean, it's not like TV—those suckers *bleed*. Completely destroyed a very fine black velvet painting of a matador from Mexico. So I thought, 'Why should I make a lousy job for some cleaning lady who never did me any harm, just because I want to off myself?' I thought maybe the bag would contain the mess, you know? Only I'm not sure it would work. What do you think? If the bullet went right through, it would probably just rip a big hole in the bag, am I right?

"Of course, in a larger sense, why should it bother the cleaning ladies? Cleaning women? Cleaning persons? I don't know what the hell you're supposed to call them nowadays—probably Domestic Technicians. Anyway, they dust all the time, and you know what dust is? Household dust, I mean? Mostly dead human skin cells. I read it in *Smithsonian*, I think. We may not have been created out of dust, but dust is definitely created out of us. So it's all the same, right? Dust and blood and brains?

"Where'd I get the gun? I bought it in a pawn shop when I was living in Chicago. Wanted to protect my valuable person."

Carl sat and looked at him.

"Don't sit there looking compassionate, you Calvinist. I am a rational, autonomous adult. I choose to take my own life. It's a considered, adult choice, protected by the Constitution, and I stand by it.

"Only I couldn't stand to pull that freaking black bag over my head.

"So I put my fist through the door. Hole in the head, hole in the door, it's all the same thing . . . isn't it?"

"You ought to get that hand looked at," said Martell.

Corson looked at his knuckles, put them to his lips. "Nothing wrong with my hand," he said. "They make those doors out of pressed Post Toasties."

He opened his bottom desk drawer and, just like a hard-boiled detective, pulled out a bottle. "A man should always have one of these handy," he said, fishing in the drawer and coming up with a fat glass tumbler. "You want a slug?"

Martell smiled. "You hit me on the right night. Have you got another glass?"

"You take this one. I'll use the bottle." Corson poured a healthy shot and passed it over. They drank together solemnly, like members of a last-man's club.

Corson picked up a sheet of white paper. "I've got a memo here," he said. "It's from the Head of the Department. It says all personnel will be required to attend an inservice workshop on Literatism. Know what Literatism is, Carl? It's the oppression of those who can't, or won't, speak and read grammatical English by those of us who can. They're going to show us how to teach English without expecting anyone to learn English, and how to grade English classes without giving an unfair advantage to anyone who actually knows how to use the language. It begins to dawn on my chemically clouded brain that my life's work has been for nothing, nothing, nothing at all.

"I ever tell you about my dad?"

"Not that I recall."

"He ran a men's shop in Saginaw, Michigan. It wasn't ever much of a concern, and as our neighborhood deteriorated it dwindled like a congressman's ethics. But Dad hung on, because he believed in Brotherhood. He said it was a matter of principle.

"Anyway, there was this old Hispanic ragpicker who used to work the neighborhood. He was quite a show—crazy as an art instructor—talked nonstop, a running commentary on every house and business he passed, pushing his smelly cart down the sidewalk, blocking people's way.

"For some reason he had it in for Dad. He'd stop that cart right in front of the shop, and he'd yell for ten, fifteen minutes about the gringo and his cheesy, overpriced clothes that fell apart. He'd say half the rags on his cart came from my Dad's suits, only a week or two old. Crazy things. And somehow he got the notion that Dad was hot for Latin women, and how everybody'd better watch if his wife or girlfriend went in there, because everybody knew what he'd be doing.

"Dad understood the old man was crazy, of course. But a guy can only take so much.

"One day he just blew. He stormed out the door and kicked that old man so hard he bounced. Then he kicked him again and again, halfway down the block, until the old man left his cart and ran off, screaming. And Dad stood there yelling at him, telling him to take his stinking rags and his stinking cart and his stinking filthy mouth and never come near his shop again.

"Note what happens next. There was a newspaper stringer on the street that day, shooting pictures of something or other, and he got a whole roll of shots of my dad kicking that crazy old man. The paper printed one of them, and *LIFE* magazine picked it up and ran it in a special feature on racism in America.

"Well, just the local part hurt Dad. But when he saw himself in *LIFE*, and knew people all over the country were seeing it, I think it just broke him. It didn't matter what he tried to do after that—the one mark he'd leave on history was a picture of white-on-brown violence. People would see that picture, doing research, going through the stacks in libraries, reading microfilm, for hundreds of years. It would be his monument, and he couldn't handle it.

"The night before he killed himself he said, 'Roy, I don't know what to tell you. You try to do right, you try to do wrong, it all comes out the same. Maybe it's entropy.' Sometimes I think people like my dad are our culture's substitute for human sacrifice."

He looked at Martell, sagging to starboard. "You've never been married, have you, Carl?"

Martell shook his head. "I've found other ways to stay poor."

"Wise man. Are you gay?"

"No."

"Being gay might be wise too. Never tried it. I imagine it's pretty much the same as straight sex, though. Which is to say undignified and messy.

"When I was a young buck, I used to believe in sex, Carl. I mean, it was my *religion*. In those days— you remember the sexual revolution?—we figured that if we could just get more and more people to score more and more sex with more and more varied combinations of partners, it would end all the world's problems, because frustration was the real cause of all the trouble. Funny how it never occurs to you when you're eighteen that an eighteen-year-old's problems aren't the only problems in the world.

"You know who knew the score? The Church

Fathers—your Augustines and Origens. They said the sex urge should be buried, suppressed, mortified, and used, if at all, under carefully controlled conditions, like plutonium.

"Maybe I'll become a monk. Do they let agnostics become monks? The church is pretty broadminded nowadays."

Martell looked at him.

Corson swung his chair around to profile, studying the damaged door.

"Sally's having an affair," he said.

Martell dropped his eyes. He could almost taste the truth, with its essential tang of tragedy. "I'm sorry," he said.

"Second marriage, Carl. For me, I mean. Sally's first, but not her last. Six years—I thought we'd been through the worst. I thought I'd learned from my mistakes. I read all the right books, I tried to be supportive and affirming and nurturing—you know how to get along with a woman, Carl? Learn to crawl. Start each day with an apology. 'My dear, I beg your pardon for five thousand years of intolerable male oppression, and for my own appalling bad taste in being born with a Y chromosome.' Don't you ever believe any married man who puts you down for being single, Carl. You can bet your bagels he envies you right down to his hair shirt.

"When I was a kid, a real man was John Wayne. Later, a real man was Phil Donahue. And everybody called that progress.

"But everybody missed the point. Here's the point—this is what sexual politics is all about—a man needs a woman more than a woman needs a man. Emotionally, I mean. And neither John Wayne nor Phil Donahue allowed for that.

"Personal fulfillment. Independence. It's all crap. I *need* Sally. I'll crawl, I'll eat crow and eat quiche,

I'll do whatever I need to do to keep her. Maybe that's where *macho* comes from. Who could blame a guy for trying to compensate for a condition like that?

"You know, now I think of it, I never met a Don Juan in my life who wouldn't tell you, when he'd had a few drinks on a slow night, that he was only tomcatting to fill in time, until he found that right girl.

"Then there's you, of course. The last of the rugged independents. How do you manage that? Are you made of iron? Stop too many lowballs playing baseball as a kid?"

Martell frowned. "I found the right girl. Unfortunately she was looking for the right guy. So I learned to do without. It's like losing a leg, I suppose. You narrow your horizons and cope."

Corson took another drink, refilled Martell's glass. "What'll I do, Carl? Knowing she's banging another guy—I can live with that. I think. I lost my pride years ago." *Lie.* "But what if she comes to me and says she needs to leave me to fulfill her human potential with her young stud? No names, Carl, but he's somebody I don't think I can compete with. He even makes more money than I do, but then who doesn't?

"I shouldn't have married a younger woman. Oldest dirty joke in the world—it was a chestnut to Chaucer. Although I suppose there's a kind of comfort in knowing I'm part of a venerable tradition.

"The cuckolds of old had it better, of course. They could just kill the pair of them and nobody'd raise an eyebrow—

"*My God, did I say that?*" Roy's eyes went wide in horror. "No wonder she doesn't want me. I'm a monster. I didn't know I was a monster . . ."

Martell said, "You're not a monster. You're a man in pain. It was yourself you meant to kill, not them."

Corson looked at the automatic. "It's still a good idea. Maybe you should just go home and leave me alone, like they used to do when they caught London clubmen cheating at cards."

"I don't think so."

It was nearly 3:00 A.M. when Martell finally walked Corson to his own apartment and tucked him into bed. He collapsed on the sofa and slept until after noon. Corson's gun he had dismantled as they walked, and dropped into a series of trash containers.

"Turning to national news, a circuit judge in Vermont has declared the Declaration of Independence unconstitutional. Overturning a lower court ruling which permitted a public school to continue posting a copy of the Declaration, Judge Beecher Whitstock ruled that the document's references to a 'Creator' and 'Nature's God' amount to an unconstitutional establishment of religion. A spokesperson for the school board said they have not yet decided whether to appeal."

"Dala horses. You know, those painted wooden horses from Sweden they sell in the gift shops," Deputy Stokke was explaining to Esther, the dispatcher, a thick, blonde woman in a uniform a size too tight. She sat in front of the radio control board, smoking a cigarette and looking tired.

"Yeah, I've seen 'em. Never saw the point of 'em."

"They're a traditional Swedish folk craft. But what I'm saying is, they actually look like carvings of Norwegian Fjord Horses."

"Don't the Swedes have horses of their own to carve?"

"I'm not sure. I think we have the horses and they have the cars."

"How come I'm not surprised?"

Deputy Stokke was working on an answer when a call came in. Esther listened on her headset, then pulled it off, saying, "It's McAfee. You'd better talk to him."

"How come? He get somebody else claiming they saw wild Indians on the streets? Tell him to do his job, for pete's sake."

"This one's touchy. He just found Mayor Sorenson walking out on County 12."

"What happen, his car break down?"

"Hard to say. He was wearing a cardigan sweater and nothing else, and singing 'Kan Du Glemme Gamle Norge.' "

"Oh boy," said Stokke. "Full Moon City."

Esther began to laugh, noisily and damply, and he didn't get it at first.

The wolf skulked from the cover of a windbreak to lap water from a low spot in the ditch, at the mouth of a culvert. The smell of man was everywhere, and wherever its own scent blew, dogs barked. The wolf was weary, but it could no longer sleep. It was hungry, but too weak to run down prey. It was frightened, but the excitement blanketed the fear.

Fenris. Fenris.

The itch in its brain had become something like a noise. A thing it could not understand, a thing no wolf had ever known before.

A thought.

The wolf had learned its name.

Chapter XII

Washing Day

Martell was awakened by the telephone. From the couch, it wasn't far to answer it.

"*Good morning, Mr. Martell,*" said a female voice that sounded familiar. "*I'm calling from KARE-TV in Minneapolis. I wonder if you could make some kind of statement on that runestone at the W.O.W. farm.*"

"I really can't improve on what I said yesterday. I believe it to be an authentic pre-Columbian artifact, but my reasons are subjective ones, which is pretty embarrassing to me as a historian. You'd do better to talk to Sigfod Oski. He's the expert."

"*We've been trying, but we can't seem to locate him. You weren't answering the phone either last night.*"

*What's going on in Epsom, anyway? We've got reports
of three car accidents, a rape, nine assaults, four major
acts of vandalism and a couple of indecent exposures
from down there last night. I thought you were a
quiet town."*

"We were, last I heard."

*"By the way, do you know anything about Ben
Goss?"*

"Ben Goss? Oh yes, the reporter. He was from
another station, I think."

*"Yes, he was. But we all drink in the same holes,
and the rumor is he's disappeared like last week's
paycheck. Did you notice anything unusual when you
saw him yesterday?"*

"No. I left before Oski did, and Goss was still there
then."

*"Well, look, if we get in touch with Oski, and we
send a crew down, would you care to be a celebrity
again for a few minutes?"*

"I'd really rather not. I haven't anything to tell you.
I'd recommend you concentrate on Oski. He's more
knowledgeable, and a whole lot more colorful."

*"Well, you think about it. We'll call you back. Have
a nice day."*

Martell hung up, looked at the phone a moment,
then unplugged it.

While he waited for Corson to wake up he washed
his dishes and read. He thought it might be interesting to go through some of the classic histories in
his library and see what parts weren't true. But his
sense didn't seem to work on them. Perhaps time had
dissipated whatever energy affected him. An original
document, like the stone, would have been another
matter. Novels gave him no impression whatever. He
almost took out a Bible, but found he didn't really
want to know.

Corson appeared at the bedroom door at last,

rumpled, bristly and sheepish. Martell gave him coffee. Neither felt like breakfast.

"Thanks for the trouble, Carl," Corson said. "No need to see me home. I'll be good. Hey, I'm a man of my times. Now that I've made it through the crisis I laugh lightly and carry on with my personal lifestyle. God, my head hurts."

"You want cream or sugar?"

"It's all the same," said Corson, but he took both. Martell let him go afterwards. He had told the truth.

Corson stopped at the door as he was leaving and turned back. "I suppose, if you want to be legalistic about it, if I had wanted fidelity I should have been faithful myself."

Martell found he had no wish to be alone. He looked unhappily at the telephone, plugged it back in, and dialed Oski.

No answer. He sighed and scratched his wounded hand. He'd said he might talk to Harry. He called him.

"Come on over," Harry said. He sounded tired. "I've made my morning visits, and as usual I don't have to prepare a sermon, and to be frank I don't feel like working today."

Martell walked up to his house, relishing the crisp air, his collar turned up.

The town looked as if it had had a rough night. Traffic signs had been run down, there was broken glass at most of the intersections, and toilet paper streamed in the wind from what seemed like every tree in town. Passing the church, he saw that someone had spray-painted in green on its yellow stone wall, CHRISTMAS CANCELLED. JOSEPH CONFESSED. SORRY.

Harry's room was pleasantly warm and dim, the piles of books unobtrusive but present, like good friends.

Harry sat by his rolltop desk. He wore a gray

sweater, inside out, and his shoelaces were untied. His face was gray and his eyes sleepy. Martell sat in a deep, sprung armchair facing him, and told him Elaine's story.

Harry frowned. "Is she lying?"

"No. She might be mistaken, but she believes what she says."

"Yes. And you say she's not a Christian."

"She made that clear."

"Would you describe her as emotionally well-balanced?"

"Who is these days? I don't think she's crazy, but I don't have any sense for sanity more than you or anyone else. I think insanity would fool me. If someone said he was Napoleon and sincerely believed it, it wouldn't ring my bell. She has to be crazy. Or Oski is. Right?"

Harry frowned and made a "hmm" noise.

Martell opened his mouth, but found he had nothing true to say.

"Something happened between the two of you," Harry said. It wasn't a question.

Martell shifted in the chair. "I didn't touch her. But I've got some bad nights coming."

"Maybe things'll be different this time."

Martell shook his head. "We're further apart than ever. But all the feelings are still there. Stupid."

"Maybe something will happen to surprise you."

"What can we do for her, Harry?"

Harry winced and arched his back. Martell looked away. He sometimes forgot his friend's constant pain.

"If it were anyone but Oski," Harry said, "I wouldn't be concerned. But that one! Tell me, Carl—is he a liar?"

"I've only caught him in one direct lie—but he *is* a liar. I feel it, in the background, even when he's telling the truth. But maybe that's just personal prejudice."

Harry frowned. "It sounds about right. Truth is the material lies are made of. A truly great liar would lie with his very being, even when his words were true."

"What do you mean, 'It sounds about right'?"

Harry waved a hand. "An idea I have. Nothing I'd care to speak of now. One thing though—if you should meet with him—"

"Oh, God."

"Please, Carl."

"Sorry."

"If you should meet with Oski, and he should offer you any food, don't eat it."

"You think he'd poison me?"

"Umm, perhaps." Harry's eyes slid away from Martell's, embarrassed at what they both knew to be an evasion. Martell didn't push the matter, but it troubled him.

Harry patted his stomach. "A fast probably won't do me any harm."

"A fast?"

"Prayer and fasting. The best I have to offer. If I were a Catholic I could light candles and say a mass, but as a good Lutheran the weapons of my warfare are prayer and fasting."

"You take it seriously? The magic?"

"Let's say I'm not afraid to make a fool of myself. Especially between friends. You can tell your lady that I'll be praying for her, for whatever my prayers are worth—and more than that, for God's grace."

"I didn't come here for this kind of talk, Harry. I came to be told there was a logical explanation, and that I have nothing to fear."

"You have everything to fear, Carl, like any other soul. If there is magic here—and I'm saying *if*—you'll need to choose sides. No-man's land is no place to be when the shooting starts."

"Well, Harry, if there is a God I hope he's noticed that I'm entirely unsuited to combat."

"I wouldn't say that too loudly. The Lord seems to enjoy singling out people who talk that way for especially hazardous duty."

"And I should believe in Somebody with that kind of judgment?"

"Absolutely. Last night our Bible Study at church got a bit out of hand, but I had intended to talk about a passage in 1 Corinthians where Paul says that most of his converts were neither bright nor successful, and then he says that God has used the weak things in the world to confound the strong, and so on.

"The idea I meant to develop was that God seems to favor using swords for plowshares, and plowshares for swords, and shepherds' slings for artillery, and cowards for heroes.

"After all, what does it prove if He wipes out an army with a bigger army? But if he uses the jawbone of an ass, as the man said, 'That's news.'

"Have you ever noticed the advertising our church PR people put out? It usually pictures the average Lutheran as somebody out of a real estate ad—young, upwardly mobile, 2.3 kids and a dog, the wife is the chairman of the board for some major corporation. Well, I don't run into that family very often on the job. Most of the saints I meet have money trouble, and weight trouble, and some kind of marriage trouble, and probably a nervous tic that drives you crazy to look at it, and now and then they're just plain bonkers. And I think those are the ones God can use, because they don't stand in His light . . . That is, as long as we let them live . . ." Harry's face hung like melting butter, and his eyes were tired.

"Is something wrong?" Martell asked.

"Nothing I can talk about. Pardon me. Go on with what you were saying."

Martell said, "So the good news you have for me is that if I come to terms with God, He'll probably set me to whatever job I want least?"

"No, not necessarily. But do you really think that, when you come face to face with Ultimate Truth, Ultimate Truth is going to shuffle through some paperwork and say, 'Well, you seem to be doing all right. Carry on'? Don't you think He's likely to ask you to stretch yourself a bit?"

"If I have to be brave to face God, then I'm afraid I'll probably just keep running."

Harry rubbed his eyes. "I'm sorry, Carl. I get carried away. God doesn't work by my formulas, or anybody's but His own."

Martell stood up. "Well thanks. I don't recall that anybody's ever given up a meal before just as a favor to me."

"I *have* said too much."

"You didn't lie."

Martell walked home, setting aside thoughts of God. The mention of fasting reminded him that it was past lunchtime. He'd been living mostly on coffee for days. He made a resolution to try and get some orange juice down.

He noticed a raven perched in one of the fir trees on his corner. Two ravens in as many days. Very odd.

He found his apartment door open. The smoke alarm was screaming and white smoke billowed out.

A fire extinguisher hung on the wall a few doors down. He ran and got it, then rushed inside.

He collided with someone. He pulled the person out the door.

It was Elaine, coughing.

He sighed. "You tried to cook," he said.

She coughed some more, and her eyes streamed tears. "You—you forgot to lock your door—you still do that, even in these times—and I thought it would be nice to make you something. I—I turned the oven off and opened the doors and windows. It'll air out. But the oven will need cleaning."

Martell laughed.

Elaine sobbed, "I wanted to surprise you! I found your address in the phonebook."

"It was very sweet. Especially knowing how much you hate to cook."

Mrs. Lindstrom from the next apartment poked her head out and asked, "Should I call the fire department?"

"No thanks. Just a burned dinner."

"It was a casserole," said Elaine with woe.

"Then it's all for the best. I hate casseroles."

When the air cleared they went back inside. Martell examined the oven and phoned for pizza. By the time it arrived they were able to close some of the windows. Martell ate a piece and kept it down without thinking to be surprised about it, and they drank beer from the refrigerator.

Elaine refused to be consoled. "I mess up everything," she said, wolfing her third slice. "Everything I touch. No wonder you hate me."

"Hate you? I like you better right now than I have in ten years, and for all that time I've been in love with you. You have no idea how the smell of burnt cheese brings back the old days."

She dabbed her lips with a paper napkin. "What's it like?"

"What's what like?"

"Not being able to lie. Is it really hard?"

"Not that bad, really. I remember I saw a movie once where the main character couldn't lie for some reason, and it was all about how impossible it is to live without your falsehoods. Like the characters in Ibsen's *The Wild Duck*. But I've found that it's a very rare situation where the truth won't serve just fine if you think about how you present it. Granted, there have been unpleasant moments, but I've only had a few of them. It's really not that terrible so far."

"It makes me afraid to talk to you, knowing you can't be gallant and spare my feelings."

"I'll be as gallant as I can."

After a moment she said, "I hurt you, didn't I?" in a low voice.

"Yes."

"That's what I'm like, Carl. We might as well both tell the truth. I'm a taker. I'd like to be a nicer person, but it seems like so much work."

"I always adored your honesty. To live with you I had to learn to be just as honest, because you always got the truth out of me whatever I did. But one thing you never spotted. You never saw how wonderful you were, how wonderful you could be. I wanted so badly to help you see yourself through my eyes."

"I couldn't be what you wanted, Carl. That's why I left. It didn't have anything to do with Forsythe. Afterwards I realized how lousy my timing had been, but by then you'd gone away."

Their hands brushed, and in a moment they were up, and she was in his arms, and it was like coming home. He held her tight and kissed her hard and wanted nothing else forever.

She looked up at him and said, "Run away with me. Run with me now. Oski's been out of town since yesterday. I don't think I was followed. We could get away."

He was ready to do it.

At that moment there was a knock at the door. He pulled free, saying, "Keep my place," and went to check the peephole.

He came back at a run.

"It's Oski," he whispered.

❖   ❖   ❖

Harry was praying for Carl, and for his own peace, when Minna tapped on his door. "It's the Buchan boy," she said. "He says he needs to talk with you."

"Send him in then."

"Well, don't forget you've got to finish your call reports. And are you going to let me cut your hair this afternoon?"

"Not possible. I've got an appointment to see the bishop."

"Will you be back for supper?"

"I'll probably be back by then, but don't make me anything until further notice."

"You're not fasting again?"

"It's been months!"

"It's been a few weeks. What's the problem now?"

"I'll fill you in later. Let Rory in now."

"You'd better. If you're going to fast, I might as well join you. Cooking for one's a waste of time."

"What's on your mind?" Harry asked as Rory sat in the chair Martell had used earlier.

"Do you have any books on witchcraft?" Rory's eyes were red and he hadn't shaved.

"I think I might have a couple. But I don't recommend them."

"I know. Witchcraft is a pretty ugly subject."

This boy's in pain, Harry thought. "That's not exactly what I meant," he said. "There are popular books on witchcraft and scholarly ones. The popular ones are usually either friendly to witchcraft, which makes them spiritually dangerous, or if they're hostile they're often a kind of sanctimonious pornography. The scholarly ones are just depressing. The church doesn't come out in a very flattering light."

Rory edged forward in the chair. "Yeah, that's what people say—but is it really true?"

"The trials are well documented."

"No, I mean—is it true that the trials were such a bad thing? Okay—maybe they could have been more humane—but have you ever wondered whether the witches *deserved* to die?"

"Rory, the witch courts of the late Middle Ages and after were industries, profiting from the confiscated property of their victims. The prisoner was assumed guilty even if proven innocent. There wasn't another reign of terror like it until the French Revolution. And putting Christ's name on it made it the foulest kind of blasphemy."

"Yeah, yeah," said Rory, "but that's assuming witches aren't real. But suppose you knew there were people out there—evil people, worse than serial killers—people who kill and pervert and poison and seduce and—"

"What's the matter, Rory? What's happened to you?"

Rory looked at the carpet, elbows on knees. "I did something," he said. "Something I swore I'd never do again. I can't talk about it now. But—then—it got all mixed up with something that happened a long time ago, the wickedest thing I ever saw. There's a man who's evil. I met him in California. And now he's here."

"Rory, if you know about something illegal going on, you should go to the police."

"They couldn't help. Not everything evil is illegal."

Harry frowned. "Does this have anything to do with the Way of the Old Wisdom?"

"I can't talk about it."

"Would you like to make a confession, Rory?"

Rory started. "I'm not a Catholic."

"Neither am I. But there are times—"

"Look—I didn't come to talk about my problems. I came to find out what my Christian duty is. I read those books of yours about the Canaanites, and frankly they weren't much help. You can sit there and say it's bad to burn witches, but you've got to admit that God disagrees with you. That's clear from the Bible."

"It's a complicated matter—"

"I don't think so. *'Thou shalt not suffer a witch to live.'* The Canaanites are practicing witchcraft and human sacrifice, so wipe them out. *'Your eye shall not spare them.'* Are you telling me God didn't mean it?"

"He meant it."

"Then why not today?"

"Will you hear me out? Promise to let me finish what I have to say?"

Rory nodded and sank back in the chair.

"Right is right," said Harry, "and it doesn't change. But our comprehension grows, like a tree. New branches, new rings in the trunk, but deep inside, the sapling is still there."

Rory opened his mouth and Harry said, "You promised." Rory settled again, frowning.

"What bothers most people about the conquest of Canaan—what bothers me—is that God told His people to annihilate the population, men, women and children. If He had sent fire and brimstone or an earthquake, it wouldn't bother me nearly as much.

"But what I have to remember is that, in a real sense, the Hebrews *were* like an earthquake. They were a force of nature. They were very different from you and me in important ways. They were happier, for one thing. Righteousness was very simple for them—plain outward obedience. They didn't agonize over sins of the heart, as we do, because God hadn't taught them about those things. And He had not told them that it was murder to kill foreigners. That lesson came later.

"So God, who has the ultimate right to take any life,

used the Hebrews in their innocence to take a great number of lives. Listen to me—this is important—He would not ask you and me to do the same thing. Between us and those Hebrews stand the towering figures of the great prophets, and of Jesus Christ himself. To act now as the Hebrews did then would be to devastate our consciences. We would have to set aside the testimony of our Lord, and that we may not do."

Rory asked, "Are you a pacifist?"

"No. I believe in just wars. But I don't believe in Holy Wars."

"Well, maybe God's told you something He never told me. Maybe He's set some people aside for . . . special work."

"Like killing people for the good of their souls?"

"I'm just saying what if."

"If I knew about people who were thinking like that, I'd be scared to death of them. Do you know what the unforgiveable sin is, Rory?"

"Blaspheming the Holy Spirit."

"Right. But what kind of blasphemy is that? Read Matthew 12, where Christ talks about it. Read the whole chapter. It's all about willful blindness—blindness so dark that you can look at good and call it evil, and vice versa. The man who can't be forgiven is the man who no longer can tell the difference, who can do abominations in God's name and call it good. When Jesus warns the Pharisees about it, he's looking toward his own crucifixion. That's the sin against the Holy Spirit. Never lie for God, Rory. Lies are always from the enemy. The enemy *is* a lie; all his power is a lie; it only works when we fall for the lie. There's nothing there. Nothing to fear. Nothing to kill."

"What if somebody's sacrificing people?"

"Then it's a matter for the police. The real battle

isn't between us and the human sacrificers. It is, and always has been, between those who believe that God has spoken, and must be obeyed, and those who think He hasn't spoken, and must be improvised. Human sacrifice is one improvisation. Witch burning is another."

Rory got up. "You believe there are mistakes in the Bible, don't you?"

"I wouldn't call them mistakes. There are errors of fact, but they don't affect the spiritual truths."

"Well, how do you know there aren't any spiritual mistakes too?"

"I believe the Bible is God's Word."

"So you think it can be mistaken about things you can check, but you're sure it's always right about the things you can't check. You know what? That doesn't make any sense at all to me."

Harry shook his head. "Think about what I've said, Rory. Think and pray. And read your Bible. There's a point where you have to leave Reason behind, but not before you come to the end of Reason."

"Yeah, well. Thanks."

"Let me know what you decide, Rory."

"Yeah." Rory went out.

I suppose I said all the wrong things, Harry thought. *I always end up preaching*. He said a prayer for Rory, but had trouble concentrating. The conversation, on top of last night's confrontation, had upset him.

Ten minutes later Minna tapped on the door and poked her head in. "Have you seen the church key, Harry? I wanted to go over and check the altar flowers, but it's not on its hook."

Harry patted his pockets. "I don't seem to have it. I suppose I could have put it down somewhere and forgot it, you know me. Here, use my master."

"All right, but you give me the other one if you

find it. I don't like having those things floating around. I'll be back in a few minutes."

"I'll be gone by then, unless I lose my car keys too."

Elaine hid in the bedroom and Martell answered the door.

Oski was smiling, showing his long teeth. Martell had never seen such teeth. Oski's nostrils flared, and Martell was sure he smelled his fear.

"Good afternoon," said Oski. "I hope you don't mind my knocking you up without telephoning first. I happened to be passing."

Dry-mouthed, Martell invited him in. The room tightened.

Oski gave him his overcoat, and Martell hung it in the closet.

"What a charming place," Oski boomed. "Where in the world can you find true comfort—comfort unrestrained by the tyranny of fashion—but in the homes of bachelors?"

"I apologize for the mess. I don't get much company. The smoke's from a cooking accident."

"Please, no apologies. I used to live in much the same style, back before my books started selling. Those were good days. I miss them in a way."

"Would you like some coffee?" *Small talk, Martell. Keep it to small talk.*

"Yes, thank you. Instant is fine, as long as it's black." He picked his way through the books and newspapers to the bookshelves.

"I love to spy out other men's libraries," Oski said as Martell put cups of water in the microwave and fumbled with saucers and spoons. "Everything worth knowing about a man can be divined from his books. And if he has no books, he's not worth knowing.

"A good collection. Yes. Yes. Yes. Of course. Even old Gibbon. Your Tacitus is worn—it's actually been

read. Oski, but that goes without saying. And my old
friend Snorri.

"It's all about stories, you know. Tales. Each man
is a tale—a saga—made in part of the tales he's heard,
with something extra that each adds for himself. Sometimes it drives me mad that, old as I am, I can never
live long enough to learn all the tales worth knowing.

"And what's this?" He turned to the Viking painting. "A true Norseman. No silly horns on the helmet.
No unnecessary fur. But he has the sea in his eyes,
and you can see that he fears nothing below the gods.
Who painted this?"

"A student of mine, a few years ago. She's a commercial artist in Minneapolis now. I suppose she had
a crush on me. She got over it, but she painted me
that Viking before she graduated."

"You must give me her address. I'd like to be
painted by this woman."

Martell nearly dropped a spoonful of coffee crystals.

"Will you do that, Martell? Give me her name and
address so I can commission her? It could be salu-
tary for her career."

Martell watched the crystals dissolving in the cup,
like blood in a bath. "I don't think I could do that,"
he whispered.

Oski walked toward him. "What was that?"

"I don't think I could do that."

"No? Whyever not?"

Martell couldn't look at him. He couldn't find
words.

Oski was very close now. Martell felt his skin
contract.

"I wonder what you could have against me, Martell?
Have I ever shown you anything but friendship?"

Martell forced the words out. "You were vicious
to my friend Harry."

"Herr Pastor? Come now, such men enjoy being

baited by apostates. It feeds their martyrdom. It must be something more, surely, that makes you think me a danger to the young. Could it be something you've heard from Elaine?"

Martell swung to face him, spilling the coffee over his trouser leg, and knew as quickly that his eyes had been read. Fear stoppered his throat.

"I've known Elaine longer and more intimately than you did," said Oski. "Do you think she could have made a rendezvous without my knowledge?

"Oh, for God's sake, don't look at me like a gaffed halibut. Do you think I'm some kind of Victorian husband? You met in a church—I very much doubt you'd have the panache to do the deed in that setting. The secrecy was amusing though. Poor Elaine is quite terrified of me."

Martell breathed again. Oski might not know Elaine was here. "Why don't you set her free then?" he asked.

"Elaine may leave whenever she likes."

Lie. But Martell didn't have the courage to throw it in his face.

"Do you really believe," Oski asked, "that I'm holding her by force? Women as individuals are quite interchangeable to me. It's the principle of the Female that matters. Only Elaine has developed this extraordinary notion that people who cross me tend to have accidents. The woman should really get professional help. I've suggested it often."

Martell stood speechless. He dared not call this man a liar. Especially while he was hiding his mistress in his bedroom.

"Why am I here then, you ask?" said Oski. "To cultivate you, Martell. You intrigue me."

"That doesn't make any sense." Martell was sopping coffee off his leg with a wet towel.

"Why not? I liked your articles. You wouldn't have

published them if you didn't think they had worth. I happen to agree with you on many points. I wish you'd publish more. You're one of the soundest men in the field. Unlike the children of this age, you have a feeling for the power—the magic—of words. Of truth and lies. All you need is to learn arrogance and bald assertion and you'll rise swiftly."

It's difficult to keep up your defenses with someone who calls you one of the soundest men in your field. Martell let himself relax a little and handed Oski the surviving coffee cup on a saucer. They sat, Oski in an easy chair, Martell on the sofa.

"Since I've met you," Oski went on, "you interest me even more. I'm a judge of men, and I see in you great things. You don't lie, do you?"

Martell looked at Oski quickly, but read nothing in the gray eye. "No," he said.

Oski smiled, sipping his coffee. "I care about the truth," he said. "It's a virtue I don't possess, so I demand it in others. I visited Conan Doyle's grave once, at Minstead in the New Forest. Do you know his epitaph? '*Steel True, Blade Straight.*' Marvelous. I love that word, *true*. We spell it *t-r-o* in Norwegian, and we use it as a noun, but it means much the same. Etymologically it goes back to the image of a tree—straight as a tree trunk. And of course trees are central to everything. Even the Christ climbed a tree.

"In old Norse cosmology the very universe is a tree, *Yggdrasil*. Do you know why that is, Martell? It's simple when you think of it. Each man's universe is his own mind. And the mind *is* a tree, with roots down deep in the evolutionary past where dragons gnaw. A straight, reasonable trunk, more or less reasonable according to the individual, then a jungle of forking and twining and twisting nerves carrying thought out in every direction, and out beyond thought to the tiny shoots and leaves which are the imagination. All kinds of creatures, the creatures of the imagination, run to and fro among its branches in ceaseless activity. And when the wind of the gods blows in those branches they cross one another and touch and—crack!—an idea is born like a spark. There is much to learn from myth, Martell, for those who have ears to hear."

He sipped his coffee again. "Do you dream, Martell?" he asked, tipping an eyebrow.

"Like anyone else, I suppose."

"I'll tell you why I write of Vikings as I do. It's because of my dreams. The research, the study, the revision and dog-work, they all have their parts, but it began with dreams. To dream is to climb the tree.

"When I was a boy I dreamed of Vikings. I saw the ships, the houses, the clothing, the weapons and tools. And would you believe, Martell, nothing I have learned since has essentially contradicted those dreams? When some 'fact' in a learned article seems to do so, I know the historian has gotten muddled. It's proven so often enough in the past to give me confidence for the rest.

"I wonder—have you ever had such dreams, Martell? Your guesses are so often right."

"No, my dreams aren't like that."

"Perhaps you forget them. It would be interesting to hypnotize you. Might I?"

Martell swallowed. "I'd rather not."

"As you wish, but it's a pity. You are a Norwegian, aren't you? How did you get a name like Martell?"

"My great-grandfather's name was Myrdal. He anglicized it, or thought he did. Martell's really Old French, of course, but I suppose the extra *l* is sort of English."

"A good name, though. Strong. And honorable, if you care for heroes of Christendom. You have the true

Viking look, Martell, if you'd only put on some muscle. What color is your beard?"

"Red, when I let it grow."

"I suspected so. Would you believe me if I told you that Erling Skjalgsson looked much so? It's a thing I know."

"Erling was one of the great ones."

"He fought St. Olaf. That counts in his favor, from my point of view."

"He was a Christian. Olaf didn't want his death."

"So Olaf claimed. Olaf had a wonderful capacity to lie with style—perhaps the most underrated property of sanctity."

"It's strange to hear you talk about Olaf and Erling as if you'd known them," said Martell.

Oski smiled.

Martell's curiosity rose. "What do you know about the runestone?"

Oski set his saucer down. "I know that Paul Knutsson sailed. He and his men found that the worshipers of the old gods had fled Greenland. The Greenlanders left behind told them the renegades had sailed to Leif's Vinland. They followed them, but sailed by error into Hudson's Bay, which is easily done. As it happened, the Greenlanders had also gone that way. Knutsson's party followed the shoreline some weeks, until they came upon one mad Greenlander, a misfit who had fled the rest. He led them south, by water and portage as far as they could, then by land. After losing some men to the Indians, they set up what you call the Kensington Stone. And very near here, they closed with their prey. They made camp, and one of them, a priest, began carving a second stone. In it he set a rune, for he was a man of lore, and by that rune he meant to bind the old gods forever. Only the mad Greenlander turned and crept to the other camp and

warned them, and the Greenlanders attacked by
night. The priest finished his stone, dying, and all
the Christians were slain. The Greenlanders wandered on, finding no further help from their gods,
and at last were made slaves by the Indians, and
came to an end."

"A bloody story, and sad," said Martell. He didn't
know if he believed it or not, but he knew Oski was
not making it up.

He thought uneasily of Elaine in the bedroom,
afraid to make a noise, listening to them, no doubt
silently screaming to him to get rid of Oski. Or
wondering why he wasn't keeping his promise to ask
for her freedom. But what could he say? Oski had
declared her free to go. He had lied, but it had rather
closed the subject.

Oski said, "Do you know what happens when
you're tortured? Providing you don't let your fear
break you? You go mad. When the Nazis set to work
on me, they wanted certain information I held about
the Resistance. So I retreated into my dreams. I spent
fine days among the Vikings. I watched, I listened.
I was so fascinated that it was some time before I
noticed who *I* was.

"I was an old man. A wanderer. I looked shabby
and poor, and no one paid me mind. I wore a long
black cloak, and I carried a heavy staff. My beard was
long and gray, and I kept my wide hat pulled down
low over one empty eye socket. Do you know what
my name was?"

Martell said nothing. He felt as if the answer would
give Oski power.

"You understand, I can tell," said Oski. "It was odd,
though, that I was only the Wanderer. I should have
had another aspect, but him I could not find. And
my home I could not find, nor my wife, nor my
friends, nor my children. Then I remembered that

the time in which I walked was shortly after the death
of St. Olaf Haraldsson, and it was about that time
that I had been said to have died. So I knew my
enemy.

"And knowing that, my reason returned. I found
myself transferred to Grini, where I survived until the
liberation.

"I found that I had lost my left eye in one of the
beatings I'd taken. And I remembered everything. I
remembered who I was, and who I had been, from
the beginning.

"I took the name Sigfod Oski—it was not the one
I was christened with. I wrote my labor camp poems
down. And I began to plan."

"Plan?"

"Do you know that Cerafsky's Comet appeared in
the year 1362 A.D.? I lost something then. I was
cheated, shackled. But the shackles are gone now, and
I shall have my own back.

"A new age approaches, Martell. Not the poly-
styrene New Age of the gurus, but an age for heroes.
Civilization, as you surely realize, is a house of gelatin,
built on sand. That is doubly true of that splendid
oxymoron, the moral civilization. Let it strangle awhile
on its dilemmas and someone's bound to say, 'Enough.'
And the citizenry will sink gratefully back into comfortable barbarism. It's nearly time again. That will
be a day for men like us, Martell, the ones who've
never been at home in a world powered by engines."

"What, are you planning to bring back tribalism?"

"Do you know, Martell, some time back, in Colonial
times, they did a psychological survey of the Zulus
in Africa. They discovered an amazing thing. There
were no neurotic Zulus. Do you know why?"

"Why?"

"Because they lived in tribal groups. They barely
had a sense of individual personality. They thought

of themselves as part of the tribe, and of course the tribe was infinitely superior to all those ill-born, benighted subhuman other tribes."

"And of course that made it okay to kill, rob or enslave members of other tribes," said Martell. "It was exactly like the Viking Age."

"Precisely. Everyone wants happiness, wholeness. There's only one way to get it. Go back to the way of life we evolved from. Abandon humanitarianism. Submerge into the tribe once again."

"White against black. Yellow against white. Warfare without end."

"More than that! White against white! Black against black! Yellow against yellow! Survival of the fittest! What heroism there will be, what glory!"

"In a nuclear age? That means annihilation, if it weren't bad enough without it!"

"Ah, but I will be in charge! I will say what weapons men have. I'll dismantle the modern world. Gone will be the engines. Gone will be the telephones, the computers, the microwave ovens. I will save the environment! I will fill Valhalla with a new generation of warriors! You'll love it, Martell! It will be everything your heart ever wanted!"

"You're mad," said Martell, but his heart pounded in his chest.

"I only require one thing. A weapon. It is nearby, I know, for hereabouts I had it last. So I come to you today. Where is my weapon, Martell?"

Martell looked to see if he was joking. He was not.

"I—what are you talking about?"

Oski's eye narrowed. "Do you say you don't have it?"

"Have what?"

Oski frowned. "You're not lying. You couldn't be. It's possible you don't understand. . . ."

He rose. "Very well then. The time is not yet. But you will have the weapon soon. All the lines converge here. When you do, remember—it belongs to me. It is mine. You wouldn't withhold a man's property, would you?"

Martell could not speak.

"Speak, man, answer!"

Martell found himself saying, "I might if I knew he meant to do harm with it."

Oski stepped very close and bent over Martell. His breath was hot as he said, "Answer me three questions, Professor. First—who is the Gelding?"

The eye compelled him. "You are the Gelding," said Martell.

"Yes. Something the Nazis did, though fortunately they botched the job. Second question—are you a coward?"

Martell found himself saying, "No."

"That is my gift to you, Martell, for you must understand I wish you no ill. Third—*is Elaine in this apartment now?*"

Martell choked. His chest tightened and pain swelled under his ribs.

"Speak! You cannot lie! You are not the first, but you are the truest! Tell me!"

"Yes!" Martell groaned.

Oski cried, "You may come out now, Elaine!" The bedroom door slammed open and Elaine stomped into the room, her eyes furious on Martell.

"I'm sorry," he moaned.

"Damn you!" she said. "Damn you to Hell, Carl Martell."

Oski walked to her and she said, "I'm not coming with you!" But when he seized her arm she went visibly limp, and he led her to the front door. Oski took his coat from the closet and drew something from one of the pockets.

"I almost forgot," he said. "A little gift for you, Martell. Something exotic for an American. Tinned reindeer meat, from Norway." He set the flat can on the kitchen counter, then took Elaine out.

Martell watched them go, trembling.

He sat down and tried to get his control back. After a few minutes he got up and went to the bookshelf. He found *The Prose Edda* of Snorri Sturlusson.

He turned to the chapter entitled, "Gylfaginning," the great Norse exposition on Creation and Apocalypse. He paged through it until he found the list he wanted:

> *"Sigföd, Hnikud,*
> *Allföd, Atriíd, Farmatýr,*
> *Óski . . ."*

Sigföd meant "Battle-father." *Óski* meant "Fulfiller of desire."

He paged back in the text and found another name he was looking for. *Jälg.* It mean "gelding."

They were all names for one character—a figure which had haunted Martell since he was a little boy wrestling with books too old for him. Mad, treacherous, murderous; a liar and a black magician and a breaker of sanity, yet somehow brave and noble and strangely sad. The high god of the North.

Odin.

"That is my gift to you," Oski had said, calling him no coward. But Martell felt himself a coward as he took the can of reindeer meat in a trembling hand and carried it outside to the trash dumpster.

He knew the story, from the *Heimskringla.* The one-eyed wanderer with the hat and staff had come to Olaf Trygvesson one night at the farmstead of Avaldsness, and had kept the king up nearly all the night with one mad, glorious tale after another.

But the wanderer had been gone when the king woke the next morning. Olaf had gone to the kitchen and asked the servants if the stranger had left any meat with them. They said he had. Olaf instructed them to throw the meat out. "For that," he said, "was Odin."

Scholars still debated the precise significance of that meat.

Martell did not want to know.

MEMORANDUM

FROM: A. Carnegie Hall, Station Mgr.
TO: WEEP Announcers

RE: It has come to our attension that some of our personnels have been rumored to have televesions in their homes. This will ceace immediately. Not only is telivision an incidious menice on our moral fiber of our nation, but is the COMPETTION, and a conflict of interests.

Also, in the future ahead, any personels found to have attended the theater, movies, or dance, or any similar unspiritual entertainments, will have given cause of the termination of those personnels.

Also, the Lord has reavealed to us that so-called Daylight Savings Time is displesing in His Sight. This months change-over will be the last for WEEP. From now on all time checks all yer long will be given in good, Christian, Standard Time.

Don't bother me.

A.C.H./cak

"You know what the trouble is, Rory? I'll tell you what the trouble is. It's heathenism. I got this book in the mail that explained it all to me. It's

not the Commies, or the niggers, or the Jews—it's heathenism."

"Heathenism? What kind of heathens you mean, Pontoon?" Rory spoke into the telephone receiver cradled between his cheek and his shoulder as he loaded a CD with one hand.

"Not heathens, heathenism! It's as plain as the face on your head. This guy explained it in the book. We celebrate Christmas, but it's not Jesus' birthday, it's just a heathen celebration they've slapped Jesus' name on. We celebrate Easter, but that's just a heathen celebration too—the name comes from some old heathen goddess—"

"But Easter is celebrated pretty much when the Resurrection happened, Pontoon—I mean, we know Christ was crucified during Passover—"

"Yeah, but we use a heathen name! That shows that we're not really celebrating Jesus, we're celebrating the heathen holiday! Anything that's been used by the heathens is contaminated! Heathen idols, heathen holy places, heathen names, we got to get rid of 'em all, or else we come under their power!"

"Wait a minute, Pontoon. What do you call the days of the week?"

"What does that have to do with it?"

"Well, I read that Sunday and Monday were named after the Sun and Moon back when people worshiped them. Tuesday was named after some German god, and Wednesday after another one, and the same for Thursday and Friday. Saturday was named after Saturn, a Roman god. Then there are the months—I can't remember all of them, but I know March is named after a god, and June is named after a goddess. Are you gonna change all the names of the days and the months?"

"By golly, you're right, Rory! We've gotta change 'em all!"

"That's not what I meant—"

"*And then there's all the products out there with heathen names—Mercury cars and Peter Pan peanut butter, and Red Devil paint! Thanks for reminding me, Rory! I gotta call some people. Talk to you later—*" And he hung up.

Another red light was on, and he hit its button.

"*Hello, Rory Buchan on the radio?*" It was a woman's voice. "*I gotta talk to somebody—I've got the Virgin Mary sitting in a maple tree in my back yard, and what I can't figure out—does that make me a Catholic?*"

The next caller said he'd seen a hunting party of red Indians running down Third Street. It was one of those nights. Rory made reassuring noises to him and hung the phone up, adjusted his earphones and outcued the music. "That was Becky O'Morgan with, 'It Ain't Cheatin' If It Ain't No Fun.' This next number's a request going out to my good friend Godfrey Hanson, and his lovely wife Christine, married ten years ago Sunday at Nidaros Church in Epsom. We sure hope they'll have many more years just as good, and we hope that they enjoy listening to Walley Windemere and 'Love Beats A Suckin' Chest Wound.' " He hit the PLAY button and slumped in the chair.

It was done. Right on time. Everyone recruited by the Hands of God would know that the meeting would be 10:00 on Sunday, at Nidaros Church.

He felt no assurance that he was doing the right thing. But good or bad, Thumb and his group couldn't be any worse than Rowan. Any enemy of Rowan's was a friend of Rory's.

He thought sadly of Laura, who had once been Zippy, now Young Goat Star. He'd known her under every name but her real one. Maybe he could do something for her yet.

But Rowan . . .
It had to stop now. The evil had to end here.

The bishop's assistant showed Harry into the inner office. Harry had a sudden impression such as the poet Wordsworth must have felt when he wrote:

I wandered lonely as a cloud
That floats on high o'er vales and hills,
When all at once I saw a crowd,
A host of golden daffodils . . .

The entire room was a symphony in yellow. The walls and ceiling were yellow, the carpet and drapes saffron, the furniture finished in a gold enamel, and all the books in the pine shelves that lined the walls had yellow jackets. The bishop himself wasn't there yet, so Harry, out of curiosity, checked some of the titles. *The Joy of Actuarial Science. Fly Fishing In Argentina. Preparing for the Master Pipefitter's Examination.*

In the entire room he could not see a single Christian image.

A door opened by the desk and the bishop came in. He wore a stylish buttonless suit, his head was shaved and he wore a diamond stud in his nose. He extended his right hand, palm down, and Harry almost shook it before he realized he was expected to kiss the episcopal ring. Another innovation. Harry had never kissed a ring before.

They sat and the bishop said, "Well, Harry, what's so important you have to see me on a Saturday?"

Harry found it hard to begin. The speech he'd planned seemed overformal.

"You know I've never gotten on with Judith Hardanger-Hansen," he said. "You need to be aware—that I'm aware—that anything I say is automatically discounted because of that . . . awkwardness. I say this because I want you to understand that I know that everything I say will be taken with a grain of salt. And that's—that's as it should be. I see that. So I just want to lay this before you, because I think you should be aware of it; then you can proceed as you think best—"

"Cut to the chase, Harry," said the bishop.

Deputy McAfee lurched through the steel door from the lockup corridor, his face white. He let the heavy door swing shut behind him and looked blankly at Esther. She looked blankly back.

"Where's Stokke?" he asked.

"Out on a call. Another fight."

"Well, get him on the horn and tell him to get his butt back here quick. And call an ambulance."

"Somebody sick?"

"That kid we brought in for beating up his girl-friend. Swanson. He's dead."

"Dead?"

"Killed himself."

"My God, how? Didn't you take his belt and shoelaces?"

"He used his hands. Pulled half his face off with his bare hands. I think I gotta puke."

Esther put a call through to Deputy Stokke. *Must be the full moon*, she thought. *Or that wind.*

"I know you," said Sigfod Oski to Solar Bull. "I know what you plan, and frankly you do not impress me."

"I don't understand." Solar Bull sat across from Oski at the formica kitchen table in the farmhouse.

"Tomorrow night a solemn rite will be enacted in Troll Valley. The sacrifice will be the true birth of the Way of the Old Wisdom, and the true birth of much, much more. You will not be a part of it."

Solar Bull made noises of surprise.

"Oh, do shut up. As you Americans say, don't kid a kidder. I've told you what you want to know, now I want you to leave."

"Leave? But—but this is my house. I built this organization. I'm the High Priest."

"Enough. Be gone. '*What thou doest, do quickly.*'"

Solar Bull stared. "You can't tell me to go."

Oski sneered at him. He lifted a hand to his eyepatch and raised it.

Solar Bull screamed and ran out of the house, tripping and bumping into things as he fled.

"Thank you for seeing me, Arnold," said Harry.

"I was delighted when you called. What can I do for you?"

Arnold Stern, the poet, led Harry into his parlor. He lived in an old Tudor house in St. Paul/Paul City's Highland Park area. It was a cozy place, not too large, with leaded glass in the windows and lots of patinaed dark wood.

Harry refused an offer of coffee and said as they sat, "How does one go about converting to Judaism?"

Stern raised his eyebrows as he lit his pipe.

"What brings you to this crisis of faith?" he asked.

"I just spoke to my bishop."

"Ah well, that was your first mistake, of course."

"I went to see him because I was concerned that my senior pastor—you met Pastor Hardanger-Hansen—was teaching Extinctionism. Last night she took it to the extent of encouraging—actually helping—a young girl to take her life. The bishop informed me, rather forcefully, that the Church has no quarrel with Extinctionism or the right to die, and that it was my job to get in step. I have put up with a great deal in my time, but I cannot stomach this."

"Not interested in Final Solutions?"

"That's exactly how I see it. I can't continue any

longer in this church. Over the years I've been losing my faith, one bit at a time, and always I've told
people that I just hold all the more firmly to what
remains. Only a day comes when you discover there
isn't any faith left to hold firmly onto.

"I always believed in the Church. I believed that
God watches over it, protecting it from gross error.
But you know what? He doesn't. The Church is just
an organization, like the Junior Chamber of Commerce or the Flat Earth Society."

"Any Jew could have told you that."

"I have to rethink my beliefs. If the Christian path
has led to this, maybe it's the wrong path. Maybe your
path is right."

"I have bad news for you, Pastor. Lots of Jews are
Extinctionists too."

"How is that possible? With your history?"

"Anything is possible, Pastor, in the world of modern religion. Hadn't you noticed?"

"I suppose I didn't want to notice."

"Your problem, if I may say so, is a very common
one. You want the one thing that is not available in
the world of faith."

"And what's that?"

"Security."

"Security? Eternal security? Are you talking about
Calvinism?"

"No, I'm certainly not talking about Calvinism. I'm
talking about the *feeling* of security. The illusion that
there is a safe place in the world where you can stop
thinking, stop being alert to the work of what some
of us call the Devil. Institutions give you that illusion. You rely on the organization to be spiritually sen-
sitive for you, to tell you what's what, to walk into
the fearful presence of God for you, like Moses at
Sinai, and bring back God's messages.

"But it doesn't work like that. We could have told

you if you'd asked—we got a splendid view of your institutions from our burned-out ghettoes."

"I can't tell you how sorry I am."

"I'm not blaming you. There's been enough corporate blame on both sides.

"But you see, this is what we've learned about God—some of us, anyway. He is not in organizations. He is not in princes, sacred or secular. He is found in two places—in His Word, and in tradition, which is the community of His people."

"But isn't the community just another name for the organization?"

"No. Organizations are different from communities. Organizations have no faces. They're driven by routines and structures. They are the opposite of communities. They are built to minimize risk—the true fear of God. Communities force you to face others, to face yourself; to risk, and risk, and risk again; to lay down your life, as your Rabbi said.

"You don't want to convert to Judaism, Harry. You want to discover again what it means to be a Christian."

Harry wept then, and they sat a long time, with Stern's arm around his shoulders.

As he went out into the dark, Harry said, "You know this places a wall between us, don't you? If Christ is the Messiah, that leaves you outside."

"I know. Not for us the cheapjack unity that comes from declaring Truth a triviality. We shall salute one another from our respective sides of the wall, united in this—that we belong to the ancient fraternity of men who respect one another enough to disagree."

Harry smiled and nodded; turned to go.

"And when the boxcars come—" Harry turned back to see Stern still standing in the doorway. "When they come with the boxcars to take us all to the new camps, we'll be together there."

❖   ❖   ❖

The wolf was crossing a field, running for cover, when it met the dog pack.

Dogs. The slaves of man. Dangerous, treacherous, unpredictable. Harbingers of death.

The wolf bolted to avoid them, but there were dogs to the right, dogs to the left, and when it turned about there were dogs.

Panting, the wolf stood still. Its strength was gone.

But the dogs did not attack. They were a starved, ragged lot, scarred and filthy and high-smelling. Though the wolf could not know it, these were no men's dogs.

They waited in their circle, moon-bright eyes on the wolf, the wind flicking their fur and rejoicing in their ears.

Suddenly their leader, a big scarred German Shepherd cross, uncovered his teeth, rolled on his side, and whimpered.

This was language the wolf understood. The sign of submission.

One by one, the other dogs turned up defenseless throats and unguarded bellies, and whimpered.

What happened next the wolf could not understand. But when it continued its journey, the dogs were nowhere to be seen, and the wolf was strong again.

Fenris, sang the wind.

Deputy Stokke got a message from the dispatcher to call his wife, so he used his cell phone. He was alone in the cruiser.

"Kevin lost a tooth during soccer practice," she told him.

"Ouch. He okay?"

"Yeah, puffed up lip but he'll be all right; but Dr. Braun says he'll need an implant. Three thousand dollars."

"Double ouch! Well, good thing we've got money in the horse account. I can put off horse buying for a few more years."

"Clare, we've got about two hundred in the horse account."

"That can't be. What happened to it?"

"You remember. The roof job last spring."

"Oh jeez, yeah. Well, it'll have to go on the credit card."

"I'm getting worried about the size of our balance . . ."

"I know, I know. But what are we gonna do? The tooth's gotta be fixed. Maybe I can arrange some overtime."

"You're working too much as it is. So am I."

"Don't worry. We'll figure something out."

Silence on the other end.

"Love you," he said.

Martell had an axe in his right hand and a round shield in his left. On his head was a helmet, on his back a coat of mail.

Shouting, he leaped with the others over the rail of Erling Skjalgsson's vessel, roaring from the dragon ship grapnelled to starboard. Martell struck with his axe, once, again; he killed a man. He shouted.

Erling's men knew their doom. They sold their lives as dearly as they might.

Martell saw King Olaf take up his station by the mast fish; climbing up on a sea chest to look over the heads of his bodyguard, for he was not the tallest of men, though broad-chested as a bull. The beard and hair under his gilded helmet were light brown, his eyes hot blue. He stared fiercely forward, bracing his weight with one hand on a man's shoulder.

He was watching Erling Skjalgsson, that tall, gray old man with red in his beard, who stood in the

*forecastle under the arching prow, commander now
of two true friends, and all the world his enemy.*

And then there was one friend.

Then Erling stood alone.

And still he fought, warding off arrows and spears
with his ragged shield, striking like lightning when
an opening came. The long fighting did not show on
him, or slow the oiled efficiency of movement learned
in a lifetime of battles.

And Martell thought, This is one of the old heroes.
Never again will there be men like this one.

Others thought the same it seemed, for at last they
drew back and let the old man be. Those he struck
at used their shields, but they did not strike back.

And Erling stood at last motionless, raised above
the wall of shieldmen who crowded before his deck.
His chest heaved but his head was high. He crossed
himself, sword in hand. There was silence, except for
the creakings and bumpings of the ship, and the slap
of the waves, and the cries of gulls, and the groans
of the wounded.

The king strode forward at the head of his bodyguard. An axe was in his hand. The shield wall parted,
and the king and the farmer confronted one another.

"Today you turned to face me, Erling!"

"Eagles fight breast to breast," Erling replied,
hefting his sword.

Martell thought of seeing these two in single combat, and licked his lips.

But the king said, "Will you be my man, Erling?"

The two locked eyes for a long minute. At last
Erling said, "I will." He tore his helmet off, threw
it aside, and set down sword and shield. He walked
to the king, towering above him.

The king stretched out his fighting axe and drove
its upper horn into the old man's cheek. "Thus I mark
you a traitor to your lord," he said.

Erling turned calmly to Martell, and Martell recognized his own face, as if in a mirror, but haggard and tired, a line of blood coursing down into the beard. "Kinsman," said Erling, "you are no coward. I place myself under your protection."

Martell swung his axe and buried it in the old man's skull.

He woke, full of horror. The king's cry still rang in his ears: *"YOU HAVE STRUCK NORWAY FROM MY HAND!"*

Chapter XIII

The Lord's Day

The morning sun lit the sanctuary of Nidaros Lutheran Church through the stained-glass windows, like a tabernacle of golden cobwebs. Pastor Judith Hardanger-Hansen looked out at the 8:30 congregation. Almost half full. Not bad. Attendance had been dropping for years, but Pastor Hardanger-Hansen was a woman of principle. She would not sell her integrity for popularity, like those unspeakable, sheep-stealing Baptists and Pentecostals, who would soon get their comeuppance.

Nothing could depress her this morning. Not while the memory of Friday night's ceremony glowed within her like brandy in the throat. She could feel the goat's hot heart jumping in her hand—never before had she comprehended the words, "Washed in the Blood of the Lamb." How childish, how pitiable, her Sunday School notions seemed now!

"The Gospel for this Sunday is taken from the book of John, Chapter Five, verses 19 through 26." She read:

> *"So Jesus answered them: I tell you this in all sincerity—the child cannot do anything of her or his self, except what she or he sees her or his parent doing: for what the aforementioned parent does, the child does too. For the parent loves the child and shows her or him whatever she or he does, and she or he will show her or him greater achievements, to your amazement. For as the parent revives and inspires people, so also the child will inspire you. For the parent doesn't impose his personal morality on anyone. . . . I tell you this in all sincerity—whoever hears about what I stand for and affirms it participates in something transcendent. . . . For as the parent is the ground of being, so she or he has also given the child meaningful existence. . . ."*

She bowed her head to compose her thoughts, knowing there was no need of prayer, because the Goddess was within her. Or rather all of life was a prayer, and mere words presumptuous.

Should she open her heart now—declare the wisdom in her heart? What a glory if the congregation heard and understood—to see them leaping and dancing in the aisles in praise of the Goddess, lost in the rhythm that is the tides, that is the blood, that is Life Herself.

But no. Not yet. She remembered the words of her seminary mentor the day she had come to him troubled, telling of her confusion, frightened that she was losing hold of the Jesus she had loved as a girl.

"You're growing up in the faith, Judith," he had told her, smiling, his eyes understanding, his white hair a corona in the window light. "Every soul that passes to true maturity must abandon the Jesus of childhood. It seems hard, but you'll find you can only keep him if you give him up. Who was the historical Jesus after all but a well-meaning enthusiast, a country preacher with strange pretensions? He died, his words were lost or muddled; we cannot know him. But the spiritual Jesus you are learning to follow can never be lost, for he is being formed each day within you. Believe in him, and your potential is unbounded. He will make you truly free."

"But can I say this to a congregation?" she had asked.

"No." He shook his head, his smile was sad. "We have to teach them in figures and parables. Lead them step by step. It's the great task of the Church in our day, to dismantle the faith of the laity without panicking them.

"Get them to make small compromises, one at a time. Never use reason. Use feelings, for feelings are the only truth of the soul. There are just two kinds of people, you know—idea people and feeling people. It's the idea people who've gotten the world into the mess it's in. So if they try to pin you down with logic, don't be ashamed to resort to the weapons of the heart. Like tears. Most people, especially most Lutherans, would rather surrender any principle than cause a scene.

"Remember—our gospel is not about statements or ideas of any kind. It is about the person of Christ, who is of course whatever we say he is."

Wondering, she had asked, "We don't know *anything* about God, do we?"

"We're creating God. Create wisely, Judith."

It had been hard to give up the Jesus who "loves

me, this I know." But she had followed the way of integrity, and what freedom, what joy she had found in return!

She was strong. She could wait. She would bring her flock in easy stages, like a good shepherd.

"In the Name of the Parent, and the Offspring, and the Sustainer Spirit," she said.

Martell sat on his sofa in his underwear, looking at a Sunday morning cartoon program. A commercial made his stomach hurt, and he switched the channel on his remote. A preacher with a face like a pit bull's was saying, "*JESUS SAYS you must be born again! I didn't say it! Jesus said it! You can come to me and say, 'Well, Brother Corey, there's nothing wrong with my life! I got a nice home, I got a—'*"

"You're sincere, Brother Corey," said Martell. "I just wish it were that simple."

He switched around and found some news.

"*Reaction continues today to the Supreme Court's refusal to consider a challenge to the DRA, the Definition of Religion Act. This leaves standing the government's new criteria by which such privileges as tax exemption and freedom of assembly will be restricted for sectarian groups. In response to charges that the law permits Washington to strip basic civil rights from anyone it disagrees with, Senate bill co-sponsor Lennon Murietta of California said: 'DRA will not affect any responsible American religionist. This law is a tool necessary to protect the people from con men and cults who would attempt to exploit them.*

'For a long time a conflict has raged in the country over the nature of the Constitution. Narrow left-brain thinkers see the Constitution in a static, literalist way, ascribing the force of law to its actual contents.

Fortunately most Americans have rejected constitutional fundamentalism to embrace the dynamic Constitutional Penumbra we've come to hold so dear.

'In the past, black-and-white thinking has taken the First Amendment to mean that all Americans have the right to think and speak as they please. Well that was a very sweet idea, and it may have worked in simpler times. But this is the 21st Century.

'Some time back the courts, understanding the nature of the times we live in, accepted the establishment of a new class of crime—the Hate Crime. This was their first official recognition that there are some ideas that simply cannot be tolerated in a free society; that it is our right and duty to root out certain kinds of thought.

'America is like a rose bush. Certain buds must be sacrificed if the best blossoms are to flourish. Our precious culture, built on the Penumbra of the Constitution, designed on the principles of moral relativism, offers the world its best hope for peace and security. We cannot allow a small group of moral absolutists to divide us and spread their hate. To allow such people to vote, assemble, publish or hold office would violate the sacred principle of separation of religion and state. Such people despise the very basis of our society, and have already forfeited all civil rights. At worst they are hateful bigots who must be locked away for the good of everyone. At best they are sick, emotionally repressed victims who require institutionalization.

'The people want DRA. We have given it to them. It's the right thing for America today.' "

Martell thumbed the remote control again, and found a popular stand-up comic doing his most famous routine. It consisted of reciting the names of well-known public figures who were unpopular in Hollywood, then sticking a finger down his throat and vomiting into an on-stage trough. *Newsweek* had described his act as "brilliant, but disturbing."

Martell wondered if he should get a satellite dish. Or throw the set out altogether. But then he'd have to think of something else to do to numb his mind.

It was a little after 11:00. He hadn't slept until after 2:00 A.M. He'd gone for a night walk to compose himself, to consult Cerafsky, but the comet was silent as ever, and he had found himself frightened of shadows. He'd thought he saw ravens everywhere. It brought back memories of childhood, and old phobias. When he had slept at last there had been the dream.

He'd been lucky Friday night, caught up in Roy Corson's miseries. Fuddled with compassion and alcohol, he'd collapsed on the sofa without a thought of Elaine or Sigfod Oski.

Elaine. He hadn't wanted to think about Elaine. Elaine demanded action, the thing he was least able to give.

Of course Oski wasn't Odin. The force of the man's personality could bowl you over, even give you nightmares, but no sane person could believe such a claim. Oski *thought* he was Odin though—Martell was sure of that—and he was mad and ruthless.

I'm no match for him.

True, but winning wasn't necessary. Not if a Noble Death was to be the climax. Oski had said he wasn't a coward—now *that* was a terrifying thought.

In bed his thoughts had run like a loop of recording tape: *He's stronger than me; I have no stomach for confrontations; she never loved me anyway.*

As a boy he used to lie awake at night and try *not* to think about a man casting with a fly rod. Because whenever he thought about a man casting with a fly rod, the rod would start whipping forward and backward in his imagination, *and he couldn't stop the motion*. And when you're lying in bed alone at one in the morning, there are few distractions to rescue you from an obsessive thought.

Last night had been like that. He had tried to read, tried to watch TV, but he couldn't stand it. Exhaustion had pulled him under at last, his thoughts still whipping, and he had dreamed, and feared to sleep again.

And now it was day, and time to do things.

Why me?

He pulled his T-shirt from his chest. It was clammy; he assumed it stank.

He thought of making breakfast but the thought turned his stomach.

He thought of leaving town, running alone. He couldn't get his savings out of the bank on a Sunday, but he could run now and worry about that later.

He thought, *Am I like that?* Oski had said he was no coward. It had rung true. But he was no hero either.

He shook his head and concentrated on a cartoon cat on television pulling a fish skeleton out of a garbage can.

He remembered, for some reason, his father and the welding torch. He remembered his father saying, "I can make the weld stronger than the piece was before it broke."

His father and mother had died in an auto accident while he was in college. He wished he could call them now and ask them what to do.

Maybe there was someone he *could* ask, though. A man with influence. One last sane recourse. Maybe he could shower, and try to eat something, and make a visit in the afternoon.

Rory Buchan knocked on the alley door of a Main Street tire store. A man in a ski mask let him in, and he found himself in the shop area. It was a cramped room, not built for auto service. Piles of tires and tools large and small left little floor space. A light fuzz of black, dusty oil covered every surface. Thumb, in his black mask, sat in a battered office chair by the workbench.

"Good afternoon, Brother Rory," Thumb said. "Quite a town you got here. From what I hear on the radio you had suicides, and fights, and attempted murder, and rape, and all kinds of vandalism, and two or three fires last night."

"It's been crazy," said Rory.

"Well, maybe we can do something about it, Brother. The power of Satan is strong in Epsom, but you and us, we can fight it. We have the weapons. Did you bring the key?"

Rory said, "Yeah," but he kept it in his pocket.

Thumb looked at him. "Are you looking back from the plow, Brother?"

"Maybe, some."

"Nobody's gonna make you do something you don't want to do. But I got to remind you that what we're doing here is mighty important. Maybe the most important thing in the history of America."

"I've been praying about it, and thinking about it," said Rory, "and I just can't get my thoughts straight. So here's the best I can figure it out. I'll give you the key. But I won't go along with you tonight."

"You got to work?"

"No, this is my night off. But I'm going out to W.O.W. myself, before you do. I don't care what happens to the rest of them, but there's one person there I've got to talk to. Maybe I can bring her out, like Lot's family."

"If that's the way it's got to be, Brother Rory," said Thumb, holding his hand out. Rory laid the key in it. It had a wrinkled yellowish tag on a string that read, ChURCh. "I wish you'd come with us, though. We'd be proud to have you."

"I'll pray for you. Pray for me," said Rory, and he left.

Carl Martell stood outside President Lygre's house in the early evening, shivering in the chill wind. The forecasters said possible snow. He walked around the block a couple times. There seemed to be a lot of people out; a lot of cars on the streets. He could hear voices raised; once or twice there was a shot. He walked some more, making up speeches and rejecting them.

He feared Saemund Lygre, as he'd always feared anyone in authority. It was a symptom, colleagues in the Psychology Department had informed him, of the Authoritarian Personality. Psychologists, while agreeing that Right and Wrong were culturally determined prejudices and therefore purely matters of personal taste, also agreed that an Authoritarian Personality was nevertheless a very bad thing to be.

If he went in to talk to President Lygre, he would be taking a stand, choosing a side. He hadn't taken a stand on anything in a very long time.

But cowardice was no longer an option. Besides, he'd phoned ahead.

He squared his shoulders and walked to the door. He pushed the bell.

Ruth Lygre answered. He thought, as he always did when he saw her, what a lovely woman she was. He thought she must have looked like a pre-Raphaelite angel when she was a girl, or a willow in spring. He felt cheated that he'd never found such a woman for himself. But he probably hadn't really looked.

"Come in, Carl, how nice to see you," she said, letting him in and taking his coat. "I'm so glad you came. We don't see nearly enough of you."

"Thank you," he said. "I'm sorry I'm a little late."

She said it didn't matter and asked him if he cared for coffee. He said no, thanks. She left him in the living room and he found himself alone with Dr. Lygre. He wasn't sure whether the man had just walked in or had been there when he entered. His brown suit faded into the paneling like a prairie bird's protective coat.

"Well, Carl, what's on your mind? Sit down."

"I—I had a visit from Sigfod Oski yesterday."

"Excellent. Excellent. He told you then?"

"Told me?"

"That he wants you for his assistant on his new project. He didn't tell you this?"

"No. It didn't come up."

"Oh well, perhaps he had a reason. I guess I've let the cat out. He wants to write an epic poem about the Vikings in America. He especially asked for your help in the research phase. I said I was sure you'd be honored to cooperate. You'd get credit in the final publication, of course, and we'll be happy to adjust your schedule, reduce your class load and so forth. It will call for travel, and of course there's some money involved."

Martell stammered, "It's . . . it's quite an honor."

"I should say so. You'll accept, I assume."

Martell took a deep breath.

"I don't think I can," he said, avoiding Lygre's eyes.

"I'm not sure I understand, Carl."

"I'm afraid I can't work with Sigfod Oski. That's why I'm here tonight. To tell you—I don't know— I think he'll be bad for the school."

"I see. How do you mean, bad for the school?"

"I mean . . . he's a very . . . I'm not sure he's quite sane. Sure, you expect a poet to be a little mad, but I think he may drag the college along into something that'll hurt it, and hurt a lot of people. Nothing can make *him* look bad—people will say, 'Well, that's Oski, the crazy Viking poet.' But Christiania can't afford to look foolish."

"Do you have any specific foolishness in mind?"

"He told me—well, he as much as told me—that he's a sort of reincarnation of the god Odin. That he's bringing in a new age. He believes this. He's going to promote it, from here. Do we want to be associated with a crackpot religion, or some kind of Fourth Reich?"

Martell looked up into Lygre's eyes and found them distinct, cold and blue.

"I had thought better of you, Carl," he said.

Martell cast about for words.

"I thought you were mature enough to work in a great man's shadow," said Lygre. "Apparently I was mistaken."

"Now wait—"

"No, you wait! If you can't bear to stand beside a man who's taller than you, the least you can do is to be honest about it. Don't muddy the waters with this drivel about his religion. These aren't the Middle Ages, Carl. We do not practice bigotry at Christiania."

"That's not the point—"

"Oh, I think it is the point, Carl. We hired you under the New Horizons program. We explained that we were breaking up the Christian ghetto. You told us you were an agnostic.

"But you don't teach like an agnostic. You talk about 'moral law' and great men. You cultivate Harry Gunderson, of all people.

"You're a closet Christian; we all know it. Your conduct has been obstructionist and hypocritical. Not to mention ungrateful."

"Ungrateful?"

"To Sigfod Oski. You can't tell me you didn't know

it was his influence that got you out of that sexual harassment complaint?"

"I—Oski wasn't even here then!"

"No, but he had written ahead to say he wanted to work with you. We couldn't very well have you under a cloud for his arrival, could we?"

"But—but I was cleared. Julie took it all back—"

"Don't be naive, Carl."

"You mean I wasn't cleared? You let me off—just to accommodate Oski?"

"Carl, these are hard times for small colleges. Did you know we seriously thought about closing the whole thing down last spring? Sigfod Oski is our salvation. What you did or didn't do is of no importance beside that."

"But—suppose I'd been guilty? What about Julie?"

"One of the alumni made a substantial settlement with the family. Out of court, so to speak."

"Dear God. You think it's true!"

"For Heaven's sake, Carl, grow up. This the real world. Appearance is what matters. Perception is reality. If you want to talk about religion, that's what religion is, at bottom.

"You've got to break out of this black-and-white paradigm, Carl. It's always the believers in Truth who end up running inquisitions and death camps. You think you'd be different, but you wouldn't. You carry the seed. Until humankind frees itself from all creeds, we'll never be rid of evil. Open your mind, Carl!"

Martell stared, speechless. Forsythe's words screamed in his brain: *"I do not say you're a child-killer, Martell, but . . ."*

Panic rose in his stomach. He had to run from here.

"Of course we understand that you've had a rough time, Carl. You're not a tough-souled man. When we hired you, the University sent us your psychological abstract—we understand your limitations. It's all right—a man who killed his own brother is bound to have them."

Martell gaped. *No, no, no, no, no!* What was the man talking about? *Killed my own brother?* Every muscle in his body tensed for flight.

"Now what I want you to do, Carl, is to go home and get some rest. You look terrible. Then you can be fresh and sharp tomorrow morning to begin your work with Oski. We'll pretend this conversation never happened. And it won't have."

Dr. Lygre got up and faded out of the room. Ruth Lygre came in with Martell's coat and escorted him to the door. He followed like a trained animal.

"Don't think too harshly of him," she whispered as he reached for the door handle. "He used to believe. But they wore him down. You know how it is. People call you a fascist and a bigot over and over, and the temptation to adjust never lets up. Finally he stopped saying what he believed, and in the end he forgot he'd ever believed it."

Her words made no impression on him. Without a word he walked out into the night. It was dark now, and the wind turned his sweat to ice. There were noises and voices everywhere, like New Year's Eve, and a buzzing from somewhere that sounded like a chainsaw.

He whispered, "My brother—I never—"

But he couldn't lie. He had had a brother.

"Remember, you're the oldest; you've got to watch out for Marty," his mother had told him.

He recalled how unjust it had felt, a strong six-year-old tied to a stumbling baby of two. *"I hate you,"* he had whispered to the child.

A day had come when he had decided to take a run through the pastures. His mother would have said no if he had asked to go out there so near supper, so he hadn't asked. And Marty had followed, as he always did. And Carl had run as fast as he could, as far as he could, to leave the small shadow behind. But he had relented at last, and stopped to let his brother catch up. But Marty never caught up. Carl had run back over the hill to look . . .

He did not remember the body floating in the stock tank, but he remembered hiding in the haymow all night, shivering with fear and horror, unable to go to his parents, while they and all the neighbors searched for both, then one, of the lost boys.

And now he could do nothing but bring the monstrosity out and look at it.

"I killed my brother," he whispered through clenched teeth.

LIE! The pain bent him over.

He stood bent, gasping for breath. What was happening? He had spoken the single truth he'd hidden from all these years, and it had come back at him like a face slap, rejected.

"I did kill him! I could have protected him, and I didn't."

Better. But not precisely true.

"Then what is the truth? I was responsible!"

You were six years old.

"I could have saved him."

If you had been incredibly mature for your age. You were guilty of a child's thoughtlessness, not a man's viciousness. All six-year-olds are irresponsible. Most get through it without anyone dying. You were unlucky. Your parents tried to explain this to you, but you wouldn't listen.

It couldn't be true. It was too easy. It was . . . irresponsible.

Look at the truth, Martell. You must.

He had no way of avoiding the awful vindication.

It was the hardest thing he had ever done to bow to mercy, to accept compassion, to be made free by the truth.

All your life you have tried to shoulder a mountain of responsibility. When you failed as Truth's Defender, you could not bear the shame. When you failed as the Defender of Innocence . . .

"It was your FIRST TIME?" he had said, looking in shock at Elaine's glowing face.

"Sure. What's the big deal?"

And he had looked at her, smiling and golden in his bed, appalled by the knowledge that he had deflowered a virgin. I'm responsible for her now, *he had thought.* I must love and protect her always.

His whole life had been based on a lie, a vainglory of guilt.

Stumbling, he began to walk, the rags of his history dragging at his ankles.

He saw, without emotion, a burning house. There were firetrucks on the lawn, and he stood with the crowd to watch. Occasionally a screeching rat ran by him, fleeing the fire. Nearby two men in hunting clothes drank beer as they looked on, the flames reflecting in their eyes, the wind whipping the hair below their caps.

"Been a freakin' lot of fires last couple days," one of them said.

"That's straight. We got a firebug in this town."

"Could be. Some kid, probably."

"Like to find that kid."

"Yup. Fix him."

"String him up."

"Yah."

"You bet."

A police siren sent up a space-movie wail somewhere in the distance.

He walked some more. There were a lot of people

on the streets this Sunday night, walking, cruising in
cars. Loud people, laughing, shouting. Keyed up.
Waiting for something to happen.

He passed three young men leaning on a car,
drinking beer. They were students from one of his
classes.

"Hey, Mr. Martell! Have a drink."

He looked at them as if he didn't understand the
language they spoke. "What?" he asked.

"Have a drink! What's the matter, you too good to
drink with us?"

He recognized his surroundings then—this was
some bad movie he'd wandered into. The next shot
called for him to refuse the beer. Then they would
beat him up.

He spoiled the continuity by taking the offered can,
drinking it, thanking them and wandering off again.

Somewhere, another fire siren howled.

Responsibility.

If it was true that his own actions weighed so little,
then he need not be as careful in the future. His
options would be greater, his choices harder. He'd
have to be . . . more responsible.

This would take some thinking about.

He hardly noticed the hunting party of Native
Americans, in breechclouts and buckskin shirts, carrying bows and arrows, who passed him on Third
Street, or the beer wagon, pulled by a pair of Percher-
ons, on Moss Avenue.

At last he found himself in front of Harry's house.
It was after ten now. There were still lights on.

For some reason he had avoided this house. He
felt vaguely that to enter it would be an irrevocable
step, as with a man in a tale who enters a fairy mound
and comes out to find thirty years passed in a night.
He shivered. The wind seemed to have gotten into
his ear canals.

A farmer in overalls and a gimme cap, quite drunk, came lurching down the sidewalk at him. He walked up close, caught Martell by the sleeve and breathed in his face.

"What I wanna know is, where's my dog?" he demanded.

"I don't know anything about your dog," said Martell.

"Ain't just *my* dog," the man went on. He chose his words carefully, his face full of concern. "Lotsa dogs been disappearin' the last coupla days. My dog, Howie Benson's dog, Ivan Munson's dog—lotsa dogs."

"Maybe you should go to the police."

"Whadda you know about it?" The man stalked off.

Minna answered Martell's knock and told him he could wait in the front room. Harry was talking to Stoney Berge. He sat on an old sofa and resigned himself.

It came to Rory Buchan, as he drove out to the W.O.W. farm, WEEP playing on the radio, that he couldn't be a party to what the Hands of God was planning. Maybe, when in doubt, the thing to do was to be merciful. You might be wrong, but you'd never sin against the Holy Spirit by showing mercy. He pulled the car over and stopped.

The police, he thought. *I'll tell them about the Hands of God. They'll protect Laura.*

He was looking for a driveway to turn around in when he heard his Sunday night stand-in announce a new record. He was surprised at that. He usually premiered new releases himself, on Saturday nights.

"*We've got a brand-new one for you from the Beaurivoir Brothers,*" the announcer said. "*This is a goody, and I think it's gonna be a real big one for them. You see what you think. It's called, 'Why Don't You Finish What You Started?'*"

Rory stiffened. Here was the sign he'd waited for. As he had always believed they would, the Beaurivoir Brothers had reached out in his moment of need to tell him what he was called to do.

Harry Gunderson came storming out of his room and stumped down the hall, pulling his overcoat on. Stoney loped behind him. Harry paused by the front room arch and looked in at Martell.

"I just dropped in—" Martell said.

"Well, come along. We'll talk on the way. Stoney here tells me something fishy's going on at the church."

"Maybe I should come back another time."

"Nonsense. Come on. It could be interesting. We might have to roust some people out."

"What?"

"Stoney picked up a rumor that there's a meeting at Nidaros tonight. Only there's nothing scheduled. Everybody knows Lutherans don't come out on Sunday nights."

Martell followed them out.

"People goin' crazy these days," Stoney observed as they stepped into the wind. They heard an ambulance siren. "Ever since they started cookin' with microwaves."

Chapter XIV

"I want to thank you all for taking time to be here tonight," said the man at the podium. He was a brown-haired, unremarkable, fit-looking man nobody could recall seeing before. He wore a denim jacket and jeans and a western shirt and boots. He stood on the small stage at one end of the basement Fellowship Hall of Nidaros Church, a maroon curtain at his back. The hall was crowded with people sitting on folding chairs—farmers with seed-company caps and laced-up boots, and a few of the fairly young and fairly old of various other callings. Mostly men. They listened politely, because this was church, but they fidgeted.

"Of course," the man continued, "it shouldn't be any hardship to gather in the House of the Lord. But we all know that to many people it seems to be. And that's why I believe that all of you are good people,

Christian people, the kind of folks who'll understand the importance of what I've got to say.

"I think you all know what this meeting's about. You all have some idea of the danger that faces us, of the craziness that's breaking out in your community, and of some of the reasons why it's happening here."

"Communists!" someone whispered, but his neighbors shushed him.

"I want you to listen to a tape recording," the man on stage said, "just so you'll know I'm not spreading stories."

He pulled a cassette player from behind the podium and pushed a button.

"*. . . the price Earth demands.*

"*And growing up under their fist, we are all made little. Lost is the beauty, lost is the terror, of the true earth, of life.*

"*Come back with me, children! Do not fear the night, do not fear the fire, do not fear the blood. All these are Woman, all these are the Goddess—your mother and your lover.*" Someone in the church gasped.

"*Will you follow me?*"

"*Yes.*"

"*Can you touch the Night?*"

"*Yes!*"

"*Can you embrace the Fire?*"

"*YES!*"

"*Can you drink the Blood?*"

"*YES!*"

"*THEN BRING THE GOAT!*"

The man snapped the cassette player off.

He leaned forward across the podium. "That recording was not made in Africa, my friends. It was not made in Haiti or South America, or California or any other heathen place. That recording was made not five miles from this very spot, at a place you know well.

"This abomination—this ritual of blood and sacrifice, was performed on our own American soil, under the protection of what some people call freedom of religion. An animal was slaughtered, my friends, to appease the Devil himself. Depraved and degraded acts followed, with which I will not offend your ears.

"Now you may say to me, 'Friend, how do you know this to be true? Where did you get this tape; how do you know it's genuine?'

"And friends, that's a very good question. You're intelligent people, fair-minded people. You don't want to take rash action without some kind of proof. That's why I'm going to introduce you to somebody. Somebody I'm sure you never expected to see in this place.

"May I introduce Solar Bull, the former leader and High Priest of the Way of the Old Wisdom!"

As the crowd buzzed, Solar Bull stepped from behind the curtain. His face was haggard and the light in his eyes was like a dying cigarette next to a spilled gas can.

"I have been in Hell," he said. "I have been a criminal, a drug dealer and a pimp and a murderer. I started a religion for money, then came to almost believe it myself. But I never understood the supernatural forces I played with, or the power of Hell, until I met a man you all know of. . . ."

Laura came to the gate to vouch for Rory, and the guards let him in.

"I had to come and talk to you," he told her when they had moved down the driveway a few yards. "You've got to get away from here tonight."

Laura looked at him but didn't seem to hear him. "Hamster," she said. "I had my purse when I got to the bus station, but . . . but . . . I lost it someplace. All my money was in it, and my ID."

"What are you talking about?"

She seemed to focus then. "Rory. I'm glad you came. I've been thinking about you a lot."

"I've been thinking too. You all right?"

"Sure. No problem. Everybody's a little weird tonight, that's all. We had a great ceremony last night, and nobody got much sleep. And the wind, too. And the comet. Crazy times—don't you feel it? A natural high."

"We've got to talk."

"Yeah. We'll go back up to the observatory."

"I don't think that's such a good place."

"It's the best place, Hamster—Rory. Believe me, things'll seem clearer there! I promise I won't try to make love to you. Not if you don't want me to. I swear it by the Brisinga Necklace!"

"The what?"

"Something Sigfod Oski told us about. Please come."

She looked childlike in the flat glare of the yard light, and the wind blew her tangled hair against her face. Rory said yes. There was time.

She led him up to the platform. At the top she stood with her back to him, her windbreaker blowing tight against her, looking off towards the west, where the clouds were moving in. The moon was full and Cerafsky burned brighter than the stars.

"There's a cold wind from Canada," she said. "Some people say it'll snow tonight."

"Could happen."

"It won't last though."

"I hope not. I'm not ready for winter."

She turned to face him. The flat light was at work up here, too, and the wind pushed her curls around, and Rory felt the wanting again, remembered how smooth her skin was.

"Are you ready for me, Hamster?"

"How—how do you mean?" He found he had moved closer. He stepped back.

"Could you handle it if I said I was in love with you?"

He looked at the clouds. He said, "I've been thinking a lot about the other night, Laura. I'd be a liar to say I didn't enjoy it, but—it wasn't right. I'm not like that anymore.

"You don't believe what I believe, but you understand about believing—about doing what's right, not just what you want to do.

"We're too far apart, Laura. I believe in Jesus and you believe in—whatever you believe here. One of us would have to change and, I'm sorry, it's not going to be me.

"Can I tell you what Jesus means to me, Laura?" He looked down and found her much closer, gazing at him, her hands behind her back.

"It's okay, Hamster," she said softly. "It'll make it easier this way."

"Easier?"

"Do you hear the wind, Hamster? The wind has her own song, and only her children can hear it."

"It's just a noise to me."

"Like you say, when you believe you have to do what you believe, even if it isn't what you want. Sigfod Oski says you have to give the thing you love most to the gods."

She brought a hunter's knife out from behind her back.

An old street instinct made Rory swerve as she rushed at him. Her momentum took her past him over the parapet, and she sprawled on the edge for a moment, scrabbling for a handhold with her empty hand.

Rory reached for her. She went over, but he caught her left wrist, his elbow nearly popping as it took her weight, and the parapet hit him hard in the chest, tight under his armpit.

He reached down with his free hand. "Hold on, Zippy," he said. There was a concrete foundation down below, and it looked like a long, long fall from the top.

Laura swung her knife up and stabbed the arm that held her.

"The Way of the Old Wisdom was a lie, a fraud and a scam," Solar Bull told the crowd. "I made it up out of tail ends of old anthropology books with a sprinkling of New Age. But it wasn't bad as phony religions go. It wasn't the truth of our Lord Jesus Christ, which our good brother here has shared with me since, but it was a good, decent human religion with a lot of the golden rule and live-and-let live.

"But that's not what Sigfod Oski is teaching there now. I've told you what he did the other night, and I've told you what he told me in private.

"He has power, but it's power straight out of Hell. When I left the farm last night, I was pursued by things I never dreamed of in my worst nightmares. I have cuts and scrapes all over my body. I was more scared than I thought a man could be and live through it, until, by God's mercy, I ran into my good brother here, who showed me the truth. Thank God there's mercy for even a sinner like me."

Voices said "Amen."

"But out at that farm, Satan's in control. Evil from the deepest pits of Hell has burst forth in Troll Valley. For your own sakes—for your children's sakes—for the sake of everything good—you've got to do something about it. And you've got to do it soon."

Solar Bull left the podium and sat down in a folding chair. The crowd buzzed. The brown-haired man took center stage again.

He spoke in solemn, measured tones. "There are times," he said, "when a hard lot falls on God's people. Our call, our commission from the Lord, is to live in peace. We are called to bear all kinds of abuse and violence; to submit; to love our enemies and pray for them.

"But what about a threat to our children? What about a threat to our neighbors, to our country? Can we sit by—do we dare to sit by—and let foul wickedness destroy everything? Will we allow blood sacrifice, and pagan immorality, and worship of devils to exist side by side with our churches, our homes, our schools? Does freedom of religion extend to that? Will we allow America to be dragged back to a dark age of savagery when people live in fear of devils, and place whatever they love, including their children, on the altar to appease them?

"NO! I tell you no!"

The audience chorused *"NO!"*

"NO! Today Christians in America are being stripped of our freedom of religion! Should we extend it to devil worshipers? Tolerance is not for those who would destroy the soul! There is a time when the Christian must take up the sword, and that time is now!"

Somebody in the audience was standing up, shouting, "Amen, amen!" Others began to stand too, saying one thing and another, not listening to each other but mostly agreeing. Stoney Berge moved around toward the back of the crowd.

That was when Harry Gunderson, whose entrance no one seemed to have noticed, swung up the three steps to the stage. Out of habit, the audience quieted as he limped to the podium. The brown-haired man moved aside for him, arms crossed, one eyebrow cocked.

"As our guest has said," Harry began, "there are

times in history when the Church comes under special Satanic attack.

"Think of it as a battle, friends. The Church on one side, the forces of Hell on the other. Satan has determined to attack, to carry part of the line, capture territory. Tell me, what does he do first?"

"He brings in witches!" someone yelled.

"That's right, he brings in witches! And why? Because witches are so easy to spot! Because our sentries can see them far off, and smell their fires and hear their loud music! Now think, my friends—what does it mean when your enemy parades his loudest, most colorful, garish battalion before your eyes? Why would he do that? Why would he want to *attract* your attention?"

There was mumbling, but no one answered aloud.

"I'll tell you why! It's a diversion! He wants you looking at those terrible witches, and talking about those terrible witches, and torturing and burning those terrible witches, so he can attack you *somewhere else!* Some really important part of the line, like Charity, or Justice. And you won't be prepared for that attack, and he'll hit you with disguised, camouflaged troops—much more dangerous, much harder to spot, and far stronger.

"Don't be fooled by a diversion! If these people mutilate animals, get evidence—let the law do its job. As for human sacrifice, there are laws against that too, and do you really think people would be foolish enough to try it? Would you be in their place?"

From the side of the stage, the brown-haired man said, "And when one of our children is kidnapped, will you comfort the family, Reverend?"

The crowd applauded. Cries of "Amen!" and "That's telling him!" rose.

"You think you're fighting human sacrifice?" Harry roared. "If you go out there with weapons, you're

serving the devil of human sacrifice! You become
heathens yourselves, killing because you're afraid of
the dark!"

Shouts drowned him out.

Martell stood with his arms folded over his stomach. He wanted to be sick. He had always run from
situations like this, and the air was full of lies. Yet
Harry Gunderson was his friend . . . he had a responsibility. . . .

He straightened and went up the stairs as up a
scaffold. Harry still stood at the podium, trying to be
heard. Martell put his hand on his shoulder. Harry
glanced at him, then stepped aside.

Martell stood and looked at the yelling faces. Sometimes, when he faced a rowdy class, his silent stare
had quieted the students. Surprisingly, it worked now.
As he looked at the audience he noticed Stoney talking in low tones with a middle-aged woman he didn't
know.

When the people were hushed he said, "I teach
at Christiania. Before that I taught at the University.
I sometimes used to debate people, and I used to
defend Christianity, or at least Christian civilization.
Until one day a very capable cynic cut me into little
pieces in public.

"His main point went like this: If Christianity
teaches love, and makes people nobler and better,
then why have so many Christians burned and tortured heretics, and Jews, and witches? Why did the
Church do so little to prevent what happened in
Hitler's Germany? One picture of a child at Ausch-
witz, one description of the torture of a witch in
Medieval France, weighs more in the mind than a
thousand acts of charity.

"Friends, I beg you, don't bring another shame on
the name of Christ! Don't give the scoffers more
ammunition! The people of Salem, Massachusetts,

repented of the witch trials when it was all over, but it was too late for the ones they hanged, and it was too late to save their good names. They'll always be remembered for one thing."

Someone stood up and yelled, "Who are you to tell us about Christianity? You're one of those college teachers! You don't even believe in Jesus!"

"YES, I DO!" Martell found himself shouting back. No one was more surprised at the thing than he. He glanced to the side and saw Harry staring at him.

"Yes, I do," he repeated. "I believe that Jesus Christ is the Son of God. I think I have for some time."

He was so shocked at the discovery that he forgot the people shouting at him for a moment.

The brown-haired man spoke from where he stood. "This is very touching," he said. "I know we all praise the Lord for you. But I think you and the pastor are missing the point. The killing has started already. Or it will soon. A child is missing."

"*LIE!*" shouted Martell before he had time to think.

Shouting, the audience seemed to flow up at him. Hands clutched his ankles.

"WHAT I WANT TO KNOW IS, IS THIS THE BEGINNING OF THE GREAT TRIBULATION?"

The voice was Stoney's, from one side of the crowd. He had plugged a microphone into the speaker system. The crowd seemed to stop for a beat.

"I don't know," said the brown-haired man, taken aback by the loud voice.

"Well, what do you think?" asked Stoney.

"It may be—it's hard to say—"

"It can't be the Great Tribulation," cried Maxine Ohlrogge, from the other side of the room. "The Great Tribulation doesn't start until after the Rapture!"

"No!" yelled somebody else. "The Rapture comes

first! When you look at the Book of Revelation from a Dispensational perspective—"

"No, no, no!" shouted a woman. "The Rapture comes mid-Trib!"

Then the fighting began. Martell couldn't see who threw the first punch, but he moved back from the podium, and felt Stoney's hand on his arm. The custodian pulled him, and Harry, out a side door and up the stairs to the utility room, where Maxie joined them a few moments later.

"Did I do well?" she asked.

"Like gangbusters," said Stoney.

"That was rather a cynical trick," said Harry, adjusting his coat without effect.

"I figured the way everybody's been goin' nuts lately, it wouldn't be hard to turn the herd."

"But why? I would have thought what that man said was right up your alley."

"Not when it gets popular," said Stoney, without a trace of irony in his voice.

"It's getting loud in there," said Martell. "What if they start hurting each other?"

"Got it covered," said Stoney. He opened a control panel and flipped a switch.

"What did that do?" Harry asked.

"Turned on the sprinklers in the basement."

"What?"

"It'll cool 'em off. Then they'll go home to get dry. Once they've been out in the wind, all wet, most of 'em won't be itchin' to go out again tonight."

"Do you realize what the Women's Group will say when they see their basement water-damaged and the piano ruined?" asked Harry.

"They'll say thank God the sprinkler system kept the fire from spreadin', an' I won't tell 'em different, because in a way that's what happened."

"Don't expect me to support you in that."

"Doesn't matter. This is my work. You've got your own work to do. Better get to it before they start comin' up."

Harry turned to Martell. "He's right," he said. "We've got to go out to the W.O.W. farm and warn those kids. Some of these people won't be stopped by a shower. We'll take my car. Be careful, Stoney."

They went up to the foyer and outside. Martell looked up at the sky. Cerafsky shone at the edge of a mass of clouds surging out of the northwest. He needed no word from it now. "Sigfod Oski will be there," he said. Nothing remained but a Noble Death.

"Come on," said Harry.

Deputy Stokke entered the Sheriff's office sweating a bit. He wasn't called over to Faribault very often, and he prayed he wasn't going to be told the department would be cutting back. He needed the overtime.

Sheriff Heikenen was a stocky, square-faced woman with short gray hair and a smoker's voice. She asked him to sit down, which he did, balancing his Smokey Bear hat on his knee.

The sheriff wasn't much for small talk. "McAfee tells me you've got problems with the Dangerous Sectarians List."

Stokke's mouth went dry. He'd never been good with words, and he didn't want to have to figure out how to explain his feelings on this subject.

"Well, do you have a problem?"

"I—I guess it seems a little . . . un-American to me."

The sheriff leaned back in her padded chair. "How do you mean?" She lit a Camel.

"I don't know—it seems like the sort of thing we'd be getting in trouble for if we did it with any other groups."

"You think you know the law better than the Supreme Court?"

"No."

"You a religionist yourself?"

"No, but I was raised in the church . . ."

"What church?"

"Nidaros Lutheran in Epsom."

"They're NAPC, aren't they? North American Protestant?"

"Yeah."

"Well, no problem then. The NAPC supports the DRA all the way. They're a legal registered religious group."

"Yeah, but we're supposed to write up people who hold Bible studies in their homes. My grandmother used to have Bible studies in her home. It would be like—like writing up my grandmother."

"Would you have a problem with that?"

"With what?"

"Writing a report on your grandmother."

Minna Gunderson awoke, instantaneously alert. Some noise must have roused her, but these wakings happened more and more as she grew older, and she knew it was useless to try to sleep again. She set her cushion on the floor and knelt on it, using the time productively.

It may have been a half hour later—she had lost track of time—when she heard a pounding on the door downstairs. She pulled on a robe and went to answer it.

She found Maxine Ohlrogge weeping on the doorstep. "They hit him!" Maxie sobbed. "They hit him and kicked him while he lay on the ground!"

"Calm down, Maxie! What are you talking about? Come in."

"Those people at the church! Well, not all of them—

most of the ones I know just wanted to go home and take a hot bath I think, and I'm sure they would have, but then the others came, and I don't know who they were, and I think it's just a shame—"

"Maxie, what happened?"

Maxie took a deep breath. "They were holding a secret meeting at the church, but the pastor stopped it, or rather Stoney turned on the sprinklers, but then these men came—I don't know who they were—but they had cars and vans, and they just started organizing everyone and pushing them into the cars, and when Stoney tried to stop them they started beating him up. I left him lying on the grass. He told me you had to call and warn them!"

"Whom should I call, Maxie?"

"The old Tysness place—what do they call it— W.O.W., of course! The pastor and that professor are on their way out there, but these people from the meeting are heading out there now to attack those young people! Stoney says you've got to call and warn them that there's no more time! And I've got to get back and drive Stoney to the hospital—his head's bleeding."

"All right," said Minna, understanding enough. "I'll call. You see to Stoney."

Mrs. Ohlrogge hurried out and Minna went to the phone.

She dialed directory assistance and asked for an Epsom number, the Way of the Old Wisdom.

"There is no listing for the name you requested," said the recorded voice.

Chapter XV

Martell and Harry found the farmhouse empty but unlocked. "Tonight's lesson, unlawful entry," said Harry, and he pushed the surprisingly heavy storm door open and led the way inside.

They entered a squarish "mud porch" built into an angle in the house's structure. One set of steps led up to the kitchen, another down to the basement. They went up into the kitchen, through a heavy steel door.

The place reeked of incense and mold.

Apparently the Way of the Old Wisdom hadn't yet worked out the logistics of communal housekeeping. The place was chaos. Crusty dishes sat in the sink and on the counters. Pots and pans nested inside one another, all unwashed, on the range. In one corner an ancient Frigidaire vibrated. Someone had set a stainless steel thermos bottle on top of it, and the cylinder had walked itself close to the edge. Harry limped over and took it down, setting it on the floor to one side. "That's a good bottle," he said. "Hate to see it cracked."

Martell made the circle of sun porch, living room, dining room and back to the kitchen. "Look at this place," he said. "It's like a fortress. The doors are steel. They've put up steel shutters on the inside of all the windows. And these little framed mottos on the walls—they cover loopholes for shooting from. They must be expecting a siege."

"Very prescient of them," said Harry, limping into the living room. He switched on an expensive stereo system and pushed the PLAY button on the cassette deck. A rhythmical chanting hummed from the speakers, not professional quality.

"They must have taped their ritual music," he said, and hit the OFF button.

"I don't suppose we could just stay here and wait for them," said Martell.

"No, I think we'll have to go out and look for them. Down in Troll Valley, I suppose—that's where the fellow said they held their ceremonies. I hope I can make it. My leg's hurting me a bit."

There was a knock at the door, and they looked at each other. Martell went to answer it. Harry followed as far as the kitchen and sank into a chair.

Minna Gunderson was there, shivering in an overcoat over her bathrobe and nightgown, slippers on her feet. Her face shone.

"What are you doing here?" Martell asked, but she pushed past him.

"Harry!" she cried, rushing up into the kitchen. "The most wonderful thing has happened! But first—wait—first I have to give you my message. The message first. The people from the meeting are coming. They're coming sooner than you thought, and there's more of them than you thought."

"Are Stoney and Maxie all right?" asked Harry.

"Maxie's fine. Stoney took a crack on the head or something, and Maxie's taken him to the hospital. I tried to call here, but do you know they haven't got a telephone?"

Harry asked, "How did you get here? I took the car."

She beamed. "I flew, Harry! Believe it or not, I flew!"

"Flew?"

"Just like the prophet Ezekiel! One moment I was in my room, the next I was—in the air! I went to a place—it was full of light, Harry, and there was music, and there were two old men. They were doing—I know this sounds crazy—but they were on a stage, doing a—what's it called?—a vaudeville routine. They wore striped coats and straw boater hats, and they were dancing a soft-shoe and juggling. They looked familiar to me, but I couldn't place them at first. Then I recognized them from the pictures in church. They were Oskar Frette and Haldor Bendikson, the men who founded Christiania!"

"Dancing? Frette and Bendikson?"

"That was my reaction. They started talking to me, and they said that this was their discipline—they wanted to be very clear that it was different from Purgatory, they don't believe in Purgatory at all, but the Lord had told them that it would be good for them to learn something frivolous. They said the hardest thing about Heaven for them was how much fun it was. They'd never learned to have fun on earth, and that left them unprepared for eternity."

"Minna—"

"I know—I know it's forbidden to contact the dead. But there's one time when we all have to contact the dead."

"You mean—"

"Yes, I'm dying, Harry. It's all right. I'm not upset about it. But I have to tell you what Frette and Bendikson said.

"They were sort of cute—Bendikson did the talking, like everyone says he did when they were alive. But Frette kept interrupting him and correcting him. So the whole thing took about twice the time it should have, though by my watch the whole thing didn't take more than a couple of minutes, and all the time they were going through their routine. They were very good, too.

"They said they were—well, in essence they were closing down the franchise. Or rather God is. Christiania College and Nidaros Church have moved so far from the things they were built for that the anointing is being taken away.

"There's going to be a kind of shaking out. Some people are being removed from the situation, partly as judgment and partly to spare them what's coming, you and me among them—"

"Me?"

"Does that really bother you?"

"No, I guess not, but—"

"Harry, I can't begin to tell you how wonderful it is! It's what I've been waiting for all my life. I don't mind anything now—not losing Wesley, not the lonely years, not the children I missed. It's all right. It's—it's very well. Harry, I rose up on wings as of eagles!"

Harry hugged her. She felt as alive as ever.

She pulled away, wiped her face with her sleeve and said, "I have a message for you too, Carl Martell. From Frette and Bendikson. They said you have to go down into Troll Valley, and quickly. Don't worry about finding the way. There's a thing that needs to be done, and only you can do it. And you have to do it alone. Harry won't be able to keep up."

Martell looked at them. He didn't doubt her story. "Oski's there," he said. "Do you know who Oski is?"

"I think he's Odin," Harry said.

"Am I a man to defy the gods?"

"There's only one God, Carl, and you've made your choice about Him. You'll have to see the thing through."

Martell nodded, looked away. "The logic of the story," he said. "A Noble Death."

"Perhaps. But I've found that God is rarely so predictable. He's a better artist than that."

Minna said, "You know, Carl Martell, there's a sin called Despair."

Martell said, "I know. I've always expected, somehow, that the truth of things would be unbearable."

"It isn't for those who bear it," said Minna.

Martell turned to the door. "We'll see. Will you two be all right? I guess that's a pointless question. Is this goodbye?"

"For now," said Minna.

"You've been good friends," said Carl. "I'll miss you."

They broke through their Norwegian reserve, smiled and hugged one another in turn.

"I don't like to think of leaving you to that mob," said Carl.

"We'll close these shutters up," said Harry. "Maybe we can persuade them the young people are in here, and give you time while we negotiate."

"And if you can't negotiate?"

"I'm a preacher. I'll bore them to death."

Martell smiled.

Harry reached out and put a hand on Martell's shoulder. "Carl," he asked, "do you sincerely repent of your sins?"

Martell looked in his eyes. He nodded. "Yes, I do. With all my heart."

"The Almighty and merciful God grant unto you, being penitent, pardon and remission of all your sins, time for amendment of life, and the grace and comfort of His Holy Spirit."

Martell took a deep breath. "Thanks," he said. "God bless you. You know, I don't think I've ever said that before." He went out.

Minna sat across the table from Harry. "We have a lot to talk about," she said, "and not much time."

Martell went out of the house and stood, shuddering, in the wind. He wished he'd worn a hat. The promised snow blew about him, damping all sound but the whistling in his ears. It was dark as only country dark can be, like velvet, the only light a faint glow through the clouds and the distant flares of farmers' blue yard lights.

"We who are about to die salute you," he whispered, and made the sign of the cross, another novelty. Only a Christian a short time, he hadn't decided whether he was high or low church. A bird swooped down, flapping near enough to startle him, and buffeted off.

There seemed to be a sort of gleam under the willow trees to the northwest, beyond the old chicken coop, on the way to Troll Valley. It would do for a beacon.

He walked to it and became aware, as he approached, of the figure of a man, outlined in swirling snow and lit from within. The flakes moved continually, but the man-shape was constant, like a glass statue full of fireflies. Only this statue moved.

A moment later Martell found himself on his face in the snow. He'd read Biblical accounts where people who saw angels collapsed in fear. He'd never understood why until now. It was as if he'd had the chance to view history as it happened, and to compare it to

his own articles, discovering for the first time all the
ways he'd been wrong. The very existence of this
being made the ground beneath his feet unstable. Its
height denounced his values. The set of its shoulders
was a reproach to his character. If this was an angel,
a messenger of God, then almost nothing he had ever
valued or counted on was of any moment. He'd paid
out the budgeted coin of his life for gimcrackeries.
No wonder prophets had responded to theophanies
by abasing their bodies and wailing over their sins.

"Get up," said the angel. "I am only your fellow
creature. Let's not waste time."

Martell rose by way of his knees. "What should I
do?" he asked.

"Follow me. You must get your sword."

"My sword?"

"Follow." The angel turned to walk westward, and
Martell came after. He left footprints; the angel did
not. "There was a sword forged to slay Odin," the
angel said. "Three men, of whom you have heard,
carried it. They did not understand its use, or understood too little. But the last of them passed it on."

"To whom?"

"To you."

"To me? I don't have a sword."

"A comet runs above us," said the angel. "A comet
is one of the many things men know less of than they
think. The ring of the comet's journey is a kind of
loop in time, and if we are in the appointed place
in a few minutes, we will cross the past. No hurry."

"Can I ask why me?"

"Why does a tree bear fruit? You talk so much of
freedom—can't you see that the only freedom worth
the name is the freedom to do what one is made
for?

"The sword is yours because you *are* a sword. From
childhood you have been forged hot and hammered

hard. Once you were broken. Lately you have been made true."

"I see—I cannot tell a lie."

"The sword that slays Odin must be the truest in the world. As legends say, it was broken and must be reforged. When the pieces come together, there will be a true sword. Truer even than its maker intended."

They made their way westward through the willow grove, walking parallel to the fence that fronted Troll Valley, and passed through an open field gate. Martell tripped in a gopher hole, falling face forward in the snowy grass. He felt the stitches open in his right hand. The bandage was wet and bloody. He pulled it off and threw it away. The angel turned back to him and said, "Come now."

"Is everybody a sword?" Martell asked, feeling fire in his hand.

"What a dull creation that would be."

"What's Harry Gunderson?"

"What is that to you? Follow me."

They went on a few more yards through the grass.

"Stop now," said the angel. "This is the place."

They stood about twenty feet from the fence row, old wooden posts with glass insulators strung with smooth electric wire, barbed wire tacked on below. The snow fell on wide fields all around, glowing in waves as the moonlight came and went. The roiling sky seemed suddenly to loom large in Martell's sight, the angel anchored at its base.

"It is time," the angel said.

The snowflakes that defined him stopped suddenly. Looking around, Martell saw that all the snowflakes had stopped, as if caught in a photograph. He put out a finger and touched one. It went where he pushed it and stayed there.

Then there were voices and shouting, and he turned to the fence, but there was no fence. Instead he saw a mass of men, facing each other in uneven rows. The men struck at one another with swords and axes and spears. They wore tunics and hose, and hooded cloaks of a thick, shaggy gray material Martell recognized as Iceland *wadmal*.

He shouldered his way through the snowflakes to the fighters. When he was nearer, the snowflakes disappeared, and he knew there had been no snow that night in 1362.

This night.

His line of sight was along one end of the battle line. To his left, at the rear of the better dressed force, one man in monk's garb carved fiercely at a gray stone with a hammer and chisel.

The man closest to Martell in that line feinted with his sword, dodged a blow and cut down his man. Another enemy, a tall man in ragged leather with a long gray beard, rushed in to attack him, wielding a long spear.

The defender lifted his sword, then seemed to pause. He looked around him, ignoring the graybeard.

His eyes fell on Martell. They were blue eyes, and Martell felt a stab of pity for a man dying, six hundred years gone.

Pale-faced, the man threw his sword to Martell. Martell caught it one-handed.

Screaming, the gray-beard struck the unarmed man down. He roared and turned to face Martell, spear poised.

He had one eye.

Instead of casting at Martell, the gray-beard raised his face to heaven and bellowed. The earth shook and the stars dimmed.

The gray-beard swung his spear back over his shoulder and threw it skyward. Following its flight with his eyes, Martell saw, fierce and clear among the stars, Cerafsky's Comet.

Then there was snow on his face, and the battle was gone, but he had the sword.

He looked on the weapon and loved it. It was a perfect Viking blade, shining pale in the moonlight. Runes were carved along its center groove, and the silver-chased grip with its short, curved guard and cocked-hat pommel fit his hand perfectly.

Too perfectly.

He turned to the angel. "I can't let go!" he said. "It's as if—as if it's burned to my hand!"

"It is welded, at the place where it met your blood. It is the nature of metal to wed its like."

"I heard that once." Martell took a deep breath. "That's it then. I can't live this way. I must die tonight."

"Feel the sword, Carl Martell! If you must die, can you be sorry, regaining the limb you've always missed?"

Martell looked at the blade again, and seemed to feel his blood pulsing down its bright length.

"It's alive," he said. "It's a part of me."

"Follow me," said the angel.

He led Martell back the way they had come, to a place where there was a gate in the fence, and a path leading down into Troll Valley.

The angel said, "Now is the time for you to do the work you were forged to do. I am permitted to tell you this—there is only one proper use for a sword. The others missed it."

"A riddle," said Martell. "That's all that was missing. Will you come along?"

"There is no need. The sword will find the gelding."

"It's dark down there. I'm frightened."

The angel's face hadn't the definition to show emotion, but Martell felt his pity—a heavy, exquisite thing like a jewel flower. "It must be very hard," the angel said, "to will a thing without wanting it."

"Almost beyond bearing."

"Your life is not what you think. You suffer such

loneliness, yet it is always an illusion. You mistake your shame, and you mistake your glory. You make such tales, you men!" The snow went random.

Martell started down the path, under the trees, his heart pounding. He had no trouble finding his way. The sword tugged at his arm like a dog on a leash. The snow fell more gently among the trees, the flakes descending like the wreck of a pillow.

He grew aware of a glowing that brightened through the trees and brush as he descended. Moving closer, he saw a crowd of young people in a ring around a stone altar, in a wide place along the river bank. The wind whipped at the fire on the altar and strewed sparks about an ash tree that overhung it, and about Sigfod Oski, clad in a brown robe and holding a spear, and about Elaine, also robed. A rope was around her neck, hanging slack, looped over a branch of the ash. Her arms were bound behind her.

"Carl Martell!" Oski shouted. "From time's morning it was carven that you would come to this place on this night with that sword—is it not a joy to find one's destiny?"

Pastor Gunderson sat alone in the Tysness house, on a sofa in the living room. He had worked his slow way around, closing the heavy shutters and bolting them. Minna had gone as she had come. He had switched on a light, and felt strangely cozy.

Now he was watching old Jack Tysness pottering about the place, heavy-handed and sour-faced. He knew Jack was dead. He did not believe in ghosts, but he let the apparition be. The bands of time seemed loosely fastened tonight.

For a moment he saw his Joanna. She stood facing him, wearing a dress he remembered, and she smiled. He smiled back.

Someone knocked at the porch door. He sighed

and got up. He switched on the stereo, and sounds of chanting filled the house.

He stumped across the kitchen linoleum, saying, "I'm coming, I'm coming." He closed the kitchen door and went down the steps. He opened the storm door and saw Solar Bull's face through the screen. Out in the yard were cars with men in them. He opened the screen door.

"They're here?" Solar Bull asked. "They haven't left for the ceremony yet?"

"That's their singing."

"You a hostage?"

"No. I'm their protector."

"You're standing with the Devil's children against God?"

"The Devil has no children. All children are God's. If they reject Him, I'm sorry. But I won't reject them."

"We can come in there and bring you out, Reverend."

"Perhaps. But you've lived here. You know the security built into this house. Do you think you'd get out of this porch alive?"

Solar Bull looked uneasily up at the loopholes.

"I'd rather have you with us than against us, Reverend," he said. "You serve the Church. All right, so do we. Some of us here belong to an order more than a thousand years old. They aren't mentioned in any history book, but whenever there was danger, whenever quick money was needed, whenever somebody had to be got out of the way, these guys have been there. They do the ugly work so you preachers can keep your hands clean. If there are still prophets, this is where you'll find them. Today, their task is to burn this house. *Thus saith the Lord! Choose ye this day,*' Pastor!"

Harry boomed, "All right! Let's see who's a prophet!

You think you can glorify God by burning this house
and killing these children?"

"If we have to. Unless the witches come out and
surrender to the justice of God."

"Then listen to me—I will stay in this house, and
if you want to burn it, you'll have to burn me too.
That's *my* word from the Lord, and I'll put my body
through the flame to confirm it. Will you do the
same?"

Solar Bull stared. "You're crazy!"

"Are you afraid?"

Solar Bull grabbed Harry's left arm and pulled.

Harry took hold of Solar Bull's wrist with his right
hand and easily pulled it loose. He squeezed the wrist,
his face showing no strain. Solar Bull's face went
white, and he gasped three times.

Harry let him go, and Solar Bull lurched away,
letting the screen door slam behind him. He ran
hunched over, one hand cradling the other.

"Our strength," Harry whispered, "always surprises
them." He saw Solar Bull rush to one of the waiting cars. There were four of them, and three or four
men and women got out of each. They opened the
trunks and brought out red gasoline containers.

Solar Bull shouted, "You think we won't do it,
Preacher, but we will!"

Harry closed the storm door and bolted it.

He labored up to the kitchen and picked up the
thermos bottle he'd moved earlier. He unscrewed the
cap and found it clean and dry inside. He carried it
to the table, sat down, and went through his pockets for a piece of paper. He found an old grocery list
and unfolded it, turning the blank side up.

To be sure of himself, he unstrapped his artificial
leg and tossed it across the room. Then he uncapped
a fountain pen and began to write.

❖   ❖   ❖

"Is it not a joy to find one's destiny?" Sigfod Oski cried.

Something like a pile of rags moved near Oski's feet. It rose to become a woman who struggled up, and Martell recognized Pastor Hardanger-Hansen. She was scratched and bruised and bleeding, and she ran hunched over, clutching her torn robe. She stumbled forward and crouched a few feet below Martell, shivering and sobbing. "Help me—help me—"

Then she convulsed to her feet and ran around him, away up the path and into the darkness.

"What did you do to her?" Martell cried.

"I raped her, of course. Then I gave her to the congregation. She was keen to learn the history of religion, and I thought the lesson should be a comprehensive one."

"You egregious bastard," said Martell. "How dare you be Odin? How dare you make Odin contemptible?"

"It appears you need a history lesson yourself, Martell. You at least should know better, but then Hell hath no fury like a Romantic disillusioned."

"Let Elaine go."

"I intend to. But for now we'll keep her as she is, as an incentive to you."

Martell felt the presence of a lie, more palpable than any he had ever felt before, though he could not isolate it. And in his belly he felt the fear he had lived with so many years. But the fear had changed, as if a cog that had been rattling loose in a machine had suddenly fallen into place and begun to do its proper work.

"Do you feel your fear?" cried Oski, reading his thoughts. "Do you know its name? Its name is Anger! All these years the thing you've feared most has been your own power! Set it free, Martell—you shall be as the gods!"

"What do you want from me?"

"Do you know how gods are made, Martell? You've read the *Hávamál*—

> '*I know that I swung on the wind-swept tree*
> *Nine long nights together,*
> *Spear-wounded, a sacrifice to Odin,*
> *My self to self devoted.*'

"It's true!

"I was a chieftain then, patriarch of a tribe of nomads in the Caucasus. We practiced the old custom of kingship—when the king's ring of years had closed, he was sacrificed for the health of the land. I remember little of that life now, but I can't forget the fear as they stabbed me with the spear and hoisted me, bleeding. But dying I found the magic, and I struck the bargain by which gods are made.

"I reigned as a god many hundred years. I drank deep of the blood of sacrifice, I established law, I gave men the mystery of the runes, and other secrets. Until at last the White Christ pushed me back into my northern fastnesses. Then my last kings began to turn on me. Haakon the Good. Harald Bluetooth. Olaf Trygvesson. How I mourned my Olaf!

"My power failed as the sacrifices ebbed. I knew a way to renew it though. The power is in the blood, Martell, and the greatest sacrifices yield the greatest power!"

"Human sacrifices?" asked Martell.

"Divine sacrifices! Do you think me some petty imp, Martell? Do you think I'd accept the deaths of slaves and prisoners, and not my own death?

"I came to Olaf Trygvesson in my Wanderer's guise, thus—" A sort of veil fell over Martell's sight. A light shone for an instant on a bearded old man in hat and cloak, with a heavy staff. Then darkness again, and the fire, and Oski.

"I told him—which was true—that I could forge a weapon to slay Odin. I did not tell him that in taking a human body and dying in it, I would be reborn to godhead. I had found a man to possess, nor was he unwilling. A man will die for power.

"Olaf gave me a smithy to work in. I thought a sword the proper weapon, for Olaf favored them. I forged it—you hold it now. If you knew the words I spoke over it and the bath in which I tempered it, it would crack your mind.

"I gave Olaf the sword, and made my plans to meet him in battle, but the fool made his mad trip to Wendland and let the Danes trap him, and drowned himself. So I hid the sword and waited for another man of the same forging, for not every man can wield that weapon.

"Then came the second Olaf. It was a task to get near him because of his priests, and I had much business with my own worshipers, but at last I reached him and offered the sword, and he took it eagerly enough. But the farmers drove him to Russia, and there he prayed, and was warned against it. He gave it to one of his men and bade him throw it in a lake, and went off to die at Stiklestad. The man, being no fool, hid the sword instead, but he too was killed, and not even I knew its hiding place.

"By then my power was bled so thin I could do little but cling to the body I wore, and trade it for another when it wore out. I wandered and waited with the years, and made a new plan. I turned my thoughts to the western land the Greenlanders had found. I thought that if I could set people of my own in Vinland, and endure the rite of rebirth among them, I could thrive among the many gods and return to my own lands when I was stronger.

"But first I needs must find my sword. I searched long and long, hundreds of years, and found it at last in Russia, as I knew I must, its beauty undimmed.

"When I walk as a man, I can still travel as a god,

if I let my host fall into a trance and do not leave
him too long. I flitted to Greenland, where many of
the desperate survivors of the Western Settlement
greeted me gladly. There was battle, and my people
killed the Christian men, packed the women and stock
into boats, and we sailed for Vinland. I took them
by way of Hudson's Bay, and far inland, where no
chance Icelander blown astray might find them. I
lacked but one thing—a proper sword wielder.

"So I flitted back to the body I'd left in Norway,
and I went to the king. I told him a tale of apos-
tasy in Greenland, and roused his blood for a cru-
sade. I found my sword-man in Paul Knutsson, and
it was not hard to persuade the king to send him on
the holy mission.

"I have told you of the expedition. I gave the sword
to Paul Knutsson, bidding him use it mightily against
the heathen. I flitted to Vinland and possessed a one-
eyed man, and in his skin met the explorers and
guided them. I set the two parties on each other and
entered the fray myself. But Knutsson feared magic,
and distrusted the sword. When a vision came to him
in the battle he took it as a sign, and cast the sword
away, choosing death.

"In my rage I flung my spear to the heavens, and
by ill luck it struck the comet you call Cerafsky,
sticking fast in it. With it went the greater part of
my remaining power, for of course it was *Gungnir*,
the staff of my strength, forged by dwarfs. Worse,
a monk among the Christians had carved that stone
we've seen, and bound me with my own magic. I
could not even touch the stone. I had barely strength
to flit back to my own lands again, and since I have
wandered in countless bodies, little more than a base
magician. But I knew that one day the stone must
be broken, and when next the comet returned I
would be prepared to take my power again. Here

I am. And here you are. And I see now how good
it was that I was prevented so long, for of all the
sword-men I have seen, you are the truest, Carl
Martell!"

"You want me to kill you?" Martell asked.

"Why not? Am I not hateful in your eyes? What
shall I do to earn my death? Rape another woman?
This one, perhaps?" He gestured to Elaine, whose
eyes pleaded.

"You can't make me your tool, Oski."

"Can I tempt you with glory? You are a sword, and
a sword's proper work is to rule. Both the Olafs were
swords. When I come to my own, there will be a new
order in this world, a more virile age. It will need
great men. You can be their chief!"

Martell only smiled.

"Would you be a god, Martell? My brothers and
my children must be reborn too. They will need hosts.
A man who is a sword could well be Tyr, god of war.
Think of that, Martell!"

"I have a God."

"You have no power lust? What of knowledge
then? I can tell you things that would set your mind
blazing. I can tell you where to dig to find the greatest undiscovered hoard of Viking loot in the world.
I can tell you legends long forgotten—would you
know how Arthur of Britain came to Norway, and
what he did there? I can tell you that story and show
you how to prove it. Or I can give you the power
to walk in your dreams as I walk, and see and hear
and feel the past as it happened. Tell me I do not
tempt you!"

"You tempt me." Martell shivered. "What of it?"

"Not even that? Then think on this—this self-
devouring nation has made a law now to suppress the
very belief you've embraced. And mark what I say,
this is only the beginning of the persecution. In my

world you'll have an honest enemy, one who'll fight you fairly and not gas about openmindedness while outlawing every opinion but its own."

"You speak well, and you have a point, but I can't do anything to stop what my government is doing. You I can stop."

"I am sorry. I would have had you for friend and sword-brother. I would have called you son. I am a chieftain who gives great gifts."

"I know a greater."

"Then I must descend to threats. Either I will be the sacrifice, Martell, or this woman will. I think your greater God would not honor your integrity if you let her hang just to protect it."

Martell opened his mouth but found no words in it.

"You know I'll do it! Come, you wish my death and so do I—why should we be at loggerheads?"

He strode nearer the tree and took up the rope end.

"Why waste time, Martell? I've left you no choice. That is the way of gods." He pulled up the slack.

Something in Martell screamed, *"LIE!"* There was a lie here, and he needed to name it.

"The sword, Martell! Use the sword!"

Martell said, "What you want is false. I can't perform a false act. I am a sword."

Oski cried, *"There is no man so true as a sword, and no sword is wholly true!"*

"YES!" cried Martell, and he saw it at last. He raised the sword, and beheld his reflected face shining in the blade. Looking deeper, he probed the heart of the thing and—yes!—*the sword had a flaw.*

"It's true," he said. "I am flawed, and the sword is flawed. My flaw is my own fault, but the sword's flaw is yours. It cannot be wholly true because *you* are a lie!

"I may be no god, or king, or hero, but I am more than a lie.

"I am your master!

"You think you know who you are, but you have no inkling! How could great Odin be a thug and a bully? Only by being a lie. Poets know who you are, and any ten-year-old with a book of legends knows who you are, but you don't!

"There was always a high Odin and a low Odin. The high Odin inspired poetry and bold deeds, while the low Odin deceived and lied and buried his face in corpses with the ravens. As you dwindled through the centuries, you lost the glory that once reflected your Creator. There's nothing creative left in you now—all you can dream is destruction. The poems Sigfod Oski made were his own—without his genius you couldn't have made a limerick. You are a parasite. You are, in truth, a gelding. You've become merely Loki. Loki was always Odin's separable soul—a lecher and father of monsters. He walked among the gods but was never of them, for he could not raise his eyes higher than his belly. He held godhood in his hand as a child holds a weapon, dangerous in his ignorance.

"You don't know what you're for, Odin, and you don't know what I'm for, and you don't know what a sword is for! I am a sword, and I am my Master's, so I know. A sword is for breaking!"

Martell raised the sword heavenward and looked upon it, channeling his truth sense into it, bearing down, seeking the flaw with prehensile thought.

"You are a sword, Martell!" cried Oski. "Break it and you will surely die!"

"True," said Martell, and the sword exploded in a thousand gleaming shards, and Martell bowed to his death.

And it was as if he fell from a great height, and

*time was stretched, and he saw Odin standing beneath
the ash, tall and gold-helmed and night-cloaked. And
the wolf came leaping down the hillside toward him,
howling his joy.*

*And when Odin saw the wolf, a weird light kindled
in his eye, and he stood, arms stretched wide, to
receive the beast.*

*And it seemed to Martell that Odin's mouth gaped
wide, wider, impossibly wide, and straight into his
mouth the wolf leaped, with a kind of nuptial cry,
one at last with his god, whose name is Fenris, whose
name is Loki, whose name is Odin.*

*And Odin stood, tall and alone, and he screamed
as he loomed taller and taller, and he was changed,
and he became the Wolf, Fenris, who had pursued
him across the miles and the centuries, as all creatures pursue themselves.*

*With a howl, the Wolf leaped heavenward. Above
it waited the comet, and the spear, and the last circle
of all.*

Rory Buchan steered his Golf back toward the
farm, along the edge of the woods, with one hand.
The car seat was sticky with blood.

He'd found Laura crumpled at the bottom of the
silo. She had cracked her head on the foundation, and
as with all head wounds the bleeding had been frightening. He couldn't revive her, and there was no telephone, so he had gently carried her to his car and
driven her to the hospital in town. They had stitched
and bound his arm, and a doctor had told him Laura
was in serious condition, refusing to say more.

A middle-aged woman in the emergency waiting
room had been noisily telling everyone about a mob
that was going out to attack the W.O.W. farm. He
thought he'd better go there.

When he was about a mile from the place, a tall

figure moved out of the woods and waved him down. In the headlights he recognized the bearded man called Solar Bull, who would always be Rowan to him.

He pulled over.

Rowan opened the passenger door. "Brother Rory! Thank the Lord it's you!" He got in, panting. "The cops caught us torching the house. I nearly got arrested."

Rory stared into the black eyes. He was still in shock, and the combination of a face he knew under one name with a voice he knew under another fuddled him.

"You're Thumb!" he gasped.

Rowan did a double take and made a motion with his jaw as if he had something in his mouth too large for it. "Ah-yeah, that's right," he said, slowly. "You haven't seen me here before without this, have you?" He pulled a black ski mask from his jacket pocket.

"All you said—and all the time you were the High Priest of W.O.W.!"

"I was God's agent, Brother! I had to be on the inside to know what they were plotting!"

"You led them. You lied to them like you lied to me. There wasn't any Satanic plot. Just you, stirring up trouble for trouble's sake!"

"I do the Lord's work, Brother! Listen to me! It wasn't long after—after what I did to your friend—that I saw the evil of my ways and gave my life to Jesus. And believe me, nothing weighed on my heart more than the memory of that wicked deed. You may not believe it, but I didn't kill many people. I was trying to gain respect, to make a reputation. It stayed on my mind, and it hurt me bad. I learned who you were and swore to the Lord that if I ever had the chance, I'd make it up to you.

"The Hands of God recruited me because I knew the ways of the Enemy. And when they sent me here, think of my joy when I turned on the radio to a Christian station and heard your voice and your name!

"I invited you to join us. I wanted to take you under my wing, to teach you, to show you adventure and glory in the Name of the Lord! We can still do it, Brother! Help me get away! I'll find a phone, and the Hands of God will have us out of here in twenty minutes, and there'll be other days, other battles to win! We'll fight the good fight together!"

"You killed Heather," said Rory. "You killed Heather, and you messed up Laura so bad that she may die. And I don't know what happened on the farm tonight, but I suppose you killed somebody there too."

"Only one, as it turns out. But he was a son of perdition, trying to use his office as a shield for Satan."

Rory leaned his forehead against the top of the steering wheel. He felt sore and tired. "Rowan, you're the sinner against the Holy Spirit. Don't ask me to be like you. I hate it, but I've got to forgive you. I forgive you, and I'll pray for you, but you'd better get out of my car now, because I'm not gonna help you run from justice."

Eyes closed, he did not see the big fist that slammed into his temple.

Rowan dragged him out of the car, rolled him into the ditch, and drove away.

Epilogue

The Following Sunday

The Rev. Judith Hardanger-Hansen stood strong and fearless, wearing her best white vestments with green stole for the Pentecost season and leading the congregation in the Creed.

"I believe in God, the parent inscrutable, ground of all being. And in Jesus Christ, the only Offspring of our leader, who was conceived by the Sustainer Spirit, born of the unwed Mary, suffered under Imperialism . . ."

She still felt weak and sore from her ordeal in Troll Valley. Her ribs hurt when she coughed, but she had made the decision not to see a doctor. She had a purple eye and a bandage on her cheek, but she'd explained to people that she'd fallen while walking in the woods.

"*. . . was oppressed, crucified, dead and buried.
The third day he transcended human categories; he
disappeared into everlasting Mystery . . .*"

It was all best forgotten. Once again she had
trusted a man; once again she had been exploited.
It did no good to obsess about mistakes. The main
thing was to go on; to be strong. All truth was a
construct—if you believe something, then it's the truth
for you. She would believe that none of this had
happened.

"*. . . and became united forever with Deity in the
mind of the Church. His principles will one day lib-
erate Humanity. . . .*"

A thought picked at the hem of her mind. Something she had always told rape victims she'd coun-
seled . . . something about seeing a doctor . . .

No. The matter was closed. She had the right, as
an autonomous Soul, to construct her own reality, and
her reality admitted no consequences for events that
did not fit her Paradigm.

"*I believe in the Sustainer Spirit; the Holy Catholic
Church, containing but not limited to the community
of Christian believers; Karma, the transcendence of
the Universal Mind, and progressive Evolution. Amen.*"

She climbed into the pulpit and faced the congregation.

Congregation?

"*I gave her to the congregation. . . .*"

She closed her eyes and breathed deeply, concentrating on her spiritual center. The congregation would
think she was praying.

When her spirit was quiet, she turned to the
Winnowed Bible before her and scanned the page for
her text.

Where's my text? she wondered to herself. She
looked up and down the columns but could not find
the words she meant to preach on.

She said it aloud: "Where's my text?" The congregation began to fidget. People glanced at one another.

This wasn't good. Still, such things happened. The secret was to be calm, not to let on that anything was wrong. *I make my own truth. I will make this moment what I wish it to be.*

She had her sermon notes. She would go straight to them, and quote the text from memory.

What was her text?

Something about blood, said a voice from within her.

No, that wasn't right! She never preached on blood. Nobody preached on blood nowadays. We'd gotten beyond that, thank God.

"Something about blood!" said a voice, and to her amazement she recognized it as her own. What was happening to her?

"Blood!" she repeated, to her own horror. "Blood and more blood! Rivers of blood, and lakes of blood! Blood feuds, blood oaths, and menses! Blood brothers and blood will out! The blood of innocents, the blood of martyrs, the blood of the Lamb!"

Suddenly she knew, as she struggled to take her tongue back, that some other Judith, some Judith she had buried with contempt long ago, had grown over time like a seed in the silent earth and chosen this moment of trauma to rise again. Some inner Justice, some secret Solomon, had spoken the terrible words, *"Divide the living child in two."* And now a light had gone out somewhere in her mind. Some interior passageway had been bricked up. That other Judith, now unjustly strong, had taken control and was pushing her back, ever back; back into some dark, gridded cell of her mind where she could scream forever and no one in the universe would hear. . . .

"My womb," her mouth said quietly. "They took my womb away. They said they'd put it where I could have it when I wanted it again, but now they won't give it back!"

Down in the pews, a deacon edged forward in the north aisle and whispered to another deacon. They went up quietly, and one of them took Judith by the hand and led her back to the sacristy while the other assumed the pulpit.

She went without a struggle, and before the sacristy door closed her voice could be heard, pure and sweet, singing, *"There is a fountain filled with blood. . . ."*

Monday

Dear Carl,

I hope you get this letter. I trust that, packed in the thermos and protected in the refrigerator, it will survive the fire. It seems possible that my way of going will trouble you, and I'd like to set your mind at rest.

I told you once that I wanted to prove that orthodox Christians were not by nature persecutors. I think I've found a way. Like all God's arguments, it is at once simple and unthinkable.

I will set my body between the burners and the witches. I trust that with the time I buy, you will be able to carry out your task and—this time at least—the burners will fail.

I might add that, now that it is upon me, death—even death by fire—is not as terrible as I feared. This is a good way to die. I'm grateful for it.

I'm sorry to leave you at a turning point in your life, but our Lord must have plans of His own for your nurture. I trust Him.

That you will survive I am reasonably sure.
I think one killing is sufficient for this night.
    Fram!

                    In the Beloved,
                    Harry Gunderson

Martell finished reading the letter, then laid it on
the bedsheet with his left hand. He looked up at
Deputy Stokke, who sat in a chair by his hospital
bed.

"Thanks for bringing that," he said. "I'd have been
sorry to miss it."

"You want to make any changes to this statement?"
Stokke asked, referring to his notebook.

"No. I realize it's all pretty fantastic, but it's what
happened and I've kind of gotten out of the habit
of telling lies."

Stokke said, "The thing is, if I submit this the way
you dictated it, you're gonna have to go on the
Dangerous Sectarians List."

"The what?"

Stokke explained.

"That sounds like a list I belong on."

"Yeah, well, that may be true and all, but I've had
to put lots of people on the list since that night at
Troll Valley. Most of those yahoos deserved it, and
some of 'em are going to jail, but I don't like it."

"I wish I could let you off the hook."

"I'll let myself off the hook. I'm gonna do some
rewriting on this thing. You went down into the valley
to stop Oski, and you had an argument with him, and
a riot broke out, and somebody set off some kind of
explosion, and Oski died. That's not a lie. I'll just leave
out the part about the god and the wolf and the
sword."

"Can't you get into trouble that way?"

"Sure can. Someday I'll lose my job, I suppose. Someday you'll get on the DSL, and they'll do to you whatever they're gonna do to the ones who won't conform. But it's not gonna be today. I'm not gonna do it to you today."

"Thank you. God bless you."

"Your pastor friend was a brave man."

"He was a true hero. Oski never guessed it."

"They found his sister dead in her bed that same night."

"I figured."

"And we haven't caught that Solar Bull guy. The car he stole was abandoned in South Dakota, but there's no sign of him. The kid he stole it from's just down the hall here."

"I know. He's all right—he'll be released today too. But I guess he won't go anywhere—he just stays at the girl's side in intensive care."

"The church people took the lady pastor away and put her in some kind of care program. And the church janitor'll be okay. Anything you need here?"

"No, I'm fine, I think. Somebody's coming to give me a ride home."

"You know you made the national news? The president mentioned Troll Valley in his radio address yesterday. He said the tragedy of Sigfod Oski's death just shows how much we need the DRA." Deputy Stokke got up, said goodbye, and went out.

As he left Elaine walked in, casual in the manner of a runway model. Martell watched her, amazed at his own dispassion. *She's a beautiful woman,* he thought. *But just a beautiful woman. The pain is gone, and with it the love. Incredible.*

"How's the arm?"

Martell glanced at his right arm, bandaged at the wrist where the hand used to be. He didn't feel like an amputee. "Phantom limb," the doctors called it—

the mind's insistence that the lost member is still in place.

"Not too bad," he said. "I guess I won't play the violin again."

"The days you were in that coma I felt so responsible." Martell looked up at the word, to see her staring at the floor. "I still do. I got you into all this."

"No. It was Oski's plan. Like you said, he saw everything and planned everything beforehand. And I'm not sorry. I'm well, Elaine, for the first time in years. Small price to pay."

"I can't help feeling guilty—leaving after all I promised you."

"You can't stay with me just out of gratitude."

She avoided his eyes. "I never said I loved you, Carl. I have so much to think about. I've got to make some sense out of all this. I've got to get away. Maybe I'll make my peace with Jehovah like you. Then, if you still want me . . ."

Martell had no idea whether she was lying or not. "What'll you do, Carl?"

"With Oski gone I find I'm not very popular here," he said. "Especially since I'm linked to his mysterious death. And of course my new faith is grounds for dismissal. They're letting me resign. I wouldn't stay anyway. I'll try to find some kind of work. I had thought about seeing if there was an opening back at the University—face my fear—but that's out of the question. So I'll face the fear of unemployment and homelessness instead. It'll be a kind of vacation after Christiania. What'll you do?"

"Oski left a will. He was generous."

"Viking chieftains always were."

"Maybe I'll go back to school. Finish my degree."

"Good for you."

She stood up. "Can I kiss you goodbye?"

"I don't see why not." She bent and kissed him lightly on the lips. It was just a kiss.

"I'm a very screwed-up woman, Carl. You can do better," she said.

"Goodbye, Elaine. I hope you find everything you're looking for."

She smiled. "Nobody lives that long." As she turned away her face caught the light from the window. For the first time, Martell noticed that there were crow's feet at her eye corners, lines on her throat. Then she was gone. He watched the slow door close behind her.

As she went out, Harry and Minna Gunderson came in. Martell was just thinking how nice it was of them to stop in when he remembered, with a shiver that ran down his entire body, the fundamental law of the world. They were a merry pair of cosmic felons though, dressed in white and walking lightly. It was the first time Martell had ever seen Harry move without pain.

"How are you, Carl?" they asked.

Martell could not speak.

"We're not restless spirits, Carl. We're just two old friends, stopping to say goodbye before we go Home."

Martell managed to whisper, "Why are you here?"

Harry sat down on the unoccupied bed. His body looked solid, but the sheets didn't crease. "First of all, to say well done. You will be mentioned in dispatches. Secondly, to give you guidance."

"Guidance?"

"You're wondering what you'll do with your life, aren't you?" asked Minna, standing by the foot of Martell's bed.

"Yes."

"Well, don't."

Harry laughed. "What Minna's trying to say is that you'll have plenty to do. Don't think that the DRA is the end of the story for the Church in America. This is just where things start to get interesting. I'm rather sorry I won't be around for the fireworks."

"What's going to happen?"

Harry laughed again. "You don't think I'd tell you, do you, even if I knew? How do you think I'd have felt if I'd known beforehand that I'd die by fire? I'd have gone crazy with fear and depression. God shielded me with ignorance beforehand, and with His presence when the time came. It's the same for all of us."

Minna said, "What we can tell you, Carl Martell, is what you already know. You are a sword. What do you think a sword is for? For breaking, yes, but afterwards for being reforged better than before. There will be need for a sword, *'piercing even to the dividing asunder of soul and spirit.'* There must be resistance to the new order; a resistance that's not led by the men who burned Harry."

"That sounds like lonely work."

" *'I have left me seven thousand in Israel, all the knees which have not bowed down unto Baal.'* " said Harry.

"I always loved heroism," said Martell. "But I never much wanted to be a hero myself."

"Guess what, Carl Martell?" said Minna. "Life isn't about what we want to do. It's about what we're called to do, and whether we say yes or no."

"I've already said yes. I won't turn back. But I'm only Carl Martell. I was never known for courage. I wish I had something—some sign or something. I'll quote Scripture to you too—*'The sword of the Lord, and Gideon.'* Gideon asked for a sign, and he got one. I know that's selfish after the things I've experienced, but faith—and courage—are new to me. I could use some help."

"There's always help, Carl, if you know where to

look," said Harry. "Well, it's time we went on our way. Ready to go, Minna? Say, Carl, I could use a drink for the road. Could I have some of that water?"

Martell poured water from his carafe into the glass on the side table, a little confused as to why a spirit would need a drink. It took a moment before he realized he was seeing yet another fundamental law broken.

He was pouring with his right hand. The phantom one.

The carafe hung steady in the air, draining its contents. He could feel it in his hand. Only he could not see the hand. It was just like movie special effects. His mouth fell open and the glass overflowed.

He turned to Harry and Minna, but they were gone. Only Harry's words remained, as much a memory as a sound: *"There was the hand, and there was the sword in it, both of them parts of you. The sword will be there again in the day of your need."*

Ten minutes later a nurse with a wheelchair arrived and Roy Corson followed her in. "How you doing, Carl?" he asked.

"I'm ready to go. Dressed and everything."

"Good, the car's waiting. Arm okay?"

Martell held it up. "Call me Tyr," he said, smiling. "I put my hand in the wolf's mouth."

"Just the kind of idiotic thing you'd do, too. You having trouble shaving with one hand?"

"I'm growing a beard."

"Curiouser and curiouser. You're going off the deep end, you know that? This is how it starts. First you get religion, then you grow a beard, the next thing you know you're teaching Sociology."

Martell sat in the wheelchair. "I won't be teaching anything," he said. "You know that."

"Nice time to become a religious fanatic." The nurse

pushed the chair out the door and they proceeded down the hallway.

Martell said, "It is, isn't it?"

"Is what?"

"A good time to become a believer. These are the times when God does wonderful things. This is when the hypocrites get winnowed out, and the corruption of power is gone, and church starts looking like Christ. How many times have I heard you mourn your radical days?"

"Hey, don't get me into this!"

"Why not? You're part of the Establishment now, and it drives you nuts. Join us, Roy. Be a subversive again."

As they waited for the elevator, Roy said, "Christ," and it was impossible to tell how he meant it.

END

Appendix

The Kensington Runestone Inscription

8 Goths and 22 Norwegians on
exploration-journey from
Vinland through the West We
had camp by 2 skerries one
days-journey north from the stone
We were and fished one day After
we came home found 10 men red
with blood and dead AVM
Save from evil

have 10 of by the sea to look
after our ships 14 days-journey
from this island year 1362

(Source: Holand, Hjalmar H.: *Norse Discoveries & Explorations In America*, pages 982-1362. © 1968 by Harold Holand. Republication by Dover Publications, Inc., New York)

Afterword

There was once an Epsom, Minnesota. It existed—
barely—a few miles west of my home town of
Kenyon, just off Highway 60, until some time in the
1930s or '40s, I think. My grandfather and uncle
helped tear up the track on its railroad spur. There's
nothing left there now, but it remained on the maps,
through some oversight, until the 1970s. When I
started this book I looked forward to using a map
to vouch for its authenticity, but the cartographers
finally got around to erasing it and spoiled my game.
I like the name anyway.

If you happen to know Waldorf College, Forest
City, Iowa, where I spent two happy years, you may
note some resemblance to Christiania. This resemblance is only cosmetic.

Experts are unanimous in rejecting the Kensington
Runestone as a clumsy fraud. For the purpose of this

fiction I have imagined the experts mistaken. It has been known to happen.

Special thanks are due to Jim Baen, John Brekke, and to my agents, George Scithers and Darrell Schweitzer, for their comments and suggestions on the manuscript. Also (posthumously) to my mother, Gladys Walker, for proofreading.

Lars Walker
New Hope, Minnesota

THE SHIP WHO SANG IS NOT ALONE!

Anne McCaffrey, with Margaret Ball, Mercedes Lackey, S.M. Stirling, and Jody Lynn Nye, explores the universe she created with her ground-breaking novel, The Ship Who Sang.

PARTNERSHIP
by Anne McCaffrey & Margaret Ball

"[*PartnerShip*] captures the spirit of *The Ship Who Sang*...a single, solid plot full of creative nastiness and the sort of egocentric villains you love to hate."
—Carolyn Cushman, **Locus**

THE SHIP WHO SEARCHED
by Anne McCaffrey & Mercedes Lackey

Tia, a bright and spunky seven-year-old accompanying her exo-archaeologist parents on a dig, is afflicted by a paralyzing alien virus. Tia won't be satisfied to glide through life like a ghost in a machine. Like her predecessor Helva, *The Ship Who Sang*, she would rather strap on a spaceship!

THE CITY WHO FOUGHT
by Anne McCaffrey & S.M. Stirling

Simeon was the "brain" running a peaceful space station—but when the invaders arrived, his only hope of protecting his crew and himself was to become *The City Who Fought*.

THE SHIP WHO WON
by Anne McCaffrey & Jody Lynn Nye

"*Oodles of fun.*"
—**Locus**
"*Fast, furious and fun.*"
—**Chicago Sun-Times**

ANNE McCAFFREY:
QUEEN OF THE SPACEWAYS

*"Readers will find themselves riveted by the
nonstop action adventure that constantly surpasses
even the most jaded reader's expectations, and by a
relationship as beautiful as it is indestructible."*

—*Affaire de Coeur*

PARTNERSHIP ☐
by Anne McCaffrey & Margaret Ball
0-671-72109-7 ◆ 336 pages ◆ $5.99

THE SHIP WHO SEARCHED ☐
by Anne McCaffrey & Mercedes Lackey
0-671-72129-1 ◆ 320 pages ◆ $5.99

THE CITY WHO FOUGHT ☐
by Anne McCaffrey & S.M. Stirling
0-671-72166-6 ◆ 432 pages ◆ HC $19.00 ◆ PB $5.99 ◆ 87599-X

THE SHIP WHO WON ☐
by Anne McCaffrey & Jody Lynn Nye
0-671-87595-7 ◆ HC $21.00 ◆ PB $5.99 ◆ 87657-0

And don't miss:
THE PLANET PIRATES ☐
**by Anne McCaffrey,
with Elizabeth Moon & Jody Lynn Nye**
3-in-1 trade paperback edition
0-671-72187-9 ◆ 864 pages ◆ $12.00

If not available through your local bookstore send this coupon and a
check or money order for the cover price(s) to Baen Books, Dept.
BA, P.O. Box 1403, Riverdale, NY 10471. Delivery can take up to
ten weeks.

NAME: _____

ADDRESS: _____

_____

I have enclosed a check or money order in the amount of $ _____

MERCEDES LACKEY
Hot! Hot! Hot!

Whether it's elves at the racetrack, bards battling evil mages or brainships fighting planet pirates, Mercedes Lackey is always compelling, always fun, always a great read. Complete your collection today!

The Bardic Voices series:

The Lark and the Wren, 72099-6 ✦ $6.99 ☐

The Robin & The Kestrel, 87628-7 ✦ $5.99 ☐

The Eagle & The Nightingales, 87706-2 ✦ $5.99 ☐

Four & Twenty Blackbirds, 57778-6 ✦ $6.99 ☐

The SERRAted Edge series:

Born to Run (with Larry Dixon), 72110-0 ✦ $5.99 ☐

Wheels of Fire (with Mark Shepherd), 72138-0 ✦ $5.99 ☐

When the Bough Breaks (with Holly Lisle), 72154-1 ✦ $5.99 ☐

Chrome Circle (with Larry Dixon), 87615-5 ✦ $5.99 ☐

Bard's Tale novels:

Castle of Deception (with Josepha Sherman), 72125-9 ✦ $5.99 ☐

Fortress of Frost & Fire (with Ru Emerson), 72162-3 ✦ $5.99 ☐

Prison of Souls (with Mark Shepherd), 72193-3 ✦ $5.99 ☐

Bedlam's Bard (with Ellen Guon), 87863-8 ✦ $6.99 ☐

The Fire Rose, 87750-X ✦ $6.99 ☐

Fiddler Fair, 87866-2 ✦ $5.99 ☐

Available at your local bookstore. If not, fill out this coupon and send a check or money order for the cover price + $1.50 s/h to Baen Books, Dept. BA, P.O. Box 1403, Riverdale, NY 10471.

Name: _____

Address: _____

_____

I have enclosed a check or money order in the amount of $ _____

" SPACE OPERA IS ALIVE AND WELL! "

And DAVID WEBER is the New Reigning King of the Spaceways!

The Honor Harrington series:

On Basilisk Station

"...an outstanding blend of military/technical writing balanced by superb character development and an excellent degree of human drama.... very highly recommended...." —*Wilson Library Bulletin*

"Old fashioned space opera is alive and well."

—*Starlog*

Honor of the Queen

"Honor fights her way with fists, brains, and tactical genius through a tangle of politics, battles and cultural differences. Although battered she ends this book with her honor, and the Queen's honor, intact."

—*Kliatt*

The Short Victorious War

The families who rule the People's Republic of Haven are in trouble and they think a short victorious war will solve all their problems—only this time they're up against Captain Honor Harrington and a Royal Manticoran Navy that's prepared to give them a war that's far from short...and anything but victorious.

continued ☞

DAVID WEBER

The Honor Harrington series: *(cont.)*

Field of Dishonor

Honor goes home to Manticore—and fights for her life on a battlefield she never trained for, in a private war that offers just two choices: death—or a "victory" that can end only in dishonor and the loss of all she loves....

Flag in Exile

Hounded into retirement and disgrace by political enemies, Honor Harrington has retreated to planet Grayson, where powerful men plot to reverse the changes she has brought to their world. And for their plans to suceed, Honor Harrington must die!

Honor Among Enemies

Offered a chance to end her exile and again command a ship, Honor Harrington must use a crew drawn from the dregs of the service to stop pirates who are plundering commerce. Her enemies have chosen the mission carefully, thinking that either she will stop the raiders or they will kill her . . . and either way, her enemies will win....

In Enemy Hands

After being ambushed, Honor finds herself aboard an enemy cruiser, bound for her scheduled execution. But one lesson Honor has never learned is how to give up! One way or another, she and her crew are going home—even if they have to conquer Hell to get there!

continued

DAVID WEBER

On Basilisk Station 0-671-72163-1 ◆ $6.99	☐
Honor of the Queen 0-671-72172-0 ◆ $6.99	☐
The Short Victorious War 0-671-87596-5 ◆ $5.99	☐
Field of Dishonor 0-671-87624-4 ◆ $5.99	☐
Flag in Exile 0-671-87681-3 ◆ $5.99	☐
Honor Among Enemies (HC) 0-671-87723-2 ◆ $21.00	☐
Honor Among Enemies (PB) 0-671-87783-6 ◆ $6.99	☐
In Enemy Hands (HC) 0-671-87793-3 ◆ $22.00	☐
In Enemy Hands (PB) 0-671-57770-0 ◆ $6.99	☐

For more books by David Weber,
ask for a copy of our free catalog.

If not available through your local bookstore send this coupon
and a check or money order for the cover price(s) + $1.50 s/h to
Baen Books, Dept. BA, P.O. Box 1403, Riverdale, NY 10471.
Delivery can take up to 8 weeks.

NAME: _____

ADDRESS: _____

_____

I have enclosed a check or money order in the amt. of $ _____

EXPLORE OUR WEB SITE

 BAEN.COM

VISIT THE BAEN BOOKS
WEB SITE AT:

http://www.baen.com
or just search for baen.com

Get information on the latest releases,
sample chapters of upcoming novels,
read about your favorite authors,
enter contests, and much more! ;)